THE WEIRD OF HALI
DREAMLANDS

NOVELS BY JOHN MICHAEL GREER

THE WEIRD OF HALI

I – Innsmouth
II – Kingsport
III – Chorazin
IV – Dreamlands
V – Providence
VI – Red Hook
VII – Arkham

OTHERS

The Fires of Shalsha
Star's Reach
Twilight's Last Gleaming
Retrotopia

THE WEIRD OF HALI
DREAMLANDS

A fantasy with tentacles

JOHN MICHAEL GREER

FOUNDERS HOUSE PUBLISHING LLC | 2019

The Weird of Hali: Dreamlands
Copyright © 2019 John Michael Greer
Published by Founders House Publishing, LLC
Cover art by Matt Forsyth
Cover and interior design © 2019 Founders House Publishing, LLC

First Paperback Edition: April 2019

ISBN-13: 978-1-945810-30-5
ISBN-10: 1-945810-30-0

For more information please visit
www.foundershousepublishing.com

Published in the United States of America

THE WEIRD OF HALI
DREAMLANDS

Down through the years, the memory remains:
An autumn evening in my childhood room.
Familiar shadows fade to deeper gloom;
The rain drums hard upon the windowpanes.
Sleep comes, and I approach the hidden door
That opens onto unfamiliar places
Across a tapestry of times and spaces
I crossed and recrossed a thousand nights before.
The rolling hills of timeless Ooth-Nargai;
The thousand gilded spires of ancient Thran;
The jasper terraces of fair Kiran—
In dream-sent journeying I passed them by,
In wanderings by land and argosies
Across the rolling oceans of the night
To ruined temples in the moon's pale light
Where once arose forgotten litanies.
But on that autumn night of drumming rain,
The hidden door of dreams, by some decree
Of gods unknown or known, was closed to me,
And never has it opened up again.

— "The Door of Dreams" by Justin Geoffrey

ONE

The Rats in the Walls

D octor Chaudronnier," said Miriam Akeley. Jenny's thin plain face was a study in delight. She fumbled for words, gave up, and flung her arms around the professor. Miriam returned the hug; lean as a heron and silver-haired, she stood more than a head taller than her pupil, and so patted her indulgently on the shoulders.

Around them the cavernous space of Halsey Center, Miskatonic University's indoor athletics building, rang with voices and bursts of applause. The commencement ceremony had just ended, and forty-one newly hooded doctors, their faculty advisers, families, friends, and casual onlookers, half-filled a space more usually given over to basketball, indoor soccer, and the occasional overpriced rock concert. There had been fewer graduates this time than in previous years, fewer in fact than in any year since Miriam first came to Miskatonic, but declining enrollment was a problem every university in the country had faced for the last decade and more, with the economy stuck in permanent crisis, student loans a thing of the past, and state and federal politics both mired in increasingly intractable deadlock. Even so, each year's crop of

1

doctorates always felt to Miriam like a promise for the future.

The thought that this might be the last Miskatonic commencement she would ever attend twisted in her, hard. She shoved the thought away, forced her attention back to the moment.

"Do you have a few minutes to spare?" Jenny asked then, drawing back. "My family's come up from Kingsport. They'd like to meet you—and I really want you to meet them."

"I'd be delighted," Miriam assured her. "Besides, thanks are in order."

Jenny smiled, turned and led the way, and Miriam followed her.

Meeting Jenny's family—that, Miriam thought, had a definite interest. During the five and a half years Jenny had been her research assistant, "my family" had been an opaque label behind which Miriam could see next to nothing. The Chaudronniers lived in Kingsport, the little tourist town on the coast ten miles southeast of Arkham; they had money, a good deal of it, which was why Jenny was able to keep working for Miriam when the last university funding for research assistantships in the humanities had been cut; they included a great-aunt whose name Miriam didn't remember, and whose death two years back left Jenny silent and withdrawn for weeks; they had relatives in France, and one of those, a Dr. Emmeline Grenier, helped Miriam get access to certain unusual documents during a sabbatical there. That was all she knew, and it had occurred to her more than once that Jenny had been at some pains to keep things that way.

Doctoral robes and hoods billowed around the two of them as they wove through the crowd. Both hoods had the white trim of their discipline, history of ideas, though Jenny's was lined with Miskatonic orange and black while Miriam's had the blue and gold of her alma mater in California. Another thought forced its way in, reminded Miriam of the contrast between the plain robes, hoods and caps of students at the *collegia* of the Middle Ages, who'd launched the tradition on its way, and the impractical abstractions they'd become as the centuries slipped past.

All at once Jenny darted ahead with an inarticulate cry. Miriam, who'd heard the same cry many times before, slowed her pace, gave her former student time to fling herself into the arms of her family and get through the tears and congratulations that followed. It was a minor vanity of hers to time her arrival exactly, so that she was there when her student turned to introduce her, and not a moment before. She managed it this time with perfect grace, lingering just long enough on the stair and then walking up to the little knot of people around Jenny.

There were four of them, all dressed with the sort of quiet elegance that spoke discreetly of old money: a stocky man in his early fifties, maybe, with hair and a neat moustache that had once been brown and now were going gray; a woman perhaps twenty years older, with stark white hair, a round face, and a ready smile; a woman a little younger than Jenny's twenty-six years, with brown hair and an uncertain look; and a man around her age, black-haired and dark-eyed, with that indefinable look that distinguishes the European from the American.

"Miriam," Jenny said, turning to find her adviser standing a precisely measured distance behind her. "My uncle Martin; my great-aunt Claire; my cousin Charlotte, and her husband Alain d'Ursuras." She turned. "Dr. Miriam Akeley."

"A definite pleasure to meet you," said Martin, taking her hand. "I trust it won't be too off-putting if I mention that we've heard a lot about you."

Miriam allowed a sly smile. "That depends entirely on what you've heard."

He laughed in response. "Very good. Shall I be hopelessly

3

redundant, and say that none of it was off-putting?"

She laughed as well, gave her hand to the others in turn.

"Before we turn to the serious business of congratulating Dr. Chaudronnier," Miriam said then, "I'd like to thank you for being so generous about the cost of her education. She's not the only one who's gained from that—I've had the benefit of a really gifted research assistant, even though the university's had to eliminate funding for assistantships. She's been of immense help to my work, and I'm deeply grateful that you made that possible." With a little laugh: "I'm still not quite sure how I'll get by without her."

Jenny blushed. "You've got Will to help you out," she reminded Miriam.

"It's been our pleasure," Martin said. "And also our privilege. The family's been sending students to Miskatonic for a good many years now."

"Are you one of our alumni, by any chance?" Miriam asked him.

"Yes—though it's been more years than I like to think about." He turned toward Jenny. "But I think we're neglecting the serious business you mentioned a moment ago."

The next five minutes or so went to that pleasant task, and Miriam, at Claire's insistence, recounted enough of her pupil's considerable academic achievements to turn Jenny's face bright pink. In the midst of that, Claire turned to Martin with what was clearly enough an unspoken question; he glanced at her and nodded fractionally, and in the next pause in the conversation, said, "Dr. Akeley, are you possibly free this evening? I'd planned a little dinner at a restaurant here in town, and we'd all be delighted if you joined us."

It was a familiar offer, and one that Miriam usually deflected with an excuse. This time, though, indecision seized her. "I certainly don't want to intrude," she said.

"You're not intruding," Claire told her with a smile.

"We're inviting."

Before she could answer, Alain said, "*Voyons, Madame!* How else are we going to hear all the embarrassing stories about Jenny you're too polite to tell in a place this public?"

Jenny turned and mimed a swat at him in mock outrage, and Miriam started to laugh. "*Bien*," she said. "*Bien*. Thank you, and I'd be delighted."

OUTSIDE, AFTERNOON STOOD poised on the brink of evening. The buildings of the Miskatonic campus stood tall against high thin clouds, the signs of years of deferred maintenance all too plain to the eye. Further off rose rounded hills mantled in greenery, their peaks dotted with ancient standing stones. The milling crowds beneath seemed transitory, a thing of dream.

Miriam and Jenny had reclaimed their garment bags from the cloakroom and shed their academic robes, to reveal Miriam's signature black dress and white sweater, on the one hand, and on the other, a wine-red day dress that managed to make Jenny's mouse-brown hair look less drab than usual. Talking and laughing, the six of them flowed with the crowd out the main doors of Halsey Center. "See you there," Alain said then, and he, Charlotte, and Claire headed off across the parking lot. Martin led Jenny and Miriam to the curbside and simply waited.

Not much more than a minute later, a black Cadillac easily half a century old slid up to the curb. The driver was a short man in an old-fashioned black suit, with hair the color of polished steel and an oddly expressionless face. He got out and opened the rear door for Jenny and Miriam, then got their garment bags stowed in the capacious trunk, while Martin went to the front passenger door and got in without further ado.

A few moments later the Cadillac pulled out onto Federal Street and glided south past the campus buildings. A gap caught Miriam's eye: a flat gravel-covered space next to the street where a building had been. That stirred worries she didn't want to face just then, and she glanced at Jenny, who had leaned back against the seat and closed her eyes. Just for a moment, she could glimpse something of what Jenny would look like as an old woman. It was an unsettling thought, and Miriam looked away. By then, fortunately, the empty space had slipped behind the flat brick face of Morgan Hall; the bulbous masses and clustered spires of Wilmarth Hall rose behind that, and the Gothic arches of Orne Library loomed ahead.

She'd guessed already where they were headed, and the route confirmed it: a block west to Peabody Avenue, across the Miskatonic River and then uphill into the older half of town, where colonial houses with sagging gambrel roofs stood cheek by jowl with tall Victorian buildings. Most stood empty now, fretted by a century of urban decay, but the failing light made it possible to ignore that. A left turn took the Cadillac onto High Street, and half a dozen blocks later it burst out of the old town into what had been a wealthy suburb in the 1920s and farmland not too many decades before that. A few more blocks, and High Street ended at a cul-de-sac, a parking lot surrounded by neatly clipped hedges, and a big Federal-era farmhouse of whitewashed stone. A sign alongside the front door read RESTAURANT LA FRENAIE.

Miriam had been to Arkham's best restaurant all of twice in the twenty-two years she'd taught at Miskatonic. The last time, a wedding dinner for an old friend the week after Massachusetts legalized same-sex marriage, was a good many years in the past, but nothing seemed to have changed but the faces of the waitstaff.

The maitre d'hote came over at once with an effusive "Mr. Chaudronnier! A pleasure, a very great pleasure, as always."

"Thank you, Jules," said Martin. "We'll need one more setting."

The maitre d's sniff announced how little that concerned him. "One of these days," he said, "one of these days—mark my words, Mr. Chaudronnier—you will actually manage to do something that will inconvenience me. This is not that day." He turned to a waitress. "Eleanor, you heard? Good. See to it." Turning back to Martin: "Please come with me."

They ended up, Miriam noted with some amusement, in the same room where she'd dined after Michael Peaslee's wedding. The paintings on the walls, decent copies of old masters, and the heavy wooden table and solid comfortable chairs remained unaltered, a little space of permanence somehow set apart from the wrenching changes of the decade just past.

They took their seats; the sixth place setting made its appearance, promptly followed by water, rolls, wine, and a platter of hors d'oeuvres in which escargots played a notable role. The soup was consommé, pleasantly chilled, and the salad was green, crisp, and enlivened with goat cheese. All the while, Claire and Alain extracted as many stories about Jenny as Miriam was willing to tell. Charlotte hid her laughter behind a hand, Martin looked on with a fond smile, and Jenny herself blushed and laughed by turns.

"I want to know what she got up to in Vyones last summer," said Claire.

"You'll have to ask Dr. Grenier about that," Miriam replied.

"I did, and Emmeline insisted that Jenny spent the whole time with her nose in books."

"She was telling the truth," Jenny interjected. "*The Book of Eibon* was quoted by dozens of thirteenth- and fourteenth-century authors, and I had to read all of them."

"That's what your dissertation's about, isn't it?" Alain

asked. "*The Livre d'Ivon?*"

"*The Influence of the* Liber Ivonis *on Medieval Metaphysical Thought*," Miriam quoted. Then, with a sly sidelong glance at Jenny: "It'll have a catchier title sometime soon, though."

Jenny gave her a puzzled look, then, as recognition dawned: "You didn't tell me!"

"I just heard from Jane Dyer this morning," Miriam told her. "I figured you had a few other things on your mind, and you'll be getting an email in a day or two." To the others, who were giving her puzzled looks: "Miskatonic University Press has accepted the English version for publication. Mrs. Dyer—she's the acquisitions editor for history and humanities—said to me that it's one of the few works of real scholarship that's come across her desk this year."

Jenny blushed yet again. "The English version?" Claire asked.

"There's also a French version," said Miriam. "Editions d'Isoile in Ximes is looking it over right now. I haven't heard anything back yet, but my guess is they'll snap it up. It really is an impressive study."

Jenny's blush turned bright pink. Fortunately, the waiter arrived just then with the main course. The wine steward followed moments later, and by the time plates were on the table and wine glasses were comfortably full, she'd regained her composure. Miriam had mercy on her then, and asked the others about Emmeline Grenier's doings. From there, the conversation wandered from there into equally harmless paths.

As dessert arrived—La Frenaie was famous across Massachusetts' north coast for its chocolate mousse—Alain said, "And so now you have done the thing; you are a doctor of philosophy. What next?"

A decade or two ago, that would have been settled already. Miriam couldn't help but think back to the days when the students she'd helped along the road to a Ph.D. would already be hard at work looking for a teaching position somewhere, with an eye toward a career in their academic field. That was a fading memory these days, though, with hiring all but nonexistent and most universities laying off more staff every year. "I'll second the question," she asked Jenny. "Have you made any plans?"

Jenny laughed. "Ask me that when it's finally sunk in that I've graduated." Then, with a more serious expression: "Back home to Kingsport for the summer—I have friends coming to visit, and a lot of catching up to do now that I'm not spending every waking hour on the *Book of Eibon*. After that?" She shrugged, and laughed again. "I'm sure I'll find things to do."

Something in Jenny's voice in those last words left Miriam feeling troubled. It sounded much older than the young woman facing her; it spoke of grave troubles surmounted and others still to come. Miriam managed to keep her reaction off her face, though. She smiled and said, "That I don't doubt at all."

THEY DROVE HER home in the Cadillac—her new place was only about a dozen blocks from campus, and she'd walked there in the cool of the morning with the garment bag rolled up and hanging from a shoulder strap. At the curb, by the light of a flickering streetlamp, Jenny gave her another hug, promised to stay in touch, and made her promise to do the same thing. Then Miriam unlocked the door to the building, made sure it latched behind her, and started up the three flights of stairs to her apartment.

She heard, or thought she heard, puzzling noises from outside as she went up the stairs: running feet, a flurry of short sharp sounds that might have been gunshots if they had been louder, a voice calling out something that didn't seem to be in English, and then flapping noises, a little like sheets on a clothesline in a strong wind. When she let herself into her apartment and looked out the window onto the street, though, all she saw was the Cadillac, which was just then pulling away from the curb. Light from the streetlamp shone through the rear window, showed Jenny's mop of mouse-colored hair and Martin's neater gray-brown, side by side in the back seat.

Imagining things, she told herself, and stood there until the car rounded the corner, then went to the light switch and turned it on. The room around her was small, and not particularly well maintained. The walls had been painted that unappealing color that a college friend of hers used to call "landlady green," and the floor was covered with a dingy brown carpet frayed on one side. Overhead, a broad gap showed to one side of the little square light fixture, where a bigger circular fixture had been taken out and replaced without benefit of plasterwork. It was a good deal shoddier than the apartment where she'd lived for the previous eight years, but also a good deal cheaper, and these days, that mattered.

A faint scurrying sound told of something living inside one wall: a rat, no doubt. If you lived in Arkham, you got used to hearing rats in the walls. It was just one of those things, and she'd long since learned the tricks of keeping them from getting to her food and garbage, so they stayed out of her living space. The scurrying sounded again, and then went silent.

The apartment didn't feel like home yet, but then she'd only moved in three days before, taking advantage of the gap between finals and commencement. A few boxes not yet unpacked sat here and there in the corners of the living room. She knew herself well enough to guess that a few months, maybe, would cover its flaws with a layer of comfortable familiarity. She took her garment bag into the bedroom, made sure the robe and hood were properly arranged in it, and hung it in its place in the closet, then changed into a loose knee-length sleep shirt for comfort. Barefoot, she came back out to the living room, put a jazz CD into the player on one desk, picked up a book from the other desk, and flopped onto the couch.

She'd intended to read a little and then go to bed, but despite the long day, sleep felt further away than the Ghooric zone. After a few minutes she got up, put the book where it had been, and crossed to the battered Governor Winthrop desk in the far corner of the room. She stood there for another minute in indecision, as she usually did, then fetched a chair, got an ornate key from its hiding place behind her H.P. Lovecraft books, and unlocked the desk.

The leaf swung down. Behind it sat an elderly computer she'd bought for cash at a yard sale, and systematically stripped of every device that might allow it to share data with the outside world. She pressed the start button and went to get a glass of white wine while the thing whirred, chattered to itself, and finally brought up a desktop image she'd lifted from an old issue of *Weird Tales*. A sip of wine, a sigh at her own imprudence, and then she opened the documents folder and doubleclicked on one of the files. A long-obsolete word processing program booted, and brought up a page with an improbable heading:

MEMOIRS TO PROVE THE EXISTENCE OF CTHULHU

How long had it been?

The question was purely rhetorical. Five and a half years had gone by since the sudden appearance of an unlikely letter, and the equally sudden disappearances of two of her graduate assistants, forced her over a line she'd hoped never to cross: five and a half years since she'd taken her first tentative steps toward a field of research that could terminate her career instantly if word got out. To study H.P. Lovecraft as a literary figure, that was harmless; to study the old strange legends and obscure tomes he'd used as raw material for his stories, that was marginally acceptable—but to ask if there might be something more to the forgotten ages and unhuman powers described in those legends and tomes than mere superstition? That was utterly beyond the pale. Scholars lived and died by their reputations, and there were subjects you didn't touch unless you wanted to put your career in jeopardy or end it outright.

Five and a half years ago, an hour after meeting Jenny for the first time, she'd stood at the window of her office in Wilmarth Hall, staring moodily at the gray bulk of a parking garage and the brown leafless trees of the hill beyond, and finally asked the question nobody was supposed to ask: why should such questions be forever off limits to scholarship?

She'd found the beginning of the answer four months later in a bin of bound periodicals that were being discarded from Orne Library's collection. The letters on the spine, PROCS. AM. ARCH. SOC. 1906-1910, stirred a faint chord of memory. She'd opened the volume at random, and found herself staring at names she'd always been told were inventions of a horror writer—George Gammell Angell, W. Channing Webb, and John Legrasse, a deputy inspector of police from New Orleans—and a photograph of a small stone statue that sent chills down her back. She'd left with the volume surreptitiously tucked into her shoulderbag.

Research followed. The American Archaeological Society, she discovered, was a onetime rival to the better-known Archeological Institute of America, founded in 1877 and dissolved, after decades of unusually bitter academic politics, in 1948. A copy of the annual proceedings had been sent each year to Brown University's John Hay Library, though they had been discarded quietly once the AAS folded. That was where H.P. Lovecraft had found them, and gotten the details that put a fictionalized but recognizable account of the 1908 AAS meeting in St. Louis in the pages of his story "The Call of Cthulhu."

From there, step by step, she'd followed up one lead after another, and though most petered out into empty air, one in twenty, maybe, gave her a scrap of data that couldn't be ignored. A newspaper clipping from a long-defunct Virginia weekly, the Gainsville *Democrat*, mentioned the puzzling disappearance of local resident Harley S. Warren in the cypress swamps east of town, and noted that his friend Randolph Carter, of Boston, was being interviewed by the local sheriff; an Arkham town directory from 1922 listed Crawford Tillinghast, 118 Benevolent Street, inventor; an article in the June 1907 issue of *American Inventor* magazine described a "telepathy machine" and mentioned in passing its successful use with a patient in a New York State institution for the criminally insane on February 21, 1901. None of them offered her more than a scrap or two of information, but all of them pointed to the same uncomfortable conclusion that Lovecraft had all too often mixed a good strong dose of fact into his fiction.

An hour later, having copied down certain notes she'd found in an unpublished manuscript of George Angell's, she turned off the computer and locked the desk. So far, thankfully, nobody else seemed to have noticed the direction in which her research had strayed. Even Jenny, who'd assisted her more than once in getting obscure documents in roundabout ways, hadn't guessed that her interest in Lovecraft's sources had become more than a matter of literary scholarship. She must never know, Miriam told herself. Not even after I'm gone.

Tiredness descended on her suddenly as the CD finished playing. She blinked, finished the last of the wine, used the bathroom and went to bed. As she settled down, the scrabbling noise sounded again in the wall, fainter than before. Good night, rat, she thought at it. Don't you dare keep me awake.

Moments later she'd drifted off into sleep: deep and dreamless at first, and for some time thereafter. In the small hours of the morning, though, she rose slowly into dreams of wandering through dim landscapes dotted with great gray stones carved in a script she could not read, a writing of spirals and whorls incised in delicate lines. She walked on, climbing a long uneven slope past stone after stone, as the light slowly brightened around her.

She reached the crest of the hill, and stopped in wonder. Below her, a city blazed golden in evening light. Houses and temples, colonnades and arched bridges of luminous marble caught the glory of the setting sun's rays. To one side, broad streets lined with fountains and delicate trees and urns full of flowering plants reached toward a harbor that glowed like hammered bronze. To the other, red-tiled roofs and old peaked gables climbed steep slopes, across which little lanes of grassy cobbles wound here and there.

She had been to that city sometime in the distant past, she knew, or would be there sometime in the far future, she could not tell which. She stood there for what seemed like a long while, and then sighed and turned to leave.

ALL AT ONCE noise jolted her out of the dream: a sudden dull thump, as though something had fallen from a height. An instant later came a prolonged high-pitched cry.

Disoriented, Miriam pulled herself out from under the covers, fumbled with the bedside lamp and got it turned on. It took her a moment to realize that the cry was coming from the living room. She stood up, went to the door and switched on the light.

Something lay in the middle of the living room floor, just under the big gap where the light fixture didn't fit the hole:

14

something alive that moved weakly, as though in pain. At first she thought it was a rat, one of the big brown wharf rats Arkham inherited from its seaport days back in the eighteenth and nineteenth centuries. It was the size of the biggest of the Arkham rats she'd seen, its body maybe a foot long and its hairless tail about the same, and its filthy brownish fur could pass for a rat's easily enough.

It didn't have a rat's head, though. The eyes were too big, and the flattish face reminded her of a monkey's or, worse, a human being's. The proportions of its body weren't right for a rat, either, and the four paws that scrabbled feebly on the wooden floor had opposable thumbs and looked for all the world like tiny human hands. The thing that clinched matters, though, was the cry the thing made. It wasn't a rat's cry, or anything like it. It was a high terrified keening that sounded uncomfortably like a child's.

Miriam stared at it for a long moment, her mouth open. Was it some kind of exotic pet? If so, she decided, it must have run away from its owner months or years back. It was starving, that was certain. Even through the matted filthy fur, she could see the lines of its ribs.

She went to the hall closet and got one of the spare towels she'd set aside for cleaning. That went into a corner of the kitchen. Oven mitts from a hook above the stove offered some protection for her hands, in case it decided to bite. She pulled them on, and then went back to the living room, where the creature was still keening.

It saw her as she approached, and went silent; the big yellow eyes widened in obvious terror. It tried to crawl away, without effect. "It's okay," Miriam said, hoping her voice might soothe the thing. "It's okay. I'm not going to hurt you." She knelt, scooped it up in both hands and lifted it from the floor. It let out a desperate cry, and all four paws—hands?—clutched feebly at the mitts. Its body was terribly frail. Even through the mitts, she could feel its heart pounding.

"It's okay," she repeated, and carried the creature to the towel in the kitchen. It cried out again as she lowered it, but relaxed a little as it felt the towel underneath it. Miriam drew back, and the creature stared up at her as though bewildered.

"I wonder what you eat," she said aloud. "Maybe some milk—"

The creature's eyes went wide, and not in fear.

"You know that word, don't you?" Miriam asked it. "Milk?"

The hopeful expression on its face left no doubt in her mind. She found a bowl, filled it with milk from the refrigerator, and set the bowl down next to the towel, as close to its head as she could. The creature managed to pull itself the necessary inch or so, and its pink tongue darted in and out, lapping up the milk with frantic haste.

She stood up, considered the strange little creature. No doubt it had been a pet once, and had gotten lost or been abandoned by its owner. She'd read about exotic animals turning up that way in the oddest places. Once she figured out what it was, she decided, she could contact whatever owners' or breeders' association there might be, and find it a proper home. In the meantime, it gave her something to think about besides the questions that haunted her.

It finished most of the milk and settled back onto the towel. She refilled the bowl with more milk in case it wanted another meal later in the night. Then, on an impulse, she reached down and pulled a stray length of the towel over it for warmth. The creature gave her another bewildered look, then nestled down, pulled the towel close with one paw and closed its eyes. She watched its belly rise and fall with its breath for a while, and then turned out the kitchen light, returned to her bedroom, shut the door tight and went back to bed.

TWO

Brown Jenkin's Folk

She woke to the sound of church bells the next morning, got up, and went into the kitchen to check on the creature. She'd wondered while dozing off if she'd find a stiff little corpse in the morning, but it was quite alive, curled up under the fold of the towel, its belly still rising and falling steadily. The bowl next to the towel was entirely empty. As she watched, the creature blinked awake, saw her, gave her a long look, and then let out a tentative chirring noise worlds away from the terrified keening of the night before.

"Good morning," Miriam said to it. "More milk?"

It gave her a hopeful look, and she laughed. "I thought so." She poured it another bowlful of milk, then left it to its meal while she washed, pulled on shorts and a baggy T-shirt, and got a pair of English muffins toasting for breakfast. By the time she'd spread butter and marmalade on the muffins, the milk was gone and the creature had nestled back down to sleep.

She booted up her laptop as soon as she'd eaten the muffins, and spent an hour trying to find out what kind of animal her uninvited guest might be, with no success. The handlike

17

paws with their opposable thumbs made her wonder if it might be some rare kind of monkey, but nothing on the primate websites she found resembled it. All the while, though, something in the back of her mind hinted that she'd read somewhere about a creature just like it.

Finally, frustrated, she closed the laptop and got up. Above the desk where she'd been sitting stood the shelf where she kept her copies of H.P. Lovecraft's stories—a set of annotated scholarly editions for research, another set of Arkham House hardbacks for sheer enjoyment—and it was when she glanced at them that she realized what she was trying to remember.

She pulled down a volume, flipped it open to "The Dreams in the Witch-House," and paged through to the passage she remembered. A few steps brought her back into the kitchen, where the little creature was sound asleep once again. The almost-human face, the paws like little hands, the ratlike body: yes, it was nearly a perfect match for Brown Jenkin, the familiar of Arkham's famous witch Keziah Mason. She'd read the court records from Mason's 1692 trial in Salem, and so had Lovecraft—even the scholars who dismissed his tales most superciliously admitted that he'd gotten most of the furnishings of his horror fiction by way of an encyclopedic knowledge of magic, folklore, and the superstitions of bygone times. The creature curled up on the towel in her kitchen was no superstition, though.

She shook her head, put the volume away, and went to get her purse. It occurred to her that the creature might be worth an article in *Lovecraft Studies* or *Journal of American Popular Literature*, but she shook her head. First things first, she told herself. Take care of the thing, find out what it is, and maybe then try to figure out what it could possibly have to do with seventeenth-century witchcraft, H.P. Lovecraft, and the mysteries at which he'd hinted.

Her ordinary Sunday routine involved walking up to Halsey Center on campus and running alternating sprints and laps on the outdoor track, but the odd little creature took precedence this time, and she was back half an hour later with a shopping bag from the venerable First National grocery on Walnut Street. The creature was awake, and there was an ill-smelling puddle on the kitchen floor not far from the towel. Miriam had expected to find the towel sodden, and adjusted her sense of the thing's intelligence accordingly. She got out two more cleaning towels, put on her dish gloves, used one towel to clean up the mess, and then knelt next to the creature and said, "You're probably not going to like this, but it's bath time."

She reached for it with the gloves still on, and though it crouched in dismay it didn't resist. Each of its paws clutched one of her fingers as she lifted it, took it into the bathroom, set it in the sink. A little fiddling with the faucets got a comfortably warm stream of water flowing in, and she stoppered the sink and fetched one of her purchases, a bottle of baby shampoo.

The creature seemed to find warm water perplexing, but didn't try to leap out of the sink, and chirred in what sounded like pleasure as Miriam worked her gloved fingers through its fur. The water in the sink turned black with dirt so quickly that she didn't bother with the shampoo at first. Only after she'd drained one sinkful of filth and refilled the sink again with clean water did she lather up the creature's fur, and it took two more fillings and drainings before the suds looked like something other than foaming mud.

She hadn't been sure how to wash its tiny face, but in a moment of inspiration she rubbed her hands together in front of it, and it copied the same motion; she mimed scrubbing her face, then, and it scrubbed its face with its forepaws. On the same principle, she got it to wash its head and all four

19

limbs. From the back of its head down to the base of its tail, though, was clearly hers to groom. It chirred and closed its eyes in obvious delight as she soaped and scrubbed its back.

Finally she finished the bath, drained the last of the rinse water, and toweled the creature off as carefully as she could. With the dirt gone, the fur was a muted golden brown with hints of red. The creature was female, and Miriam guessed that she was relatively young, whatever that meant for her unknown species. Miriam wrapped her up in the cleaning towel for warmth, carried her back into the kitchen, and set her down on the towel, and this time the movement didn't make the creature crouch or clutch at any available grip for safety. She nestled against Miriam's arm and burrowed into the towel.

The creature woke again while Miriam was cooking dinner, lapped up more milk, and ate part of a banana she'd bought at the grocery—she didn't seem to know what the banana was until Miriam peeled it and cut it into small pieces, but then picked up each piece in both of her front paws, examined it with eyes and nose, and then ate it one nibble at a time with a neatness Miriam found amusing. The creature already looked much less starved and haggard than she had when she'd dropped through Miriam's ceiling. As the creature nestled down under a fold of the towel, Miriam smiled indulgently, then laughed at herself and left the kitchen, shaking her head.

The next morning was Monday, and the alarm went off too soon for Miriam's taste. She got up to find the creature awake, and sufficiently recovered to follow her around from room to room of the little apartment, once she had breakfasted on milk and sliced banana. It was, Miriam decided, a little unnerving to be watched solemnly while on the toilet, but not ten minutes later she went back into the bathroom to brush her hair and put on makeup, and the creature was perched on the toilet, using it for its intended purpose. "You're really quite clever, aren't you?" she asked. The creature answered with a chirr.

Before she left for the university, a fragment of memory sent her digging in the dresser for something one of her students had given her years back as a half-joking gift: a little plush doll in the shape of Cthulhu, the squid-faced devil-god H.P. Lovecraft had resurrected from obscure mythologies and made the centerpiece of one of his most famous stories. The thing was acid-green and cheaply made, but it was the only stuffed toy she had in the apartment, and she thought she remembered reading somewhere that stray animals found stuffed toys just as comforting as stray children did. She handed the toy to the little creature, who examined it minutely and then embraced it, apparently pleased by it.

"I'm going to be gone most of the day," Miriam told the creature, who regarded her with wide eyes. "Let's get you some more milk." She scooped up the little furry animal and the Cthulhu doll, carried them into the kitchen and set them down on the towel. Once the bowl was full again, she said, "Don't worry. I'll be back tonight."

As though she can understand me, she thought, laughing at herself. She shouldered her purse and left the apartment.

HER ROUTE TO the Miskatonic campus ran through the heart of Arkham's old downtown. Most of it was abandoned now, the windows boarded over or simply left open to whatever wind and rain happened to wander past the fragments of shattered glass. Here and there she passed a tavern, a pawn shop, or a rundown apartment building like the one she now tenanted. A few of the old houses still had people living in them, and three blocks from her front door she was startled to find that a ground floor space, boarded up for years, had suddenly turned into a little restaurant with OPENING SOON signs in one window.

She stopped in front of the door, glanced up at the sign above it: CAFÉ YIAN, it read, and below that THAI AND ASIAN FOOD. Memory stirred; she'd seen workmen around it a few times recently on her walks to and from campus, though she'd thought nothing of it—sometimes the city government found the money to tear down a collapsing building before it could tumble down by itself and block the street in front of it. She peered through the window. The space looked shabby but clean inside, with a row of square tables covered with bright red tablecloths down one side, a narrow counter lined with tall stools down the other side, a wider counter with a cash register in back, and a menu board up above that she couldn't quite read. All in all, it looked more promising than anything she'd seen in Arkham's old downtown in years, and she decided on the spot to get dinner there the day it opened.

The rest of the way, as she walked down the slope toward the Miskatonic River, held no similar surprises. A few cars grumbled down Peabody Avenue or veered from it in one direction or the other, a few other pedestrians walked by. Newspaper vending boxes offered the morning Arkham *Advertiser*, the headline on one side of the front page yelling about New York City's flooded subways—there'd been another bad storm, the second that year, and with sea level rising so fast a lot of coastal cities were having serious trouble that way; the headline on the other side said something cryptic and unsettling about the national debt and the stock market. Miriam frowned and kept walking.

Then her footsteps rang hollow on the Peabody Avenue Bridge as the green rippling Miskatonic rushed below. The street leapt over long-disused railroad tracks, passed west of Lovecraft Park—a bronze statue of the writer faced her from the middle of the grassy square, gazing off vaguely toward the Blasted Heath Reservoir while tentacles writhed around his feet and an eye on a stalk peered up at him from below—and finally came to the edge of the campus.

First, though, she had her respects to pay. The old Arkham Sanitarium building on Derby Street, practically abutting Orne Library and the Armitage Union Building, had been turned into the Lovecraft Museum many years ago. The museum had run into financial troubles and was open only two days a week, but the bronze statue in front of it—an image of Cthulhu rising from the deeps, with one mighty fist raised to clutch at nothing in particular—had acquired a reputation of its own. Since long before Miriam came to teach at Miskatonic, campus wags had made a habit of decorating the statue with an assortment of absurdities. This morning, the Great Old One sported a straw beach hat and brandished a can of cheap beer in its upraised fist.

That sort of thing had amused her for a good many years, but more recently, as her secret project unfolded and taught her more and more about the archaic traditions and forgotten lore behind H.P. Lovecraft's stories, it had begun to make her just a little uncomfortable. For the last three months or so, for reasons she'd gone out of her way not to analyze, she'd made it a habit to pass the statue on the way to her office and repeat a certain incantation used by the Great Old One's worshippers: silently if there were others around, out loud if she was alone.

That morning, no one else was anywhere in sight as she approached the statue. She glanced around, paused, and then addressed the statue in a low voice: "*Ph'nglui mglw'nafh Cthulhu R'lyeh wagh'nagl fhtagn.*"

If the devil-god heard her, he gave no sign of it, nor did she expect anything more. As she turned to go, though, something pale caught her eye, sitting on the pedestal of the statue in front of Cthulhu's great clawed feet. She went closer, to discover that someone had placed three perfect seashells and an old silver dime there, as though in offering.

A sudden urge pushed her to add something to the little heap there, but she had nothing suitable; nor, on reflection, was she willing to go quite that far. She pulled herself away from the statue, angled across the Lovecraft Museum parking lot, and hurried through the narrow walkway between Orne Library's Gothic spires and the comfortable brick surfaces of the Armitage Union. She had no shortage of things to do that day, she reminded herself, and the morning was passing.

NONE OF THE corridors of Wilmarth Hall ran straight. Some veered sharply from side to side, others swayed as though whoever it was that laid out the floorplan had been mildly drunk when he'd took pen in hand, and all of them had a shallow rippling pattern on the walls that always made Miriam feel as though she'd somehow gotten inside some huge creature's digestive tract. The corridor that led to her office from the stairway was one of the gently swaying kind. She walked to the seventh door, unlocked it, and went inside.

Outside the tall, slightly trapezoidal window at the room's far end, summer sunlight blazed on the green slopes of Meadow Hill and cast harsh shadows from the gray stark mass of the West Campus Parking Garage. Miriam glanced out briefly, then settled at her desk, got the computer booting, and sat back in her chair, enjoying a moment of silence.

She straightened up again after a minute or so, brought up her email program and started sorting through the morning's crop of messages. As chair of the History of Ideas department, she had no shortage of questions to answer and fires to put out. She was about halfway through when a knock sounded a familiar rhythm on the door—tap, tap-tap, tap-tap-tap. "Come in," she called out; the door opened, and her not-quite-graduate assistant Will Bishop came through it.

The History of Ideas department attracted odd students, she'd learned long since, and Will certainly qualified. His broad brow and narrow jaw made his face look uncannily like a goat's, an impression not at all hindered by the brown tuft of beard on the bottom of his chin or the woolly brown hair that tumbled back toward his shoulders. Even in the hottest weather, he wore baggy sweatshirts, loose slacks, and heavy laced boots; he put on old-fashioned half-moon glasses to read, and habitually carried his books in a canvas shopping bag—his shoulders had birth defects and wouldn't handle the pressure of a shoulderbag or a backpack, Jenny had mentioned. He was an acquaintance of hers, from the country up near Aylesbury in north central Massachusetts, though how the two of them happened to meet, Miriam had never learned.

"Good morning, Dr. Akeley," he said with his usual quick grin. "Checked the mail?"

"No," she admitted. "Was there any?"

"Not a thing. Denny's playing solitaire on her computer, it's that busy."

Miriam laughed; Denise Creed-Chalmers was the department secretary, and legendary in the History of Ideas department for finding something useful to do whenever she was in the office. "No surprises there," she said. "It's usually pretty quiet until summer session starts up." Then: "Have you got your summer plans settled?"

He nodded. "I heard back from my folks Saturday. I'll catch the bus back home for a couple of weeks in July, and then come right back to town. I've got some things I want to study." His voice still held onto the old Massachusetts accent; he pronounced "catch" as though it was "ketch" and "town" on his lips turned into "taown," but growing up in a rural backwater hadn't slowed him down intellectually in the least. He'd done two years at Aylesbury Community College with a 4.0 GPA, and was finishing up a bachelor's in history at Miskatonic with similar grades before starting an MA in history of ideas in the fall. Miriam had seen some of Will's research papers already, and knew she'd have the challenge of helping to train a considerable intellect: a pleasure, that, and one that teaching didn't always provide.

They discussed the week ahead, and Miriam's current research project—Will had already taken over from Jenny in that regard, doing much of the legwork of tracking down citations and hunting up promising source material that made a scholar's life less trying. His interests as a historian of ideas had begun to focus more and more intently on the early history of mathematics, rather than anything more relevant to the writers Miriam studied in public or the archaic lore she hunted down in private, so she'd taken risks with him she never would have taken with Jenny, sending him after scraps of information that barely even made a pretense of relevance to her official studies.

His latest project for her was no exception. She'd found a reference to an article on alchemy published in a 1919 amateur-press magazine, written by a youthful Rhode Island eccentric named Charles Dexter Ward. That was the link to Lovecraft—the horror writer had written a story about Ward after the young man's 1928 escape from the asylum where he'd been institutionalized—and Miriam hoped the connection might justify a paper for *Lovecraft Studies*, but that was far from the most important reason she wanted the article.

"Got it," Will said laconically, and handed her a large manila envelope from inside his canvas bag. It proved to contain six blurred but readable photocopies. "Nobody's put it online and I don't think it's even been microfilmed," he went on, "but the guy who published it lived in Bolton, and the Bolton Historical Society has most of the issues in a box in the basement. We might want to see about getting those scanned—there are some letters to the editor from Lovecraft, and a couple of poems of his, too."

"Good heavens," said Miriam. "That's definitely a find. Thank you." She scarcely noticed his response, because most of her attention was on the article. The literary scholar in her had already noted that Ward in 1919, while still a teenager, already had a good working grasp of the basic concepts of alchemy—that would be unwelcome news to the faction of scholars that insisted that Lovecraft had invented Ward's occult studies out of whole cloth—but there was something else in the article far more interesting to Miriam. It was an acknowledgment at the end, thanking Professor George Gammell Angell for the loan of several books.

Miriam caught herself, put the article back in the manila envelope before her attention to its details attracted questious she didn't want to answer. "Well, that's going to be article fodder," she said finally. "I'll have to check my notes at home before I can give you anything else to chase down, so you'll have to content yourself with—what's the latest hare you're chasing?"

That got her a laugh. "Medieval number symbolism," he said. "Fascinating, but kind of dry. Honestly, driving over to Bolton or wherever is a pleasant break."

They chatted a little more, and then Will said a cheery good-bye and headed off. Miriam watched him go, shook her head. He was definitely an odd duck even by the standards of the History of Ideas department, and campus rumor claimed even odder things about him—for example, that he was good at picking locks, and took weekend hikes to the stone circles atop the hills surrounding Arkham. We all have our oddities, she told herself, and allowed an edged smile as she considered the consequences if hers became public knowledge.

She went back to her email, got rid of a dozen pieces of

spam offering low-interest loans and penis-enlargement pills, read and then deleted four announcements for campus events that didn't concern her and one email about the university-wide faculty meeting the next day, and then opened the last message on the list: something from someone she'd never heard of named Andrew Weeden. He turned out to be a grad student at a New Jersey college she'd never heard of either, who was in Boston on other business and wanted to swing by the next day and discuss some Lovecraft stories that had turned out to be relevant to his research.

She tapped REPLY, typed in a quick polite response agreeing to the idea and letting him know when she'd be free, and sent the email. That done, she toyed with the thought of turning off the computer, leaving the semester's unfinished chores for an hour or two, and heading down to the campus pool to get in her twice-weekly swim a little earlier than usual, but shook her head, made herself tackle the next thing on her list.

FIVE O'CLOCK FOUND her descending the long stair that wandered down the middle of Wilmarth Hall, deep in conversation with another professor. "The question Jim's raised," she was saying, "is why things shifted when they did. It's not just that most eighteenth- and nineteenth-century horror literature was embarrassingly bad—"

"'Are they all horrid?'" her companion, Dr. Michael Peaslee, quoted, in a high-pitched English accent. "'Are you sure they are all horrid?'" He laughed, let his voice fall back to its normal baritone and New England accent. "And they were."

Miriam laughed too. "What was that from?"

"Jane Austen, *Northanger Abbey*. She heartily agreed with you, by the way."

Nobody who met Michael Peaslee had the least trouble

recognizing him on a second encounter. Dumpling-shaped and fussily dressed, with a pink face that flushed easily and an unmanageable mop of gray hair that danced around his face in the slightest breeze, he clumped around the Miskatonic campus in an apparent state of perpetual distraction. Miriam was one of the few who wasn't fooled by that latter; she'd seen far too often just how little Peaslee missed.

"But you were saying," he went on.

"All of it, except for a few outliers—some of Poe's better work comes to mind—was almost suffocatingly anthropocentric. You've got your mad monks and antiheroes, by turns Byronic and moronic; you've got your dead people draped in sheets, you've got your dead people with sharp teeth, you've got your living people who turn into critters with sharp teeth, you've got your artificial people bolted together from spare parts—always people. And then, plop, Maupassant's Horla comes slithering onto the scene in 1886, and for half a century after that most of the really good horror literature is about the utterly unhuman."

"As in H.P. Lovecraft," Peaslee said.

"Yes, but not only him. Arthur Machen, Algernon Blackwood, Randolph Carter, Clark Ashton Smith, Robert Blake, Robert E. Howard, Philip Hastane—those are just the big names. All of them, and quite a few others too, tossed aside the sort of anthropocentric folklore I mentioned and started digging raw material out of ancient and medieval sources like the *Necronomicon*, and the less human it was, the better. "

They reached the ground floor, headed for the door to the quad. "But here's the point at issue," said Miriam. "Those sources were tolerably well known by the middle of the eighteenth century. They weren't common, any more than they are today, but people had heard of them—some of the horrid books Jane Austen was talking about mention their titles, for example, to add to the shiver factor. And then in the 1880s, horror writers stopped using them as stage settings and started using them as raw material. Jim's raised a valid question: why that shift, why then?"

"I wonder if it had to do with dreams," Peaslee said.

She glanced at him as the double doors wheezed open. "In what sense?"

"The 1880s were when psychologists started paying close attention to dreams," he said. "These days we remember Freud and Jung, but they built on earlier research by van Eeden, Maury, and others. That earlier work caught the fancy of literary circles in Paris and Vienna, and got them exploring dream states, trance, hypnotism, drugs—it was the era of the Decadents, after all." The two of them started across the mostly empty quad. "And dreams are one of the places where the human mind most readily encounters the unhuman."

"I suppose that's true," she said. "And it would explain a data point I'm not sure you know—Lovecraft drew quite a bit of material for his stories from his dreams."

"Well, there you are," said Peaslee. "And once writers got a taste for the fantastic by way of the dream state, old mythologies and magic would have been obvious resources at the time—the Decadents were seriously into those, too."

"That makes sense," Miriam said. "I'll toss that to Jim and see what he thinks."

For a while they walked on in companionable silence. Finally, as they turned onto the walkway between Orne Library and the Armitage Union, Peaslee said, "Have you heard anything about the faculty meeting tomorrow?"

"Nothing worth mentioning," Miriam admitted. "Kate Ashley's heard a rumor that it's going to be another resource grab by Noology—but she admits it's just a rumor."

Peaslee glanced at her. "I wonder whose department's going to get eaten this time."

She winced and said, "Don't even think that too loudly."

He was right, though, and she knew it. For the past five years, every reorganization Miskatonic had gone through had handed more resources, more programs, and finally whole departments to what was now the Noology Department—and it didn't help that nobody anywhere seemed to be willing to give a straightforward answer to the question of exactly what noology was.

On the far side of the library they wished each other a good night. Peaslee turned and headed west along Derby Street toward the condominium he shared with his stockbroker husband Phil and a brace of Corgis. Miriam, smiling, watched him go, and then turned and passed the statue of Great Cthulhu on her way to the Peabody Avenue Bridge.

The Great Old One still sported his beer can and straw hat, but the collection of offerings at his feet had increased by two shells, another old silver dime, and a pale water-smoothed stone. Miriam glanced around to make sure no one was looking, and nodded respectfully to the statue, murmuring the traditional incantation under her breath before walking on.

She got home well before dark and went to check on her uninvited guest. The creature blinked awake as she turned on the kitchen light. She was nestled in her towel, curled around the plush Cthulhu doll, and looked startled for a moment and then let out what was clearly a friendly chirr. "I'm glad to see you too," Miriam said. "Let's get you some more milk."

The creature let out a worried sound when Miriam picked up the bowl and set it in the sink, chirred again with relief when a clean bowl and the milk carton put in a prompt appearance, and the little pink tongue lapped up milk with frantic haste again. "You really have had a rough life, haven't you?" she asked. The creature glanced up at her from the bowl, and Miriam said, "Don't worry. One way or another

I'll make sure you get taken good care of."

One way or another: the phrase circled in her mind, reminded her of bleak realities she didn't want to face just then. She shoved them away, took the carton back to the refrigerator.

Banana slices on a plate went next to the milk, and then Miriam turned to fixing her own dinner, a fish burrito—she'd learned the recipe from a housemate from Veracruz her junior year at UCLA, kept it ever since as one of the few relics left of her California girlhood. Rice, refried beans, and pieces of cooked fish came out of containers in the fridge and formed layers down the center of a big flour tortilla, a healthy splash of salsa picante joined them, fold and roll and tuck into the microwave: it was practically a ritual, and by the time the thing beeped at her she'd gotten a salad assembled and a glass of wine poured, and was ready to sit down at the kitchen table, with the antics of the little creature as an additional source of entertainment.

By the time she was finished with her meal, though, the creature had nestled down to sleep again. She considered the animal for a while, the uncomfortably human face, the pink hand clutching the Cthulhu doll, then got up, took care of the dishes, and put some music on—a Thelonious Monk CD, one of her favorites. As the jaunty opening notes of "Monk's Dream" rang out from the speakers, the old Governor Winthrop desk in the corner of the living room called silently to her, but she temporized, made herself sit down at the other desk, boot up the laptop, and try again to figure out the identity of her visitor. A website hosted by a west coast university offered a beginner's guide to animal taxonomy, and she started picking her way through the living creatures of the Earth.

Step one, she thought. It has fur, and two little nipples—that makes it a mammal.

Step two, it has opposable thumbs and forward-facing

eyes—that makes it a primate.

Step three...the trail abruptly went cold. It didn't have any of the features that would have defined it as an ape, an old world monkey, a new world monkey, a lemur, a tarsier, a loris, or any of the other odds and ends the primate order had to offer. Okay, she thought, maybe it's not a primate after all, and paged back to the checklist of mammals. None of the other mammalian orders she tried to trace took her any further, and attempting a process of elimination—not a whale, not a bat, not an ungulate—promptly landed her in absurdities. Miriam shook her head, laughed, and thought about calling somebody in Miskatonic's biology department.

The thought stirred something cold in the deep places of her mind. She wondered at that, then thought: for all I know it's illegal to bring one of them into this country, and heaven knows what the authorities would do to it. That must be it.

The cold awareness remained. After a moment she shut down the laptop, unlocked the Governor Winthrop desk, and turned on the old computer. The machine chattered and whirred awake, briefly matching the jazz tune playing just then, and she sat down and busied herself with her forbidden studies.

THREE

The Closing Door

The next morning she got to Wilmarth Hall early, visited the departmental office down on the first floor to talk to the secretary and make sure everything was set for the summer break, and found a welcome piece of mail waiting for her there: a manila envelope from Brown University with the latest quarterly issue of *Lovecraft Studies*. It was photocopied and staplebound these days, a far cry from the professionally printed journals of earlier decades, but even so its arrival was a pleasant surprise—she hadn't expected it for another week.

From there, though, the day headed downhill. Wilmarth Hall's notoriously cranky ventilation system wasn't working that day, and the air in her office made it feel like a swamp; Will Bishop had left a note for her, letting her know that he'd gotten a sudden call from a friend who needed help moving, and wouldn't be able to make it in until Wednesday; and her email, when her office computer brought it up, started off with the last message on Earth she wanted to deal with just then. She'd more than half expected it, but she still clenched her eyes shut and drew in a slow breath before reading it a second time.

FROM: Kingsport Oncology Associates, LLC
TO: Dr. Miriam Akeley
SUBJECT: Latest test results

Miriam, I'm very sorry to say this latest set of scans and lab work shows continued progression. I've posted the details on the patients area of our website. Please make an appointment to see me soonest if you'd like to discuss options. G

She gave the email a bleak look, hit REPLY and typed:

Gordon, thank you, but I made up my mind two years ago and see no reason to change plans now. M

She didn't like to be so terse. Dr. Gordon Krummholz was practically a personal friend; she'd been driving down to his office in Kingsport once a month or so for six years now, and she knew he genuinely cared about her condition. Still, the two rounds of chemotherapy she'd already been through had been so excruciating, and the co-pays had pushed her so close to bankruptcy, that she'd decided to let things take their course if the cancer returned. Now it was back, and that choice seemed even more sensible than it had when it was still in the realm of maybes, but of course Dr. Krummholz couldn't see it that way. It was just as well, she decided, that she hadn't burdened anyone else with the knowledge. She considered logging into the website and looking at the details, put that off for later.

The rest of the email was a pointless inconvenience to the electrons that had carried it, but she slogged through the stack, deleted most of it, filed the rest on the unlikely chance that it deserved another few minutes of her time. She'd just finished when an unfamiliar knock sounded on the door; she glanced up sharply, then remembered the appointment she'd

36

made with the grad student from New Jersey, and called out, "Please come in."

Andrew Weeden turned out to be a muscular young man with blond hair and a ready smile. "It's a pleasure to meet you, Dr. Akeley," he said, shaking her hand. "Thanks for being willing to meet on such short notice; I'm really out of my depth here."

She said something suitably polite, waved him to a chair. "So what can I help you with?"

"It's a bit complicated," he confessed. "My dissertation's on H.A. Wilcox—I'm not sure if you're at all familiar with him."

"If you mean the artist, very slightly."

He nodded. "That's the one—the leading spirit of the Providence Decadents in the '30s and '40s. One thing I'm trying to bring out in my research is the way he relied on dreams for a lot of his imagery, and one of the profs on my committee told me that Wilcox corresponded with H.P. Lovecraft, and—well, I read Lovecraft's dream stories, those led me to your book on *The Dream-Quest of Unknown Kadath*, and that's what clued me in that Lovecraft also lifted stuff from his own dreams. I've done some literature searches on that topic, but I was hoping you could point me toward some of the more useful pieces, and, well, away from the other kind."

That got a laugh from Miriam. "Fair enough. Yes, I'd be glad to help. Did you know that Lovecraft put Wilcox into one of his stories?" Weeden's blank look answered her. "You'll want to take notes," she said then. "There's a lot of ground to cover."

She spent the next fifteen minutes or so sketching out Lovecraft's use of dream material, while Weeden tapped frantically on a tablet. "So that's the rough version," she said. "Does that cover the ground you had in mind?"

"Most of it, thanks!" he said. "There are two other points,

though." She motioned for him to go on, and he said, "I also read a piece in *Journal of American Popular Literature* by someone who I think is a student of yours, Jenny Chaudronnier."

"Was," Miriam corrected him. "She just graduated a few days back."

"I'd still like to get in touch with her, if I could. She mentioned some sources and some ideas I'd like to follow up with her."

"I'm not sure where she is just at the moment." That wasn't true, of course, but she hardly knew Weeden well enough to hand over a friend's contact information just like that. "Send me your email and I'll let her know."

"Thanks—that'll be great," Weeden said, but Miriam noticed something that might have been a well-concealed flicker of annoyance in his eyes. "The other thing—well, it's kind of strange. Wilcox talked a lot in a couple of his journals about places where you could go into the dream world without falling asleep. One of those was supposed to be somewhere up around Arkham. Do you have any idea what he was talking about?"

"He'll have gotten that from Lovecraft," Miriam said. "One of the stories I mentioned, 'The Silver Key,' has that as a plot device."

Weeden nodded. "Is that something Lovecraft got from folklore? You mentioned in your book that he did a lot of that."

"He might have," she allowed, "but I don't recall ever seeing that in what I've read of his sources. You might want to talk to Connie Rice down at Princeton—she's really the go-to person when it comes to Lovecraft's sources these days."

"Okay, thanks," he said, and made a note in his tablet, but the thing that might have been annoyance flickered again in his expression. He asked a few more desultory questions, thanked her profusely, and made off.

By then the clock was showing quarter to ten, time to head for Morgan Hall for the faculty meeting. She left her office, all but walked into Michael Peaslee in the hall outside, headed down the stairs in his company and that of two English lit professors. By the time they got to Wilmarth Hall's front door, framed in a vaguely rugose archway that always made Miriam think of certain bodily orifices, they were part of a modest stream of Miskatonic faculty that flowed along the north side of the quad to the main entrance of Morgan Hall.

Bored and distracted, Miriam replied to Michael's amusing chatter as briefly as she could without impoliteness, wished that she had the option of leaving campus and going home. With the news from the oncologist weighing on her, she wanted to be alone—a desire that somehow managed to coexist comfortably with the memory of the curious little creature who waited in her apartment. That wasn't an option; as the chair of the History of Ideas department, she had to attend the administration's occasional dog and pony show, but she hoped it would be over quickly and she could hole up in her office and then hurry home and hide from the world.

The faculty meeting was in one of the big auditorium-sized rooms that usually held first year history classes. She and Michael settled into chairs about halfway back, watched the rest of the faculty file in and find seats. Miriam knew most of them by sight and name, and a good many were personal friends. After nearly everyone else had arrived, a patrician figure with white hair and a nose like a hawk's beak came in the side door and took a seat in the first row. Miriam recognized him instantly: Dr. Carl Upham, a respected medievalist and the current president of Miskatonic's faculty senate, who'd been on the interview committee when she'd been hired by Miskatonic and helped her career along more than once since then. His presence at the meeting was a source of obscure comfort to her.

Once everyone was seated, President Ward Phillips got up from a chair to the right of the stage, climbed the steps, crossed to the podium and gave the assembled faculty a perfunctory glance. He was tall and portly and gray-haired, with the kind of face Miriam associated with corporate vice-presidents and career politicians; the regents had hired him six years back from Brown University, where he'd been the dean of the College of Arts and Sciences, and everyone knew that he hoped to leave Miskatonic for the presidency of one of the bigger Ivy League universities just as soon as he could manage.

"Ladies and gentlemen," he said. "Thank you for coming. On a day this lovely, I won't keep you any longer than necessary, I promise." He unfolded a broad insincere smile. "As you know, ours is one of only three universities in the country with a program in noology, and the only one that's seen that program rise to the departmental level. That's one of the many things that makes Miskatonic special. I'm delighted to say that we're about to implement an initiative that will take Miskatonic the next step forward and make us unique among American universities. It really is—" He brought out the smile again. "Well, I'll let Dr. Noyes explain it, as his department has taken the lead in developing the plan. Clark?"

Noyes followed the same route President Phillips had taken, shook Phillips' hand, took his place at the podium. Miriam's eyes narrowed. She'd distrusted the man since she'd first met him almost a dozen years back, before the word "noology" had ever been uttered in Miskatonic's sprawling postwar halls, when he was an assistant professor of psychology just arrived from MIT. It wasn't just the smooth calculated blandness of his face, the clothing that made him look like someone had taken a generic Ivy League professor and filed off the serial numbers, or the skill with which he'd manipulated the vagaries of campus politics to his own benefit. There was

40

something cold about him, Miriam thought. It was almost—the thought was bizarre, but she'd never been able to shake it—as though there wasn't actually a human being inside the polished shell he presented to the world.

"THE MOST UNFORTUNATE thing in the world of today's scholarship," Noyes said, "is our inability to correlate the contents of our separate disciplines." He glanced around the lecture hall, and chuckled an odd, almost mechanical chuckle; his expression did not change at all as he made it. "Yes, I know. You've all heard that before, haven't you? But it's true. We live, if you'll excuse the metaphor, on a little island of dismal ignorance in the midst of splendid seas of possibility, and it is our destiny—" He leaned forward over the podium. "It is our destiny to travel far. Much farther, in fact, than we have yet gone as a species."

Miriam glanced at Michael, who rolled his eyes.

"The Noology department, as you know, is in the forefront of interdisciplinary studies not only here at Miskatonic but in the American academic field generally. Over the last two years, in consultation with leading experts in and beyond the academic community, we've drawn up plans for a program of coordinated studies that will transform Miskatonic University from a discordant mass of conflicting and competing agendas to a single body pursuing knowledge together—all of us working in harmony toward common goals."

He talked on, piling abstraction on top of abstraction in a tottering structure so elaborate that even Miriam, who had long since mastered the art of plucking a penny's worth of meaning out of a steaming heap of verbiage, had to struggle to keep from getting lost in the flow of words. A stray phrase—"a central office directing the research of the departments"—gave her bearings again, and from there she was able to piece together the implications of what Noyes was saying.

After maybe fifteen minutes, he finished his speech, and said, "I'd be happy to take questions now, if there are any."

Miriam managed to get to her feet before anyone else. "Dr. Akeley," Noyes said.

"Dr. Noyes." She paused momentarily to frame her words, went on. "Unless I'm very seriously mistaken, what you're saying is that under this scheme of yours, professors would no longer have the right to choose their own research topics, but would have to follow orders issued by this central office you mention. Is that correct?"

Noyes' face took on a pained look. "That's an extremely crude and, if I may say so, unfair way of phrasing things. Nobody is going to be 'following orders.' The central office will help each participant in the university community find some way that they can contribute to the mutual project of learning."

A dozen professors sprang to their feet, and Miriam, satisfied, sat down. "Dr. Summers," Noyes, said, nodding to one of them. Tall and mahogany-colored, her hair a torrent of slender braids, Dr. Gwendolyn Summers was one of Miskatonic's most prestigious scholars, internationally respected in her branch of world literature, and nobody's fool. "Dr. Noyes, I presume that participation in this scheme of yours would be voluntary."

"No, the assumption is that everyone would participate."

"And those who choose not to?"

The pained look returned to his face. "That's a purely theoretical question at this point, and I trust we'll all work together to keep it that way."

That got a sudden indrawn breath across the hall. "Dr. Noyes," Summers said, "I gather the tradition of academic freedom means nothing to you."

"I would like to think," Noyes said, "that a scholar of your distinction would recognize the need to get past such purely personal and, if I may say so, selfish concerns, and put the good of the university community first." His eyes all at once reminded Miriam of the eyes of a dead thing, blank and unseeing, opening onto emptiness. She shuddered, and looked away.

More questions followed, and more evasive answers, but Miriam had trouble keeping track of them. All at once she could see the entire pattern to which the proposal belonged, the logical endpoint of trends and fashions that had swept the academic world over the previous half century: the transformation of scholarly research into for-profit activities for the benefit of the university and its corporate sponsors, the gutting of salaries and benefits, the whittling away of academic freedom, and the rest of it. The grand old ideal of the university as a community of equals, in which scholars freely pursued knowledge wherever the quest took them, had been on the far side of a closing door all through that period. Now the door would close once and for all, and what remained would be a wretchedly up-to-date arrangement in which academic employees labored at sweatshop wages, turning out assigned bits of knowledge the way workers in a factory churned out salad shooters and three-pronged widgets. Progress, she thought. The word tasted bitter as ashes on her tongue.

Finally the questions petered out. "Any others?" Noyes said. "No? I look forward to working with all of you on this very promising new initiative."

The moment he finished speaking, a figure with a shock of white hair stood up in the front row: Dr. Carl Upham. He turned his back on the stage and said, "I'm calling a meeting of the faculty senate for Thursday afternoon, to consider this proposal."

Behind him, Noyes said, "Dr. Upham, I really don't think

that's necessary."

Upham glanced back over his shoulder with a faint conde-scending smile. "Your opinion, Dr. Noyes, has been noted." He turned back to the faculty. "You may expect an email in the next few hours with the details. I look forward to seeing you all there." He turned, and without another word crossed to the side door and left the lecture hall.

President Phillips took the podium then, and said some-thing about how important it was not to get bogged down in negativity in the face of progress, but Miriam was not listen-ing. We can fight this, she told herself, and then: I can fight this. The news she'd gotten from her oncologist that morning rose to her mind, and she nodded, thinking: what have I got to lose?

THE REST OF the day, though, dragged her back down into the leaden mood that had her in its claws before the faculty meeting. She got in most of an hour swimming laps in the Halsey Center pool, then had a pleasant lunch with Michael in the faculty club, but after that she'd had to head back to her office for an appointment with another professor. Once that was done with, she spent most of an hour looking up doc-uments on college governance, everything from the current Miskatonic policies and procedures manual to the act of the Massachusetts Assembly that chartered Miskatonic Liberal Academy back in 1765.

In the process, she reviewed the last ten years or so of amendments to the university's constitution and bylaws. Uni-versities were always tinkering with their groundrules, she'd heard that from professors all over the country, but most of the resulting changes were harmless, while the Miskatonic University amendments were anything but. Individually, they seemed innocuous enough, but taken together, they weakened the faculty senate's position in the governance of the university, made it much more difficult for professors to defend the terms of their contracts of hire, and handed far too much control over crucial aspects of the university system to the President and the Board of Regents. Clearly someone had been planning this latest proposal for quite some time, and Miriam thought she could put a name to that someone.

She considered her options, sent an email to the other professors of the History of Ideas Department calling a meeting on Thursday morning at ten to discuss options, sent another to Will to warn him, then paged through her campus directory—Miskatonic still issued that in a print version, though Miriam was one of the few people who used it—and found the email addresses of two of the Regents she'd met socially. To them she sent polite notes asking them to reconsider whatever support they might have given to Noyes' proposal. Phil Dyer of the geology department, who was in Greenland doing research that summer, got a longer email explaining what was going on; he was a personal friend, but the Miskatonic Greenland Project also had close connections with the Université de Vyones in France and several other overseas schools. Other emails to colleagues followed. Maybe, she thought, with enough pressure from the national and international scholarly organizations...

She was still typing emails when answers came back from the Regents. They could as well have been form letters; they insisted, in nearly identical language, that Noyes' proposal was an important step forward for Miskatonic, and they were sure that Miriam would find the new system entirely acceptable if she simply gave it a chance.

The second one, with its air of bland self-assurance, succeeded in making her shout "Damn it!" at the computer screen. Embarrassed at the outburst, she shelved the thought of writing a sulphurous answer, closed the email window, and tried to busy herself with the tasks that had to get done now that the semester was over. That seemed even more pointless than usual, but she made herself keep at them until six o' clock, when she pushed herself back from her desk and headed toward the door in a foul temper.

Outside, the air was only a little less stuffy than it had been in her office. She hurried across campus, paid silent respects to the Cthulhu statue—a very tall man in a black coat and broad hat in the Lovecraft Museum parking lot glanced toward her when she came out from between the library and the student union building, and that kept her from saying the ancient words aloud—and set out through Arkham's streets for home.

The long slope of Peabody Avenue seemed even more desolate than usual as she climbed it; abandoned buildings and cracked sidewalks made her think of what the ancient tomes said about the ruined cities of the elder world. A flicker of red light, though, caught her eye as she turned off Peabody Avenue onto College Street. It proved to be a little neon OPEN sign in the window of the Asian restaurant she'd discovered the morning before. The front door was open, the lights were on, and a young woman was perched behind the counter. Miriam hesitated, and then decided to go in. "Excuse me," she said. "Are you open for business?"

"Just barely," the young woman said with a grin. She had short brown hair and a round pleasant face. "What can I get you?"

"I'll have to decide," said Miriam, and looked up at the menu board. After a few moments: "I'd like chicken phad Thai, please."

"Coming right up. For here or to go?"

"To go."

The young woman relayed the order through a window into the kitchen. When she turned back to the counter, Miriam said, "This really is welcome. I live just a few blocks away from here, and the only other restaurants in town these days are down by the university."

"Oh, I know," said the young woman. "We just moved here from Buffalo—we have friends in the area—and we got a really good deal on the rent for this space."

"Welcome to Arkham," Miriam said.

"Thank you." A shy smile, then: "I should introduce myself, shouldn't I? I'm Patty Shray, and my husband Larry's in the kitchen."

A brown Asian face appeared in the little window, grinning. "Hi."

"Pleased to meet you. I'm Miriam Akeley."

"I hope you won't mind my asking," said Patty, "but are you a professor?"

That got an amused smile from Miriam. "Is it that obvious? Yes, I work at the university."

"Oh, it's not that," said Patty. "Larry's grandmother knows a lot of old traditions, and she said we should open this evening, and a woman with silver hair who's a scholar would come in first and bring good luck for the business."

Miriam blinked, and said, "I'm glad to hear it."

"And also good luck for you," Patty said then. "She said the woman would be going on a long journey soon, and could use some luck with it."

"Here you go," said Larry, handing out a plastic bag with styrofoam containers in it. "Since you're our very first customer, I've put in a little treat, no charge." Miriam thanked him, paid for the meal, took a paper menu from a stack by the cash register, and headed home.

Going on a long journey, she thought, smiling and shaking her head. No time soon. A moment later, though, the smile fell from her face, as she thought of a journey she was going to make soon, feet first. She made herself keep walking, and the evening deepened around her.

THE SUN WAS drowning in a haze of clouds over the hills west of Arkham when she got back to the apartment, feeling exhausted and depressed. Scents of garlic, peanut oil, and coconut rose with the steam from the bag in her hand, contending with the stale air of the old building, as she trudged up the stair to the third floor and fumbled with the key.

The sound of the opening door apparently woke the little creature, for a chirr of greeting came out of the kitchen a moment after Miriam got inside. After the day she'd just had, the friendliness in the creature's voice was more than welcome, and Miriam went to the kitchen, turned on the light, and said, "Thank you."

The creature slipped out from under the towel and sat up on her haunches, considering her and sniffing the air. After a moment, Miriam guessed at the reason. "Don't tell me you like Thai food," she said aloud, and then thought: why not? If it's some kind of relative of monkeys, well, monkeys eat meat, vegetables, and fruit, don't they?

The animal watched her with hopeful eyes as she set the bag of takeout on the kitchen table, got silverware from the drawer, poured herself a glass of white wine. Once Miriam sat down, she came tentatively over to the foot of the table and made a little querulous noise in herthroat.

"Yes, you can have some," Miriam said. She opened the bag, tore the top off the container of chicken phad Thai—there was plenty of it, enough for dinner and a decent lunch even after the creature got a bellyfull—and spooned a modest portion into the lid. Though she'd planned to set that on the floor, she thought better of it, and reached down with both hands. The creature didn't crouch in dismay this time. She took hold of Miriam's thumbs with her forepaws and two fingers with her hind paws, chirred as though to say she was ready, and let Miriam lift her and set her down across the table, in front of the meal.

"There you are," said Miriam. *"Bon appetit."*

The creature ate the same way she had eaten the banana, picking up bits of vegetable and chicken one at a time, giving them a close examination, and then nibbling away. The noodles didn't appeal to her, but she liked the sauce on them and licked them clean, and the peanuts seemed to be a special treat. The way she watched Miriam drink the wine reminded her of another need the creature doubtless had, and she got a teacup of water and laughed, watching the little pink tongue darting down and back. For her part, Miriam sampled the phad Thai and then tucked into it with enthusiasm; it was remarkably good, as good as anything she'd had at the best Thai restaurants in Boston.

The treat they'd given her turned out to be mango slices in a sweet coconut sauce. Once again she tore off the lid, spooned a portion into it, and set that in front of the creature, who sniffed at it. The tiny face took on a dazed look; the creature let out a little wavering chirr, picked up a mango slice in both front paws and began to eat, and her eyes drifted shut in delight. Watching her, Miriam laughed again, and then sat back, considering her guest. She hadn't owned a pet in years, not since her second marriage fell apart and the question of who was going to get their two cats very nearly turned into a full-blown custody battle. She'd come to her senses and walked away from that fight, as she'd done from so many others, but at first the thought of getting another pet was too painful; more recently, she was out of the habit, and lately there was the cancer to take into account. If no one came forward to claim the little creature, though—

"I should give you a name," she said. The creature blinked out of her trance of mango-fueled enjoyment, looked up at her expectantly. "Amber," she said then, thinking of the red-gold highlights of her fur. "I'll call you Amber. I hope you don't mind."

The creature chirred at her, waited a moment longer, and then returned to her feast.

They finished their meals at very nearly the same moment. Miriam lowered Amber to the floor, watched the creature blink and make a slightly unsteady path back to the towel, where she curled up around the Cthulhu doll, pulled a fold of towel over herself, and nestled down to sleep. She watched Amber for a while, then got up, cleared away the remains of the meal, refilled her wine glass and left the kitchen. She's a charming little thing, she told herself then, but I have work to do.

The air inside the room was hot, but she knew better than to think that the night air outside was any cooler. She changed into a sleep shirt, got another CD playing—this time it was *Time Out* by the Dave Brubeck Quartet, another old favorite—and settled down on the couch to drink the wine and read the latest issue of *Lovecraft Studies*. Under other circumstances, that would have been a pleasure; among other things, there was a piece on Schopenhauer's influence on Lovecraft by Jim Willett at Brown University, the second part of a study of themes from Arthurian legend in Lovecraft's fiction by Connie Rice at Princeton, and Jenny Chaudronnier's essay on the legends of the drowned land of Poseidonis, the last part of Atlantis to stay above water. They'd both sweated blood over that paper, finding references for every assertion in modern sources—you didn't even mention the old dark sorcerous tomes in your bibliography, not if you wanted your paper to see print. Getting that paper accepted by the premier journal in their little corner of literary studies felt like a triumph, and not just for Jenny.

After the day just past, though, even Jim Willett's crisp prose failed to hold her attention. Here we sit, she thought moodily, spinning our little cobwebs in our little corners like so many spiders, and all the while the clouds are piling up and the wind's rising. Does it actually matter to anyone that Jim's found Schopenhauer's fingerprints all over Lovecraft's "The Silver Key"?

She knew the answer. To a few scholars, certainly; to some of Lovecraft's readers, maybe; to those who had money and political influence, not at all, and even less to whatever it was that she'd seen in Clark Noyes' eyes.

Just then she felt a tiny hand pull at the hem of her sleep shirt.

She glanced down, startled. Amber stood there, stretching up toward her; Miriam guessed that she was still too weak to jump up onto the couch. The little creature had an odd solemn look on her face.

"Sure," said Miriam, reached down, and helped it up.

She thought the creature would settle onto her lap like a cat, but Amber clearly had other ideas. She clambered up Miriam's left arm and nestled between her upper arm and her breast, holding onto the arm with all four paws and tail. Fingers stroking down the creature's spine got an affectionate chirr in response.

Miriam picked up the issue of *Lovecraft Studies*, then, and tried to make herself read. Amber gave her another long solemn look, and then let out a different sound, a soft throaty churr.

All at once Miriam found herself dozing off. She blinked, tried to clear her mind, but the churring sound scattered her thoughts to the winds. A moment later her eyes drifted shut and she sank into deep dreamless sleep.

When she woke up, the clock on the wall told her she'd slept for nearly three hours. Amber was still nestled on her arm. Only half awake, she got up from the couch and went into the kitchen with Amber still clinging to her arm, stroked the little creature awake and tried to put her back down onto its towel. Amber responded with a doleful little chirr of protest, though, and Miriam relented. She picked up the towel and the Cthulhu doll, took them into her bedroom, and set them on the foot of the bed.

That was apparently good enough, and the little creature settled down onto the towel. Miriam considered her for a moment, then used the bathroom, climbed into bed, and sank into sleep deeper and more refreshing than she'd known in years.

FOUR

The Statement of Randolph Carter

T hat's appalling," said Will Bishop.

"I won't argue," Miriam replied. They were in her office, and she'd just finished filling him in on the faculty meeting from the day before.

"I hope the faculty has the guts to tell Phillips where he can put his plan."

Miriam gave him a bleak look. "There's still a chance that'll happen, but not as big of a chance as I'd hoped for."

She'd come into her office most of an hour late that morning, having slept through her alarm and dashed through a semblance of her morning routine, and found a flurry of emails waiting for her. One was from Phil Dyer in Greenland, and contained a sulphurous paragraph about the news from Miskatonic and two more pleasant ones about the doings of the expedition and two mutual friends who were with it.

The others were from other Miskatonic professors. Half a dozen of them were trying to organize opposition to the new plan, and she sent them encouraging emails offering her support, but there were discordant notes. Programs that had spent years struggling for funding had been promised lavish new grants in exchange for their cooperation, restored funding for graduate assistantships was being mentioned here and there, generous retirement packages were being discussed for professors near the end of their career who didn't care to make the transition to the new arrangements, and hints were about that those who threw their support to the new plan early on would be first in line for these things, while those who opposed it would get nothing at all.

She explained this to Will, and his frown deepened. "They seem to have quite a bit of money. I wonder where it all comes from."

"That's a good question," said Miriam. "Maybe somebody should try to follow the money and see if that turns up anything. In the meantime, we'll just have to see what we can do."

"Have you considered going to a different university?"

The question brought her up sharply. How could she answer it honestly? If the cancer hadn't come back, that would be an option; she could probably get herself a job at Brown University with a few phone calls, and a talk she'd had with Emmeline Grenier one clear summer day in France had made it clear that the Université de Vyones could readily find a place for an American scholar who was fluent in French and knew her way around popular horror literature in both languages. As it was, though, how could she take any such offer when she might not live long enough to make it worth a new university's while?

"We'll see," she temporized. "Priority number one is keeping this one out of Clark Noyes' grubby hands."

Will laughed. "That's the spirit," he said, and didn't object when she changed the subject, asked him about his studies, and shook her head in amazement on hearing that, having gotten a solid reading knowledge of ancient Greek, he was about to tackle Egyptian hieroglyphics.

"It's essential," he said. "How else am I going to read the Rhind Papyrus, or any of the other primary sources on Egyptian mathematics?"

"There are translations," Miriam pointed out.

"Yes, but you know how much gets lost in translation, especially when it's from one language family to another. I figure I can get a working knowledge of Middle Egyptian by the time I finish my masters, take on the Mesopotamian languages while I work on my doctorate, and then go on to the really old stuff like Lomarian after I get a teaching gig."

"Better you than me," she said, laughing, and sorted through the papers on her desk until she found the one she needed, another odd question that might lead nowhere and might turn up something. This time it was a phrase in an unknown language, *Dumu-ne Zalaga*, which she'd found referenced once, underlined but without explanation, in one of Angell's manuscripts.

"If you have the chance, see what you can find on this. Can you come by Friday? Tomorrow's the faculty senate meeting, and I probably won't have a free minute all day." He agreed cheerfully, and after a few more friendly words headed out the door.

She shook her head again when he was gone, and the smile drained from her face. It was a good thing, she decided, that he'd never know how much time she'd put into learning the Aklo language quoted at such length in the *Necronomicon*. How could she face any of the scholars she knew if they found out she'd begun to take the ancient lore seriously?

She pushed those thoughts aside. She had emails to send, and the remarks she intended to make to the faculty senate needed drafting as well. Before she started on those tasks, though, she went to the Kingsport Oncology website, clicked on the patients' area, entered her email and password. Most of a minute passed while files loaded, and then she clicked through to the first of the scans and looked at the thing that was growing in her belly.

Dr. Krummholz hadn't exaggerated. The primary tumor was significantly larger than it had been three months back, large enough to push organs to either side and fill the gap it had opened between them. Here and there she could see the lumpy growths of secondary tumors where the cancer had metastasized. She stared at the image for a long moment, clicked to the next, and then to the ones that followed.

Finally, she made herself go to the prognosis. Much of it was written in medical jargon, and even after the years she'd spent dealing with her illness, a good many of the terms still meant nothing to her. Still, enough of it was in plain English that she had no trouble catching the meaning. *Without treatment*, Gordon had written, *hospice care will be required in three to four months, with another two to three months after that before end stage organ failure.*

Six months, maybe, she told herself. Fair enough. She signed out of the website, and busied herself with emails and paperwork until it was time to head to the faculty club for lunch.

AFTER LUNCH SHE had nothing on her schedule until four, when a committee meeting was scheduled. The last place she wanted to go was her office, and she decided instead to go to the restricted collections in the basement of Orne Library and try to chase down a few more scraps of data for her secret research. That was risky—old Abelard Whipple, the restricted collections librarian, knew the old tomes better than anyone else alive, and would be more likely to guess what she was doing than any of her other colleagues—but the news she'd gotten about the cancer left her more willing to take risks than she'd been. Though she knew perfectly well she'd likely die before solving any of the puzzles the old lore set her, they gave her something to think about other than her health and the fate of Miskatonic University, and that was enough.

"Ah, yes, Miriam," said Whipple once she'd buzzed at the intercom and announced herself. "Come in, come in." The door opened, letting her into a bare concrete room lined with gray steel shelves, lit from above by the harsh glare of long fluorescent tubes. Whipple's desk was strewn as always with sheets of paper covered with enigmatic scrawls; they had nothing to do with his published research, which mostly had to do with the proper curation of manuscripts written on unusual forms of parchment—squid skin, reptile leather, and stranger things still—in which he had a worldwide reputation. What else he might be studying, Whipple had never mentioned to her, and she'd never found the courage to ask.

The old man made sure the door was locked behind her, gave her a quizzical look with his improbably bright blue eyes, and then went back to his desk and buried himself in his work. She pulled down a volume from the shelves, settled in a chair at one of the two steel tables, and busied herself taking notes. The volume was a bound photocopy of Ludvig Prinn's *De Vermis Mysteriis*; Miskatonic had originally had its own copy of that strange tome, but that had vanished five and a half years ago, one of many things—and people—that went missing one foggy night when fire gutted the noology program's original quarters in Belbury Hall.

An hour later, having noted down an assortment of curious details about Cthulhu and the other Great Old Ones, she thanked Whipple and left the basement room to chase down lore on a different topic. An elevator took her to the top floor of the library, where books on the sciences filled row after row of long gray shelves beneath high vaults and ogive arches copied from the Gothic cathedrals of nine hundred years past. That part of the library wasn't familiar to her, so it took her a while to find the books on zoology, and more time to find the shelf where books on primates had their home.

Like so many university libraries, Orne Library had fallen into the fashionable bad habit of purging old books from its collection, and had too many volumes that had been dumbed down to current standards and too few that maintained the scholarly rigor of an earlier era. Even so, Miriam was able to find books detailed enough to be worth her time. *Singes Inconnus et Peu Connus d'Afrique*, a hefty tome by Jules Verhaeren, looked promising, and so did *Primates of the World* by Ellery W. Dexter. She tucked them under her arm, paused, and then added two more, a 1926 Miskatonic doctoral dissertation by one Matthew P. Lake titled *The Fossil Primates of North America*, and a recent book full of glossy photographs, just in case something had been discovered since Dexter's time. With that, she went to the south wall, where scarred oak tables stood beneath stained glass windows depicting the seven liberal arts, and settled into a chair.

The book by Verhaeren offered her no help—most of it was devoted to the author's theory that an unknown species of humanlike apes or apelike humans had survived in the Congo into historic times—and Dexter's book and the recent survey mostly confirmed her sense that Amber's species had somehow managed to escape the notice of primatologists. The dissertation by Lake was another matter. It traced the evolution of the primates from tiny shrewlike creatures that lived in the age of the dinosaurs, through now-rare creatures called prosimians, to monkeys, apes, and humankind. Lake was an excellent writer as well as a thoroughly knowledgeable biologist, and Miriam found herself wondering why she'd never seen anything else from his pen.

Most of the primates' evolutionary journey, Lake explained, had taken place in the Old World, but a branch of the prosimian line had crossed to the Americas on some long-drowned land bridge, and from that branch the New World monkeys or Platyrrhini were descended. Only scattered fossils, woefully incomplete, remained of the New World prosimians, and most of those seemed to be relatives of Old World lemurs, but from the remainder it was possible to guess at the probable appearance of the distant ancestors of the marmoset and the capuchin monkey.

Miriam turned the page and considered the carefully rendered ink drawing of a New World prosimian perched on a branch. It was not Amber or any member of her species, but a relative of hers? Of that she had no doubt. The vaguely ratlike body, the four delicate paws with opposable thumbs, the long prehensile tail, the monkeylike face with its large forward-facing eyes: the family resemblance was unmistakable. The one question remaining was how a prosimian from the late Miocene had turned up in an Arkham apartment building without leaving any trace of its existence through the intervening years. She shook her head, kept reading until her phone beeped at her and warned her it was time to head back to Wilmarth Hall.

The committee meeting was two hours of pointless boredom, and she was glad when it was over and she could leave the campus behind. As she walked south on Peabody Avenue past Lovecraft Park under thickening gray clouds, a curious silence gripped the old town. She tried to tell herself that it was just the time of year, the gap between the spring semester and the first summer session when one set of students was already gone and the summer-school set had not yet arrived, but it felt as though it went well beyond that. The old gambrel roofs crouched in the stifling air like beasts ready to spring.

She made two detours on the way home. The first was on the university side of the river, where she'd rented a post office box in a shipping-company storefront in the name of an elderly and nonexistent relative—one of Michael Peaslee's friends, an elderly drag queen who did a very convincing batty old lady, had helped her with that. There she sent and received mail concerning her secret studies, using the name of the nonexistent relative as cover—an extreme measure, maybe, but she wasn't willing to take risks. Weeks at a time would pass with nothing in the box but junk mail, but this time she was in luck. The box contained a big manila envelope from a correspondent in Weymouth, which might answer certain crucial questions. She left, feeling a little less battered than before.

She crossed the river, climbed the slope beyond past mostly empty buildings. On the way, a sudden thought struck her; she glanced up at the clouds, guessed that the rain would hold off a little longer, and made the second detour, veering over to the corner of Pickman and Parsonage Streets. There, she recalled, Keziah Mason's house—the witch-house of Arkham legend—once loomed up black over the surrounding buildings. It was long gone, of course, demolished in 1931 to make room for a garage and gas station, which had been pulled down in its turn and replaced by a fast-food restaurant in 1979.

The chain had gone bankrupt five years back, and what was left of the premises squatted windowless and dark on the corner, with a dumpster in its parking lot serving the bar next door. Miriam stood there looking at the building for a long moment, thinking: the prosimians might have left one trace, then. From prehistoric times to 1692, and then from 1692 to last Saturday: maybe. Just maybe.

Amber chirred a greeting when Miriam let herself into the apartment, and waited patiently while Miriam shed her black dress and slipped into a tee shirt and shorts. Miriam reached down, then, and the little creature took hold of her left arm and climbed up it onto Miriam's shoulder, where she chirred again and rubbed her face against Miriam's cheek.

Miriam laughed, and reached up to stroke the little head next to hers. "For a missing link, you seem to be doing pretty well," she said.

LATER ON, AFTER she and Amber had dined on sesame chicken, and the first drops of rain spattered against the windows, she changed into a sleep shirt, poured herself a glass of wine, got an Ethel Waters CD playing, sat down on the creaky couch and opened the package from the post office box. Within was half an inch of assorted paper, with a letter on top written on lined paper in a hand that wavered with age:

My dear Mrs. Corey,

Many thanks for your letter of the 7th last. You're quite correct that the Randolph Carter whose letter your cousin found was a relative of mine, though not any sort of ancestor. He never had children; as we used to say in my somewhat more innocent day, he wasn't the marrying kind.

That last phrase evoked a snort of laughter. She'd already suspected, from the details she'd been able to gather of Carter's biography, that he was gay. It wasn't just that he showed zero interest in romantic relationships with women in his life or his fiction, either; there were the very close relationships he'd had with an assortment of other, similarly unattached men, and the five years he'd lived with an older man named Harley Warren on what even an innocent like Lovecraft described as intimate terms. She filed away the detail for future reference.

The soft padding of delicate paws broke into her thoughts as Amber came into the room. This time the little creature managed to climb up on the couch by herself, picked her way up onto Miriam's shoulder, considered the papers spread out on the lap below, and then sensibly nestled down and went to sleep. Miriam gave her an affectionate look and kept reading.

> I do have a few papers of his, and a few other things relating to him, which I hope may be of help to you in your genealogical researches. I've taken the liberty of sending copies, as my neighbor Eddie Muñoz has scanned nearly all my old papers and taught me how to use the computer and printer. He really is a very dear young man.
>
> Please let me know if there's anything else I can do for you, and if your health ever allows you to travel as far as Weymouth, please don't hesitate to drop by for coffee and conversation.
>
> Yours sincerely,

Beneath that was an inky scrawl Miriam deciphered, with some difficulty, as the signature of Mabel Aspinwall: an elderly widow in a small Massachusetts town, who was apparently the last living relative of one of the most enigmatic figures in Lovecraft's circle. Randolph Carter had been a cousin of Lovecraft's, seventeen years older, and an important author of weird stories himself; the two of them had written reams of letters to each other, beginning when Lovecraft first started writing stories as a child, and ending with Carter's disappearance in 1926.

Few of the letters survived, to the dismay of Lovecraft scholars, for Carter was one of the members of Lovecraft's circle who also appeared in his fiction. The hero of "The Statement of Randolph Carter," "The Silver Key," and above all *The Dream-Quest of Unknown Kadath*, he was a constant frustration to Lovecraft's biographers, because so little was known about him. Even basic biographical details remained an open question. Now, though...

She set the letter aside, paged through the sheets of paper

underneath. The first fifteen pages were standard genealogical forms in which Randolph Carter appeared here and there, a lone branch on a thinning tree. After that came a certificate in French signed by a constellation of dignitaries, commending him for his service in the French Foreign Legion during the First World War, and a 1919 interview in a Boston newspaper about his wartime experiences, with a blurry photo of the man—a lean harsh face, clean-shaven, framed in dark hair, and looking at the camera as though he meant to ask it some momentous question.

Next was his will, an elaborate document handing out bequests to more than three dozen relatives and an assortment of charitable causes; she glanced through it looking for Lovecraft's name, and duly found it—the younger man had been left a modest sum of money, an assortment of books from Carter's library on sorcery and ancient myth, and a dozen of Randolph's journals.

That left one sheet of paper. That was a copy of a letter written in a crisp forceful hand:

29 April 1926
Boston, Mass.

My dear Lizzie,

Should you read these words, I regret to say that we will not see each other again in this world. Do not think, though, whatever nonsense the family may happen to say, that anything amiss has happened to me. To my very great surprise, I have discovered a possible means of regaining entry to a certain realm we once knew well:
the hidden door
That opens onto unfamiliar places,
as poor Justin put it.
I intend to put that means to the test shortly. If all goes as I hope, I will acquaint you with my discovery upon my return; but I am as yet uncertain if return will be possible. Thus this letter, which Parks has been told to mail if I have

not come home by Tuesday next.

    If you should relearn the trick, look for me in Ilek-Vad.

In any case, I hope you will always remember me as,

    Your very dear cousin,

      R.

Miriam read through the letter twice, frowning. Five and a half years ago she would have dismissed it as a prank, but she'd learned too much since then for that easy evasion to have any appeal left. Plenty of questions circled through her mind, and for a moment she considered opening the Governor Winthrop desk and searching through her surreptitiously scanned copies of the old tomes she'd gathered, but decided against it. Instead, temporizing, she stared at the bit of verse the letter quoted and tried to remember where she'd encountered it before.

The first name Carter mentioned gave her the clue she needed, and she got up as gently as she could, hoping not to wake Amber. The creature clutched a little harder with her paws, but that was all, and Miriam went to the shelf where she kept her Lovecraftian literature and pulled out a slender volume in a well-aged dust jacket—a well-worn second edition of *The People of the Monolith* by the early twentieth-century American poet Justin Geoffrey. It took her only a few minutes to find the entire poem:

THE DOOR OF DREAMS
Down through the years, the memory remains:
An autumn evening in my childhood room.
Familiar shadows fade to deeper gloom;
The rain drums hard upon the windowpanes.
Sleep comes, and I approach the hidden door
That opens onto unfamiliar places
Across a tapestry of times and spaces
I crossed and recrossed a thousand nights before.

The rolling hills of timeless Ooth-Nargai;
The thousand gilded spires of ancient Thran;
The jasper terraces of fair Kiran—
In dream-sent journeys I had passed them by
In wanderings by land and argosies
Across the rolling oceans of the night
To ruined temples in the moon's pale light
Where once arose forgotten litanies.
But on that autumn night of drumming rain,
The hidden door of dreams, by some decree
Of gods unknown or known, was closed to me,
And never has it opened up again.

It was not, she judged, one of Geoffrey's best poems, but it had seen more critical discussion than most. Most of the debate focused on a pretty little puzzle of who had influenced whom. *The People of the Monolith* had been published in 1926, Lovecraft had mentioned Ooth-Nargai in a story that saw print in 1922, but the other two place-names were in a piece of Lovecraft's that didn't get into print until 1943, long after both men were dead. Did Geoffrey borrow Ooth-Nargai from Lovecraft's tale, and Lovecraft return the favor by borrowing Thran and Kiran? Or had they both borrowed from some older source scholars hadn't found yet?

Either way, the point Carter had meant to make by quoting it was clear enough. She put the volume of poems back where it belonged, paused briefly, and then crossed the room to her shelf of Lovecraft stories, pulled down every volume that had something to say about the realm the old lore called the Dreamlands, and returned with them to the couch.

AT QUARTER TO midnight, she finished her reading, more puzzled than when she started. Amber was still perched on her shoulder, her paws holding tight to the sleep shirt and her tail wrapped around Miriam's arm; twice she'd woken, made a little soft chirr, and then gone back to sleep. The presence of the little creature reminded her of the hard core of reality that seemed to underlie a great deal of Lovecraft's fiction, and of course that was the problem.

If the letter wasn't a mere hoax, the conclusion of Lovecraft's story "The Silver Key" had not just been the product of a horror writer's imagination. Most Lovecraft scholars assumed that he'd simply come up with a colorful story in response to his cousin's disappearance in 1926, and put that into a story the way he'd woven together fact and fiction in so much else. The letter implied, though, that Randolph had actually intended to do what Lovecraft said he'd done—

And passed bodily into the Dreamlands.

The idea seemed preposterous. The broader idea into which it fit, the notion that there was some kind of objectively real plane of being that some human beings could visit in dreams, and a few could dwell in permanently—a place where myths and legends were plain facts, where cats jumped to the Moon and gods and goddesses mingled with human beings—seemed more preposterous still. Unquestionably, though, the old blasphemous tomes that Lovecraft had studied so avidly, the *Necronomicon* and the *De Vermis Mysteriis* and the *Unaussprechlichen Kulten* of that fearsome and fascinating madman von Junzt, devoted many pages to the subject. For that matter, the grad student from New Jersey who'd dropped in the day before—what had his name been?—said he'd found references to the same thing in the journals of that Providence artist he was studying. She made a mental note to have Will Bishop look into the Wilcox archives as time allowed.

The clock on the wall reminded her that she had important things to do in the morning. She spent a few minutes putting the books away before waking Amber and getting ready for bed. The two of them took turns using the bathroom—for all the world like roommates, Miriam thought, amused—and then went to the bedroom.

As they passed through the door, on the stroke of midnight, something changed in the air, or maybe in the night outside. It was subtle at first, an odd sense of wrongness Miriam couldn't place, but it didn't stay subtle for long. A cold, bleak mood gripped her with increasing force, reminded her of unpleasant memories she hadn't thought about in years. She tried to shake it off as she got Amber settled on her towel at the foot of the bed, turned down the covers and climbed in, but it brushed aside her efforts.

Turning off the light made it worse. Waves of fear and wretchedness seemed to roll toward her out of the darkness, dredging up old miseries and frustrations from every corner of her past and flinging them at her, scattering any hope of sleep to the winds. She lay there in the darkness for what felt like half of forever, trying to push the unwanted thoughts away without the least success. Every noise, from the low rumble of cars on nearby streets to the soft patter of rain on the window, jolted her nerves.

Then another sound joined them—a low, plaintive call from the foot of the bed. She nearly panicked, and then remembered that Amber was sleeping there.

Or, more precisely, not sleeping. Paws pressed down on her as the creature clambered up to her shoulder. Each momentary pressure sent sudden frantic thoughts scurrying through her mind: it's going to bite me, it has some kind of disease, it really is a rat after all—

Then, breaking through the rising spiral of panic: why am I thinking these things?

A moment later Amber was on her shoulder, and made another of the low plaintive calls, for all the world as though asking what was wrong. "I don't know," Miriam said, too upset to do anything but answer. "I can't sleep, and I can't stop thinking."

Amber chirred reassuringly, nestled in the hollow of her shoulder, and then began making the soft throaty churr that had scattered Miriam's thoughts and put her to sleep the night before. The effect this time was even more drastic. The fear and the wretchedness disappeared as though they'd never been, the tormenting thoughts went silent, and sleep washed over her so suddenly that her attempt to say "Thank you" produced only a faint mumble.

Later, toward morning, she dreamed. She was sitting on a gray plain that swept away to the horizon. Behind her rose somber mountains of gray stone half mantled in curious brown mosses, and topped here and there with low white sheets of ice. The wind blew cold, and ahead of her, low in the sky, a mottled-blue sphere a dozen times vaster than the full Moon hovered, half of it brightly lit by the sun, the other half in shadow. It looked like the Earth from space, but none of the continents belonged to the Earth she knew.

She sipped water from a little jade cup, and noticed in passing—it seemed the most natural thing in the world—that she wore sandals, a sleeveless dress of vaguely ancient Greek cut, a diadem and bracelets set with many jewels.

"There's war in my kingdom," she was saying.

"Tell me," the other replied.

Tall and lean, he wore traveler's gear: a brown leather jerkin set with bronze studs over a loose white shirt, baggy pantaloons of dark green wool, high soft boots equally suited to walking and riding. A broad-brimmed hat with a many-colored feather stuck in the band sat on the stone beside him, next to his satchel, blanket roll, and sheathed sword. Black hair framed the harsh angles of his face, grey eyes considered her.

"The enemy's already inside the gates," she said, "and

there's treachery at work. Will you advise me? I'd be grateful for it."

"Gladly," he said, and refilled her cup and then his from a water-skin. "You've readied your forces to defend the city against them, I suppose."

"Of course."

"A waste of whatever time and resources you've got. They'll already know where your strong points are and where you're likely to make a stand, and if you wait for them to move, they'll simply concentrate their forces there and over-whelm you. No, you must attack at once. Look for their vulnerabilities and strike them hard. You can't win a war by re-acting, you know—you have to seize the initiative and keep it. Surprise them, hammer them, harry them, keep after them until you hound the last of them out through the gates. Do you understand?"

"Yes," she said. "Yes, I think so."

Then she blinked awake.

She was lying in bed in her apartment in Arkham, of course, with Amber still nestled against her shoulder, sound asleep. Through gaps in the curtains, sunlight slanted down onto the scarred hardwood floor, glowed on the lurid green fabric of the little stuffed Cthulhu doll at the foot of the bed. The wretched mood of the night before was gone as though it had never been.

The dream remained in her mind, vivid as the sunlight, and before she had quite finished waking up she knew exactly what it was trying to tell her.

She glanced at the clock—it was just past seven in the morning, well before she needed to get up—and then let her head settle back against the pillow, her mind racing. Look for their vulnerabilities, their weak points, the figure in her dream had said. It was good advice, and she decided then and there to follow it, even if it came from—

All at once Miriam started laughing. Amber blinked awake, and after a moment, chirred amiably at her. She sat up, still laughing, and helped the little creature down to the floor, then sat for a moment, shaking her head in amusement. After staying up late reading Mabel Aspinwall's packet and then Lovecraft's stories, it was no wonder that she'd dreamed about Randolph Carter.

FIVE

The Nine Great Elms

President Upham," Miriam said.

"Dr. Akeley." Carl Upham nodded once from the podium. "You have the floor."

All around her the faculty senate of Miskatonic University sat listening: close to three hundred men and women dedicated, at least in theory, to the life of the mind and the cause of higher education. Some genuine scholars, Miriam thought, some careerists who'd chosen the academic life as a less strenuous alternative to a corporate or government position, some duffers who'd drifted into a professorship by way of personal connections or a big family donation to the Endowment Fund—and then there were the professors of the Noology Department, who all had the same bland smiling look as Clark Noyes and the same emptiness behind it, and whose publications were couched in an argot so opaque, even by academic standards, that Miriam had come to believe that it was deliberately meant to conceal something.

"Thank you," she said to Upham, and then: "I'd like to start by bringing up what may seem like a minor point. Dr. Noyes and the other supporters of this plan have said over

71

and over again that it's a great step forward for Miskatonic. Forward." She let the word hang in the air for a moment. "Forward in what sense? By what measure? Toward what destination? We haven't been told. I think most of us have seen that sort of vague buzzword in undergraduate papers, and when one shows up, it's normally a good sign that the case the student is trying to make won't stand on its own merits. I suggest that the same is true here."

Sure of her course in the wake of the dream, she'd discarded her previous drafts and outlined a response in a few minutes on a piece of scrap paper. She'd reviewed it again before leaving for campus, and spent the walk turning the outline into the words she wanted to say. It wasn't a characteristic speech for her; she usually took a moderate position and tried to find common ground among all the various points of view; but the dream-Randolph Carter was right. This time, she meant to take the Noology Department by surprise, and harry them right out the gates of Miskatonic University if she could.

"The word 'new' is another one that's been bandied about quite a bit by proponents of this plan. I beg to differ; there's nothing new about subjecting professors to an arrangement that assigns them research projects for someone else's benefit." Clark Noyes, two rows and a dozen seats away, made a movement as though to protest, and she glanced back over her shoulder at him. "Excuse me—as you said, they would be 'helped' to find research projects for someone else's benefit." She turned her back on him. "Most fields of study have been through the exact equivalent, whenever a few prominent scholars and their allies come to dominate a given branch of scholarship, and control access to the important journals and the sources of grant money. The result, invariably, is intellectual stagnation. The one thing that sets Dr. Noyes' scheme apart from this familiar experience is that he would impose that stagnation on an entire university by fiat. That doesn't strike me as an improvement."

When she'd met with the other professors from the Department of History of Ideas, she'd been startled by how exhausted and shaken they looked. For a moment she'd wondered how many of them had had the same kind of bad night she'd almost had, without any equivalent of Amber to chase off whatever it had been. Still, she'd arranged for Will to bring in coffee and doughnuts, given them a chance to air their worries, and tried to reassure them. By the end of the meeting most of them seemed a good deal less rattled. Once that was done, she'd gone to the Halsey Center pool and put in an hour of hard swimming, trying to drown her worries in sheer physical effort; it had helped, despite the bleak recurring thought that the cancer would put anything so vigorous out of her reach soon enough. Afterwards she'd dressed and gotten ready for the meeting as though she'd been donning armor and shouldering a halberd.

"I also wonder how many of you have thought of the reaction of other scholars in your disciplines to this plan. I'm not just talking about the traditions of academic liberty here; those are important, but they've already been discussed by several of our colleagues. I'm talking about the projects we've all done with scholars at other universities—many of them ongoing, some of them building on decades of work already done. Academic freedom is essential to that. I don't have to touch on the reactions elsewhere when your colleagues find out that you've accepted a position as a piece worker in an academic sweatshop and are abandoning your commitments to them—but I do think it's relevant to ask how many first-rate scholars will be interested in taking positions here under the constraints Dr. Noyes wants to impose on them, and how many gifted students will choose to come here when they will be denied the freedom of inquiry that other universities give masters' and doctoral candidates as a matter of course."

The dream-Randolph Carter had been right, too, about the weakness of a defensive strategy. Half a dozen elderly professors had risen to speak early on, talking about the traditions of Miskatonic University and the need to preserve that heritage, and had been neatly shot down by professors from the Noology Department and its allies in the few other departments that backed it, who had clearly prepped themselves to counter just such a defense. Miriam had been careful to speak in exactly the same overfamiliar terms in informal discussions before the faculty senate met, and the surprise, shock, and anger she saw in the faces of certain professors as they watched her told her that she'd gained the surprise she'd hoped.

"Finally, I want to say a word or two about money. There have been quite a few lavish promises bandied about over the last few days—new grants, new funding for assistantships, expanded retirement packages, and the like. It all sounds very appealing, doesn't it? But I think all of us know just how difficult it is to pry money loose for higher education these days, and it occurs to me that nobody has yet mentioned where all this money is supposed to come from. Is that money already available? Is it hoped for? Or is it simply a line of patter meant to lure the faculty of this university into approving something that none of them would accept if they were entirely in their right minds?"

She'd hoped to draw out Noyes with that last remark, and succeeded. He stood up and said, "Dr. Akeley, that allegation is an insult to—"

Upham's gavel came down hard enough to make Miriam jump. "Dr. Noyes," he said in precise unforgiving tones, "you do not have the floor. Kindly sit down."

Miriam wheeled to face Noyes. "Dr. Noyes, this entire misbegotten project is an insult to Miskatonic University and its traditions, and an intolerable power grab on the part of your department." She turned her back on him again. "And I encourage this body to reject it in no uncertain terms. President Upham, thank you."

She sat down, considered the variously startled, approving, and appalled looks her colleagues nearby gave her, and waited. If she'd done what she'd hoped—

Somewhere behind her, someone she couldn't see started to applaud.

For a moment the steady beat of his clapping was the only sound in the hall. Then another joined it, and another. The sound built until the hall rang with it; some of the professors were on their feet. Miriam closed her eyes and wished for a moment that she believed enough in the old lore to say a prayer of thanks.

As the applause died down, Noyes got to his feet, and so did another figure further down the arc of seats, a short balding man with a neatly trimmed gray beard. "Dr. van Kauran," Upham said, recognizing him. Miriam braced herself. Elias van Kauran was a literary critic of classicist tastes, and the two of them had tangled repeatedly in half a dozen journals over the value (her view) or worthlessness (his) of the popular fiction she'd made central to her academic career.

"President Upham," van Kauran said. "Distinguished scholars—and the rest of you." He met the annoyed looks around him with an edged smile. "You will rarely hear these words out of my mouth, but just this once, I am inclined to agree with Dr. Akeley." He went on, picking apart Noyes' plan with the mordant precision that had earned him the hatred and grudging respect of two generations of literary rivals, but all at once Miriam couldn't follow his words. Relief washed through her. Maybe, she thought. Maybe we really can stop this.

Noyes spoke next. His voice remained bland and calm,

but he'd clearly been taken by surprise—he had only vague generalities and promises to respond to the challenges Miriam and van Kauran had raised. When he sat down, an assistant professor of mathematics from India got up and spoke in animated tones of how disastrous Noyes' plan would be when it came to recruiting top talent for Miskatonic.

That, Miriam reflected later, was the moment when the tide definitely turned. The rules of the faculty senate mandated that each professor could speak once only on any given question, barring special permission from the chair, and Carl Upham was in no mood to give special permission to the Noology Department. One after another, junior professors rose, got Upham's nod, and tore into the new plan along lines already traced by Miriam and van Kauran. The few noology professors who hadn't spoken yet tried to stem the tide and failed. Miriam sat back and listened, thinking: I almost wish this was a kingdom at war. I'd hand the junior professors swords and shields, and we'd follow Carter's advice and harry them right out the gates.

Finally everyone had had their say. "Anyone else?" Upham asked. No one rose, and he said, "Very well, then. We have a motion on the floor, to support the proposed changes placed before us by President Phillips and the Noology Department. All in favor please stand." Maybe a fifth of the professors rose, looked uneasily around them. "Please be seated. All opposed, please stand." The other four-fifths stood. "Please be seated. The motion is defeated."

Elias van Kauran stood then. "President Upham."

"Dr. van Kauran."

"I make a motion that this body go on record as rejecting in the most forceful terms any proposal that would infringe on the freedom of scholars to pursue their own researches or give priority to any department in managing the affairs of this university."

Miriam was on her feet before he had finished. "President Upham, I second the motion." Van Kauran glanced back over his shoulder, gave her an amused look.

"We have a motion on the floor. Is there any discussion?"

"President Upham," said one of the elderly professors emeritus in the front row, "I call for the question."

Upham glanced from side to side, waited for any objection. The professors of noology said nothing. "The question being called for, all in favor please stand." Again, something like four-fifths of the professors got to their feet. "Please be seated. All opposed, please stand."

No one moved. A few professors glanced uneasily at the noologists, as though waiting for a cue, and then settled back into their seats.

"Opposed, please stand," Upham repeated, and then: "The motion is adopted."

IT TOOK ANOTHER half hour or so for the formalities of the meeting to finish up, but Miriam didn't mind. She sat back in her seat and savored her moment of triumph. It might well be a temporary victory, she knew; the the faculty senate had limited powers, and the administration might simply brush aside the resolutions and impose Noyes' plan anyway; but just then, she felt as though she'd followed the advice in her dream and, like some sword-swinging heroine in a *Weird Tales* story, led a host of warriors into battle and scattered the foe to the four winds. That they might return in force later and overwhelm the defenders was a matter for another day.

Finally, Carl Upham brought the gavel down, closing the meeting. The noologists got up and left at once without a word; others drifted out; Miriam rose to her feet after a long moment, and waited for others to clear the way to the aisle. By the time they'd done that, the aisle itself was nicely blocked with professors heading for the exit doors, and so Miriam turned and went down toward the podium with an eye toward one of the side doors.

Before she turned, Carl Upham motioned her over. "I'd like to thank you for your comments," he said in a low voice. "You and Elias, between you, said most of what I wanted to say." Then: "Are you free this afternoon?"

"I can be," said Miriam.

"Good. Some of us will be meeting in my office to talk strategy."

"I'd be honored."

He smiled. "Thank you. An hour, maybe? I'll expect you."

The air outside was sultry, with billows of cloud in the west promising another storm, but Miriam didn't care. She headed across campus toward the rugose mass of Wilmarth Hall, enjoyed the startled looks she fielded from a handful of professors whose paths she crossed and the sullen glare directed toward her by a professor of psychology who'd been vocal on Noyes' side of the dispute. For once, Wilmarth Hall's big front doors actually hissed open—the machinery had been innovative for its time, and therefore rarely worked—and she even took the risk of riding one of the elevators. It clanked and rattled alarmingly as it rose, but the doors opened on the right floor, and she headed for her office.

She was about to unlock the door when Michael Peaslee poked his head out of the office two doors down. "Can we talk for a moment?" he asked.

"Of course." She left the door locked, went into his office instead. "What's up?"

He motioned her inside. His office was as irregularly shaped as hers, with the window at the far end a slight parallelogram and the built-in bookshelves on the walls noticeably uneven. Framed art prints hung here and there, mostly Impressionist pieces; the desk had a photo of his stockbroker

husband, dark-haired and grinning, and a picture of the big
two-masted sailboat they owned, the *Norma Jean.*

"I'm not sure it was a good idea to be quite so outspoken
today," Michael said. "I'm no more in favor of this business
than you are, but there's more going on here than an ordinary
departmental power grab."

She tilted her head, looked at him, remembered all the
times he'd been right about university politics before. "What
do you think is going on?"

"I don't know. That's part of what bothers me. I talked
to a couple of dozen professors last night and this morning.
People I would have expected to fight this tooth and nail were
making plans to retire or get jobs somewhere else, and they
looked scared. Did you notice that Gwen Summers didn't say
a thing at the faculty senate meeting?"

"Yes," Miriam admitted, "and that surprised me."

"This morning I talked to her, and she wouldn't discuss
the proposal at all. She said she was looking at early retirement on account of her family."

Miriam gave him a puzzled look; he shrugged. "That's
what I know. If you feel you have to fight this thing right out
in the open, understood, but be careful. The people backing
it may be willing to go further than you expect. That's all."

She thanked him and asked after his husband and their
Corgis, and they chatted briefly about little irrelevant things
before she said her goodbyes and went to her office. All the
while she wondered if she should explain to him why she
wasn't worried about Clark Noyes and whatever might be
backing him, and didn't plan on leaving Miskatonic for early
retirement or another position, but the thought of his likely
reaction to news about her cancer made her cringe. No, she
told herself. He doesn't need that on top of everything else.

THE MEETING IN Carl Upham's office went well, though no one there was foolish enough to think that the vote of the faculty senate had settled anything. Upham spoke for them all when he said early on, "If I were a betting man, I'd bet good money that first thing tomorrow, Phillips will announce that he considers our vote purely advisory and this damned plan will be going ahead anyway." Two hours went into discussing ways of bringing pressure to bear by way of national and international scholarly associations, major university donors, and the State Assembly: all the things that come into play when university politics stops being a game and turns serious. By the time the meeting ended, Miriam's feeling of triumph had mostly trickled away, though she still clung to the memory of Noyes' face when she'd rounded on him.

They made arrangements to be in touch first thing the next day, and headed home. Most of the professors headed to an assortment of parking garages, but Miriam and Elias van Kauran both set out walking the same way, toward the Lovecraft Museum parking lot. "Now that we've been forced to agree about something," Miriam said with a sly look, "I trust you'll find a good opportunity as soon as possible to denounce Lovecraft in print."

"Of course." He allowed a precise smile. "You're far too entertaining an opponent to leave unchallenged."

"That's high praise," said Miriam. "Thank you."

"You're most welcome," he said, saluted her with the stout knob-handled walking stick he always carried, and headed up Derby Street toward the condominiums west of campus. She watched him go, paused by the statue of Cthulhu long enough to repeat the old incantation silently, and headed home.

Back at her apartment, after she'd greeted Amber and gotten dinner cooking, she slumped onto the couch and sat there for a while, waiting for the microwave bell to chime. Amber came padding silently out of the kitchen, bounded neatly up

80

onto the couch—the little creature had recovered a great deal of her strength, which was some comfort—and perched on one of Miriam's knees, looking up at her with wide eyes and a questioning chirr.

"Just tired," Miriam answered without thinking. "It's been a long day." She blinked, then, and considered the little prosimian. The bad news she'd gotten from the oncologist's website had been much on her mind on the walk home. She didn't know how much English her uninvited guest understood, but the creature kept surprising her, so she decided to try to explain.

"Amber," she said, "sooner or later—I don't know when—I'm going to go away and not come back." The creature's eyes went wide and she let out a low unhappy sound. Miriam, wincing, went on. "There really isn't anything I can do about it. When that happens, I'll make sure that someone else will take care of you—so if someone comes here to take you somewhere else, don't worry. It'll be okay."

The expression on the little face told Miriam just how thoroughly Amber disagreed with that. The creature made another low unhappy sound, then climbed up onto Miriam's arm and buried her face into Miriam's shoulder. Miriam ran her fingers through the fur on Amber's back, closed her own eyes, waited for the microwave to chime.

She'd worried that the wrongness she'd felt the night before would return again, but nothing of the sort happened, and she made an early night of it. The next morning she still had tag ends of grading to take care of before the semester was finally wrapped up once and for all, so once she and Amber had breakfasted—she on two English muffins with butter and marmalade, Amber on a bowl of milk and a quarter of an apple sliced thin—she donned her usual black dress and high-heeled shoes, made sure of her hair and makeup, and packed her shoulderbag for the day.

81

She was almost ready to leave when her cell phone rang. She glanced at it, recognized the caller's number—the History of Ideas departmental office—and picked up. "Hello?"

"Miriam? It's Denny." The secretary's voice sounded ragged.

"What's wrong?"

"I just heard from a friend at the University Hospital. Dr. Upham was just brought in. Somebody beat him up really bad."

"*What?*"

"He was unconscious and bloody all over. Whoever it was must have been waiting for him when he got out of his car. Miriam—" The secretary drew in a shaky breath. "I don't think you should come in today."

"Okay," said Miriam, still stunned by the news. "Okay, I guess." They said their goodbyes, and Miriam stood in the living room staring at nothing for a long moment. A memory made her wince: she'd fantasized the day before about leading the junior professors in a charge with swords and shields, without thinking about the all-too-physical carnage that would involve—and now Carl Upham had been on the receiving end of something not too different.

She was still trying to process what had happened when the phone rang again. The number was Will Bishop's. "Will?"

"Dr. Akeley? I have some really ugly news."

"I just heard about Carl Upham."

"Okay, good. I wonder if you'd be willing to consider getting out of Arkham for a few days. There's a pretty fair chance they'll come after you too."

"They," Miriam said, feeling suddenly uneasy. "Who are we talking about?"

"We can discuss that later. Look, I can borrow a car from a friend of mine, swing by your place, and get you somewhere safe."

"That won't be necessary," Miriam told him after a moment of stunned silence. "I've got a car, and I can go visit friends out of town for the weekend."

A brief silence. "Okay," he said. "You should stay off the freeways if you can."

"Why?"

She heard a ragged breath on the other end of the call. "Dr. Akeley, please just trust me. I know that's asking a lot, but—just trust me on this one, okay?"

Miriam stared at the phone for a moment, then said, "Okay." She glanced down at Amber then, considered taking the creature with her, then thought of the potential difficulties if the wrong people asked questions about what she was and how Miriam had come by her. "One other thing. You know where I keep the spare key in my office, right? I have a pet here at the apartment—a strange little thing. Her name is Amber. If you can make sure she's got food and water—" A sudden fear: if someone's coming here to beat me up, and they find her, what will they do to her? "Better yet, if you can put her up for a few days at your place, that would be great. She eats most human food, and she's toilet-trained."

"I can do that," Will promised. "I'll be by later this morning, once I'm sure it's safe."

"Thank you."

"Just get out of there as soon as you can, okay?"

"I'll do that." They said their goodbyes, and then Miriam closed the connection, shook her head, and then went into the kitchen.

"Amber," she said to the little prosimian, "I'm going to have to leave for a few days. Someone's going to come here later today and take you with him. It's okay—he's a friend of mine, so go with him. Do you understand?"

The odd thing was that the little creature did indeed seem to understand. Her eyes went round, and she let out a wavering chirr. Miriam knelt and ran fingers down the creature's spine, trying to comfort it. "It'll be okay. I should be back in a few days—but I have to hurry."

It took longer than she expected, though, to haul a suitcase out of the back of the bedroom closet, fill it with a weekend's necessities, make sure everything in the apartment could be left alone for a few days, and head out the door. She almost walked out the front door before catching herself and going out back to the parking lot where her battered yellow Toyota spent most of its days. It took three tries to start the thing—no surprises there, since it had been two weeks since she'd driven it—but finally the engine grumbled to life, and she backed out of the parking place and started through Arkham's narrow streets toward the old road to Aylesbury.

As she drove, something small and black appeared in her rear view mirror, hovered, and then sped off. A bird, she told herself, but it hadn't moved like any bird she'd ever seen.

SHE'D GOTTEN MAYBE ten miles northwest of Arkham, following the old winding road along the Miskatonic River, when she noticed the gray SUV a half mile or so behind her. She could only see it now and then, when the vagaries of the road allowed a glimpse far enough backwards, but it kept pace with her as she drove by long-abandoned farmsteads, dilapidated stone walls, and great ragged woodlands that looked far more like virgin forest than she remembered. A handful of other cars had passed hers and she'd thought nothing of it, but something about the SUV made her tense. It didn't help that the windows were mirror-tinted, so that whoever drove it remained completely unseen.

Don't be silly, she told herself, and kept driving.

A sudden flash in the mirror caught her attention, and she saw something long and thin protruding from the open passenger-side window of the SUV. An instant later her car lurched hard to the right and kept dragging that way. She fought for control as the right rear wheel went thump-thump-thump, shaking the car. It took a moment for her to realize that someone in the SUV had just shot out one of her tires.

She got the car off the road, flung herself out the door onto the gravel of the shoulder. Stark terror held her frozen for a moment—would they shoot her next? A bend of the road hid her from the SUV for the moment, but she could hear its engine, growing louder.

A rising wind hissed suddenly in the trees to her right. It was almost, she thought, as though *it's trying to get my attention.* The moment that thought finished crossing her mind, the hissing turned into words: *This way, this way.*

She wavered for another moment, then turned and ran into the woods. The heels on her shoes were high enough to make anything faster than a walk risky, and she paused to kick them off and scoop them up in one hand, then ran on, barefoot except for her nylons. Stones and twigs stung her feet as she dodged trees and brush, kept running as fast as she could. Her heart pounded and her breath came in gasps; stark terror made her limbs feel like lead. Even so, something she couldn't define seemed to pull her onward, kept her fleeing deeper into the woods, at a particular angle to the road behind.

She heard gravel spray and doors slam open and shut as the SUV stopped on the shoulder near her car. The sound of booted feet on the gravel followed a little later. Just for an instant, she imagined herself being beaten like Carl Upham and then left for dead in the woods, and a terrible sense of helplessness surged through her. The wind in the trees hissed louder, though, and the words in it were still the same: *This way, this way.*

She followed. A clumsy dodge around a tree sent her full

tilt into a shrubby whitethorn, and she dropped her shoes; as she struggled to free herself, her purse slid off her shoulder and the thorns shredded one side of her dress. None of that mattered, though she couldn't tell why. All that mattered was reaching—

She stopped, stared upwards. Around her rose a circle of nine huge elm trees, the smallest of them two hundred feet tall. Looking up at them, a chill ran through her, because there hadn't been elms that large anywhere in Massachusetts since Dutch elm disease came through in the 1940s. The sounds of pursuit no longer reached her—or was it just that the wind in the branches had become a roaring voice urging her onward? She walked out into the center of the grove, still staring up at the trees.

All at once the ground dropped away from under her feet.

She cried out and flailed, to no effect. Darkness swallowed her, and air rushed past, roaring. She wondered if she'd fallen down an old mine shaft—were there ever mines this far down the Miskatonic valley?—for the bottom of the pit seemed improbably far away.

Then darkness swirled and took shape before her. A vast hoary face the color of midnight bent over her, and eyes pale and huge as moons regarded her. Something that was not a voice seemed to speak: *You have come, and just in time.*

She stared at the face, sure she was hallucinating.

Listen well, the not-voice said. *You have passed into my realm, into the Great Abyss, but you shall not remain here. When you come to another realm, you must seek out a king, one who is known to you by name. When you meet him, you must command him to take you to the Oracle of the Great Abyss, where you will learn what must be done. Thereafter the two of you will go to the place of the Flame. Tell no one of this but a king whose name is known to you. A grave danger is coming, but you may be able to turn it aside. Do you understand?*

No, Miriam thought desperately. No, I don't understand. I'm falling and hallucinating and I don't even know where I am any more—

It is well, said the not-voice.

The void spun around her, and everything went black.

SIX

The Hills of Dream

She blinked awake, and wondered where she was.

The great dark elms had vanished. She lay sprawled on her back, as though she'd fallen from a height, and a half-remembered scent came from what felt like crushed herbage beneath her. Above her the sky bent blue and clear, splashing the pale sunlight of early morning over her. She blinked again, tried to fit the scene around her with the broken memories of that last desperate flight into the woods. Had she tumbled over a rocky edge, to lie unconscious through the evening and the night—and if so, how had the hunters missed her?

She flexed fingers and toes, moved her head from side to side, made sure she could feel and move every part of her body. If she'd fallen, she'd managed to land unhurt. Slowly, then, she rolled onto one side and sat up.

She was nowhere in New England, she knew that much at a glance.

The ground sloped gently away around her toward the rising sun, mantled in purple heather, soft green grass, and low gnarled cedars in which breezes hissed. Off in the distance,

89

the slope wandered down to a river valley thick with forest, and to the north of it the river emptied into a great sea that stretched away blue and dancing to the edge of sight. To the south, purple heights rose to face the morning, rank upon rank of them into the distance. Behind her, to the west, the crest of a ridge traced a ragged edge against the sky.

She blinked, rubbed her eyes, looked again. The improbable landscape remained. Am I still hallucinating? she asked herself. Or—she shied away from the thought, but it kept returning to her mind—dead?

The breeze offered her no answers. After a time, she got to her feet.

The thorns had left one side of her dress half shredded, and so little remained of her nylons that she took them off, considered them, and tucked the remnants down the front of her dress—she might find some use for the scraps, she told herself, or at least a less pristine place to throw them away. Then, picking her way around the heather, she headed for the crest of the ridge. Her one thought was to try to find some human settlement, if such a thing existed in the strange landscape around her. She'd taken classes in wilderness survival at a Camp Fire Girl summer camp when she was twelve years old, but could call to mind next to nothing of what she'd been taught in those far-off days. Since then? She'd rarely seen wilderness, much less strayed into it.

She'd expected the way to be hard on her bruised feet, but the grass felt soft as carpet. Great black bees hummed here and there, darted obligingly out of her way. All the while, as she climbed the long gentle slope toward the ridgeline, something she couldn't trace prodded at her memory, half-convinced her she should recognize the purple hills around her. Something about them stirred old forgotten images in her mind, reminded her of something. What?

Finally she reached the crest and looked down the long

slope beyond, and knew at once where she'd encountered those hills before.

She slumped to the ground, dazed, and sat there trembling in the heather with the bees buzzing around her, staring past the gentle hills below, dotted with cottages and shrines, groves and gardens of asphodel. Beyond them a river curled around the feet of a mountain capped with snow. Beyond river and mountain, a sea stretched out to unguessable distance, and where the river met the sea stood a city.

It was not Arkham, or any city or town of Massachusetts or the waking world. Walls of veined marble surrounded it, topped with bronze statues that glowed in the morning sun, and soaring towers tipped with gold rose high above golden roofs within. Beyond was a walled harbor where a hundred painted galleys lay at anchor. The river was named Naraxa, she knew, and the mountain's name was Aran; ginkgos grew on its flanks. The land she had somehow entered was named Ooth-Nargai, the ridge on which she sat belonged to the Tanarian Hills, and the city before her was, had to be, Celephaïs.

After a few minutes, she pulled herself back to her feet, and started walking down the slope toward the soaring minarets of the city. It helped that she'd published one book and a dozen papers on H.P. Lovecraft's novel *The Dream-Quest of Unknown Kadath*, another book and half a dozen more papers on other stories from his cycle of dream-tales, and supervised three masters' theses and two doctoral dissertations on that end of Lovecraft's oeuvre; it helped even more that she'd read through the stories in question less than forty-eight hours before. That made it just a little less baffling to her that somehow, her flight from her pursuers had brought her to the realm the old books of lore called the Dreamlands.

BY THE TIME she'd descended out of the purple heather into the grassy slopes below, Miriam had convinced herself that she was probably dead. One of Lovecraft's dream-stories told of a man who'd gone to become a king in the Dreamlands—king, in fact, of the shimmering marble city before her—while his mortal body lay crumpled and lifeless on the rocks below a seaside cliff. The idea bothered her less than she'd expected. The wind was cool and salt-scented, the grass felt soft beneath her feet; she'd spent six years trying to come to terms with death, and she decided that even if she and the hillside were to dissolve into nothingness in another moment, the experience was less wretched than she'd expected.

The hillside remained for the time being, though, and so did she. Ahead, Celephaïs blazed in the morning. She guessed it was maybe twenty miles off, further than she thought she could walk without rest. Closer, though still far off, the little thatched roofs of cottages dotted the landscape, and closer still—maybe half a mile ahead of her, maybe more, in the midst of a meadow in a fold of the hills—stood a little building of white marble, surrounded by pillars and topped by a gilded dome. A shrine? It seemed likely, for as Miriam came closer, she could see an altar out in front of it, with an offering of flowers upon it.

She came closer still, and realized that someone was kneeling at the altar: a woman, she guessed, with dark unbound hair and a white sleeveless garment.

She paused, then, all at once unsure of herself. How on Earth, she thought, or off it, will I explain to anybody who and what I am, and what I'm doing here? As she stood on the slope, though, looking down it at the shrine and the altar, the woman rose, curtseyed deeply, backed away from the altar, and then glanced up and saw her. For a moment neither of them moved, and then the woman called out to her. The wind swept the words past Miriam, and they seemed to make no sense, but the voice was not unfriendly, and Miriam found her courage and went down the slope to the meadow and the shrine.

The woman was young, maybe eighteen at the most. She wore sandals and a plain white garment of vaguely ancient Greek cut, bound with a cord around the waist and breasts, and she seemed to regard Miriam with utmost astonishment. Once Miriam was within speaking range, she curtseyed and said, "*Anané ai-yanesh eyi'sile uye'loroné.*"

The possibility of a language barrier hadn't occurred to Miriam. "I'm sorry," she said. "I—I don't know what you're saying."

The English words seemed to astonish the young woman even more. She overcame her amazement after a moment, though, and paused, considering, then gestured tentatively toward Miriam, then toward herself; she mimed the two of them walking together, using two fingers of each hand, and then motioned down the slope of the hill; she pointed into the distance, then used two fingers to indicate a person, gestured below her chin to suggest a beard, and then moved hands like chattering mouths, in one place, in another, in a third.

From this Miriam gathered that the young woman was offering to take her to a bearded man who spoke many languages. Guessing what gestures would communicate assent, she curtseyed to the young woman, who blushed in response, and then smiled and motioned for her to lead the way. The young woman turned, then turned back, gestured toward herself, said "Anané," and then made the same tentative gesture toward Miriam.

It was her name, Miriam was sure of it. "Miriam," she said, gesturing toward herself.

"Mee'ree'em," Anané repeated, smiling.

They crossed the meadow, started down the slope beyond it. There a spring bubbled up, and a stream flowed from it, edged by tall reeds. Beside the reeds on one side ran a trail of packed earth. That was less easy on Miriam's bare feet than the grass had been, and before long she was walking gingerly and hoping their destination was not too far.

Anané noticed, though, and gestured for her to stop. Once she did so, the young woman went to the reeds, broke off a dozen or so, sat on the grass and deftly plaited them into sandals, which she handed to Miriam with a smile. "Thank you," Miriam said, surprised and pleased, and Anané smiled at her and said *"Eleleth iyé."* A sudden startled moment, and then they both began to laugh, recognizing that they had managed to communicate.

BY THE TIME they reached the destination Anané had in mind, Miriam felt dazed and exhausted. Part of it was the length of the journey—her eye for distances had never been good, but she guessed they'd walked three or four miles from the domed shrine, and that was on top of at least as long a walk from the place where she'd awakened. Even so, it wasn't just the physical effort that tired her. The jarring discontinuity between everything she'd believed about the world, and everything her arrival in the Dreamlands implied, pressed in on her from all sides.

Finally, though, they came to a turf-roofed cottage in the midst of a garden. Anané called out in her own language, and a woman in her forties, maybe, opened the door and came out: Anané's mother, Miriam guessed, for the two looked much alike. She gave Miriam an astonished look and then said something to her daughter. The two of them conversed briefly, and then the older woman took Miriam's arm and, smiling, drew her into the cottage, while Anané said something that was probably a farewell and headed off.

Inside, everything was cool and quiet. Plastered walls,

wooden furnishings, and a ceiling held up by great dark beams reminded Miriam of colonial houses in Arkham. She let herself be led to a sturdy wooden chair by an equally sturdy wooden table and sank gratefully into it. The woman spoke to her in the kind of soft voice that calms animals and frightened children—the kind of voice, in point of fact, that Miriam had used to calm Amber when the little creature had fallen through her ceiling.

The comparison amused Miriam at first. After all, she thought, haven't I just dropped through their ceiling? A moment later, though, she thought about Amber. That made her wince, and wish there was some way she could be sure that Will had gotten the little creature to safety.

The woman busied herself at a wooden sideboard, came back with slices of brown bread, butter that smelled so sweet it had to have been churned that morning, and a brown pottery cup filled with some white liquid that smelled a little like yoghurt. "Thank you," Miriam said, hoping the woman would understand the tone of voice, if not the words. The woman smiled and nodded, and then paused, as though recalling some distant memory. After a moment, she said something that sounded like "Yi'u u'ele'kem." Miriam blinked, and realized that she'd done her best to say "You're welcome."

Astonished, Miriam considered the woman, who beamed and motioned toward the food and drink. Miriam smiled and reached for the bread, then stopped, motioned toward herself, and said her name. The woman responded in kind and said, "Ieloré."

That settled, Miriam ate buttered bread, sipped the beverage—it was made of fermented milk, she was sure of that after one sip, and mildly alcoholic—and let herself sink into the dim cool quiet of the cottage, while Ieloré went unhurriedly about the day's chores. She didn't recall dozing off, but blinked awake suddenly when the door creaked open

95

and Anané came in, leading a hale black-bearded man in a sleeveless white tunic and a brown cloak. Ieloré greeted him placidly, and he answered in a deep rumbling voice.

Miriam, guessing at the local customs, started to get up out of the chair, but the man waved her back to her place, pulled out another chair from the table with one sandaled foot, sat in it. "Mee'ree'em," Anané said, and motioned to the man: "Daelos."

"Pleased to meet you," said Miriam, as Ieloré set a cup of the white beverage in front of each of them, then poured a third for Anané, who sat at the far end of the table and watched with her chin on her hands and a look of fascination on her face.

"And likewise," Daelos answered. At her startled look, he laughed. "Aye, I know the King's language, or some part of it. I'm one of his huntsmen and speak with him now and again. Do you know where you are, milady?"

"I think," Miriam said, "that this is the kingdom of Ooth-Nargai."

"That it is," said Daelos. "Might I ask if you came here on purpose?"

"No," Miriam said. "I was—" How to explain the events that brought her to the elm grove? "Chased by enemies," she said then. "I was alone, and there were many of them. I ran into the forest and came to a grove and—fell into darkness. Then I woke up, on the hillside beyond the ridge." She gestured in the direction of the Tanarian Hills.

"Might I ask further," said Daelos, "if one spoke to you out of the darkness?"

"Yes," said Miriam. "But he forbade me to repeat his words."

Daelos nodded. "That I don't doubt. The Tanarians hold many portals to and from the waking world, or so it's said. Doubtless you came upon such a portal, and the One who guards all portals asked something of you in return for letting you pass." He drank from the cup before him. "Be that as it may, the King has commanded that anyone who comes to his realm from the waking world shall come before him, and only then be given leave to wander freely."

"I'm entirely willing to do that," Miriam said.

"Capital," said Daelos; the Englishism made her smile. "The only difficulty is that the King dwells just now in Serannian among the clouds, and will be returning shortly. If you were to sail there, it's by no means sure you would arrive in Serannian before he sets sail again for Celephaïs. So you must wait—" He calculated on his fingers. "Two weeks, I believe, is the way it would be reckoned outside Ooth-Nargai, where time exists."

Miriam considered that, and nodded. If her material body lay dead in some pit in the forest northwest of Arkham, as she suspected, two weeks one way or another would make no imaginable difference. The thought sent a pang through her, reminding her of all the people she would never see again. That was going to happen anyway, she reminded herself. This way—

A possible difficulty occurred to her then. "Where will I stay?"

In response Daelos turned to Ieloré, and the two of them talked in their own language for a few moments. "Here with Ieloré and her daughter, if you're willing," Daelos said to Miriam.

"I hope I won't be any kind of inconvenience," said Miriam.

Daelos glanced at Ieloré and said something, and she responded with a smile, a shake of her head, a few words in a tone that Miriam understood at once. "Not at all," Daelos said.

Miriam turned to her hostess and said, "Thank you."

"Yi'u u'ele'kem," Ieloré said with another smile.

IT MIGHT HAVE been two weeks before she left for Celephaïs, or two hours, or two years. Afterwards, Miriam gave up trying to guess. Lovecraft had written that in Ooth-Nargai time did not exist, and in the waking world, she had rolled her eyes at those passages, dismissing them as the sort of extravagant romanticism he'd indulged in early on, before maturity and a hard life had shaken such fancies out of him. Dwelling on the slopes of the Tanarian Hills made that skepticism impossible to maintain. Mornings and evenings happened, but in some sense they were all the same morning and evening; events took place, but change did not; neither Anané nor Ieloré nor any of the other folk of Ooth-Nargai had ever been younger than they were, nor would they ever grow older, and the rhythm of their days never wearied or palled because neither past nor future existed for them.

Both existed for Miriam, but they stood at a distance from her, somewhere off beyond the high purple ridge to the east or the glittering edge of the sea to the west, like the life she'd lived before she'd woken on the heather and grass of the Tanarian Hills. In the little cottage or the countryside around it, none of it seemed to matter much, and time stopped for her as it did for every dweller in that land. Her first day in Ieloré's house, she'd set herself the task of learning the language of Ooth-Nargai, but noticed a few days later—or was it more than that, or less?—that she was speaking it without ever having gotten around to learning it.

She got used to wearing the simple garments of the country the same way. Her shredded dress and underclothes were laid up in a chest that first day, and once the chest closed it seemed as though they had always been there and would always be there. Anané helped her put on linen shift and sleeveless woolen dress, and tie the cord just so, crosswise, so that it supported her breasts. After that one lesson, donning the garments was as natural as though Miriam had been doing it her whole life. A sturdy pair of leather sandals made their appearance, but Miriam kept the ones Anané had plaited for her in the plain but pleasant little room where she slept, and they never failed to call up a look of embarrassed delight on Anané's face when she saw them.

Every day was different and every day was the same. Some days young women came to Ieloré's house to card wool together and gossip, and Miriam sat with them, listened to the gossip—who was in love with whom, mostly, an endless round of romances that reminded Miriam of nothing so much as Renaissance pastorals—and laughed with the others at her own lack of skill with the carding combs. Once—or was it more than once?—a child came with the women, a thin blonde girl of six or so who perched by the fireplace and watched the proceedings with wide eyes. Something about the child seemed curiously familiar to Miriam, but she could never quite remember what it was.

Other days Anané took offerings of flowers to the little shrines of amiable gods and goddesses that dotted the slopes of the Tanarians, and Miriam stayed behind and helped Ieloré with such chores as she could. Still other days were times of festival, and Miriam went with a crowd to one of the temples, where the young women danced before the statues of gods and goddesses and the young men chanted and clapped to keep time. At dawn and dusk each day she saw the young men leading the flocks up into the hills and back down again, and more than once—or was it only once?—drums pounded in the distance, telling of some nocturnal rite the men enacted in the hills around a roaring fire.

Daelos came by now and then, though Miriam could not guess how often he had visited. A hunter, he roamed the

Tanarian Hills after deer, and brought gifts of venison in exchange for the hospitality he received in every cottage. He told stories, too, and had traveled outside Ooth-Nargai, east of the Tanarians and south along the coast road toward distant Mnar, where time existed. He asked Miriam, when he visited, "Are you happy here?"

"Yes," she said on each visit, "but there's an errand I need to take care of."

On each visit he nodded, smiled, and left.

Finally, one morning, he came to the house and said, "The King's ship has been sighted from the pharos of Celephaïs. Are you ready?"

"Of course," Miriam told him, and said her good-byes to Anané and Ieloré. The older woman took her hands in hers, and then placed one hand on her forehead and recited a blessing, calling on an even dozen of ancient goddesses to protect her. The younger flung her arms around Miriam and wished her well. Then Daelos led her away, down the trail that wound through the fields and groves and pastures toward Celephaïs.

"Will you miss them?" the hunter asked her as they walked.

"Very much," Miriam admitted. "But I don't think they will miss me."

He laughed, shook his head. "No. Come back after a day, or a year, or a thousand years, and to them, you will never have left at all."

They walked on. Mount Aran rose higher and higher on their right hand, and its snowy peak blazed in the noonday sun. Celephaïs spread across the western horizon, until its walls hid the harbor beyond and its towers stabbed the blue heavens. The trail joined others and became a road, on which many others traveled alongside them: traders with ox-drawn carts bringing woolen fabrics of the hill country to the mar-

kets of Celephaïs, whence they would be traded across the
length and breadth of the Dreamlands; pilgrims seeking the
turquoise temple of Nath-Horthath, where orchid-wreathed
priests intone litanies that were immemorially old before
stone was first set upon stone in the aeons-forgotten city of
Sarkomand; wanderers through the lands of dream, of whom
some few, Miriam guessed, were travelers from the waking
world; and those with petitions of one sort or another who
sought King Kuranes.

Noontide found them in a village a few miles from the
city, and there Daelos led Miriam to an inn, where they had
a pleasant meal of bread, meat, cheese, and ale, before returning to the road. Maybe half a mile further on, the swift
and bubbling river Naraxa came out from the forests behind
Mount Aran and the road curved to run alongside it. Grass
dotted with unfading flowers bordered the road for another mile, and beyond that the road passed through a grove
where the sea breeze whispered among leaves that had never
sprouted and would never fall. Past the grove a great stone
bridge bent up and over the Naraxa, and past that, tall gates
of bronze stood open in an arch of marble, with the streets of
Celephaïs a half-lit strangeness beyond.

Sentries in red and gold stood watch in the gateway, but
Daelos said, "the King's huntsman with a journeyer from the
waking world," and they uncrossed their spears and let the
two of them pass. Beyond the gate the streets were paved with
onyx from far Inquanok, and the houses and palaces were of
marble and bronze; market squares bustled with commerce;
temples to the gods and goddesses of dream, and above all
others the mighty turquoise temple of Nath-Horthath, rose
high and splendid above the streets; visible over the rooftops,
the great lighthouse of the city stood ready come sunset to
blaze a guiding light across the Cerenerian Sea. At the heart
of the city, a palace with walls of rose crystal soared pinnacle

upon pinnacle into the sky. Miriam didn't need Daelos' guidance to tell her that this was their destination.

More sentries in red and gold waited at the palace gates, and responded to Daelos like those at the city gate. In the high-vaulted chambers inside, sunlight glowed golden-rose through translucent walls on throngs of servants and officers, bustling about their duties now that King Kuranes had returned from Serannian. As they passed through a long corridor quieter than most, Miriam asked Daelos about that, and he laughed.

"The King is always returning and always departing, always in Serannian and always here," the huntsman said. "You dwell in time habitually, so you only experience one of those things—" He gave her an amused glance. "At a time, as you say."

FINALLY THEY REACHED a many-pillared hall where pale lamps in glass spheres drifted in stray breezes just below the ceiling, scores of chairs stood scattered across the floor, and a fair-sized crowd waited, a few standing, most sitting comfortably in groups. A young man in the king's livery of red and gold came to them and bowed. "A stranger from the waking world," Daelos told him in the language of Ooth-Nargai, "who seeks the king willingly in answer to his edict. Her name is Miriam." Daelos turned to Miriam then, and in English said, "Here we part for the present. If your errand allows you to remain in Ooth-Nargai or brings you back to this land, look for me." With a broad smile: "I'm always here."

Miriam thanked him and they said their goodbyes. To the young man in livery, who was obviously trying to make sense of their speech, she said in the language of Ooth-Nargai, "I can also speak the tongue of this land, if you wish."

"I thank you, Lady Mee'ree'em," he said with evident relief. "I know little of the tongue the King speaks privately, though he is pleased when others speak it to him, and I counsel you to do so if you wish him to favor your errand. You see that many have come to seek audience with the King; let me write your name, and you will be presented to him in due order. Until that happens, please be comfortable and accept such hospitality as we can offer you."

She thanked him, found a free chair, and waited. Now and again, an elderly man in the king's livery came out of a great double door on the room's far end and called out a name, and someone else went to the door and passed through it. Young pages in the same livery moved through the crowd and offered food and drink to those who desired it. All the while, the lamps drifted here and there below the ceiling, and more people came to seek audience. Since no time passed, none of it left Miriam wearied or bored.

The old man in livery came through the door and called out, "The Lady Mee'ree'em." She got to her feet and went to meet him. The old man bowed, motioned for her to follow, and led her through a long corridor lined with guards in golden armor to the throne room of the king.

Sunlight blazed golden-rose through the translucent wall behind a throne hewn of a single mighty crystal. A long carpet made of cloth of gold, figured with hippogriffs and wyverns, ran down the center of the room. More guards in golden armor and crimson livery stood at attention to either side, their spearheads gleaming in the filtered sunlight. Sages with long forked beards looked on from low chairs to either side of the throne. "The Lady Mee'ree'em, from the waking world," the old man proclaimed, and bowed again and motioned her to advance. She walked up the golden carpet to the foot of the throne, curtseyed deeply there, and said in English, "Your Majesty," before rising from the curtsey and looking up.

Kuranes, undying King of Ooth-Nargai and the Sky Around Serannian, clad in robes of crimson and gold and crowned with a circlet of white gold set with rubies, was a plump little man with watery blue eyes and a round and utterly English face somewhere between young and old, framed with hair of that vague color that never quite manages to be either blond or brown. He blinked at her, and also in English, said, "From the waking world, eh? Just gadding about in a dream, or have you some particular reason to come to Ooth-Nargai?"

"Your Majesty," Miriam said, "I was sent here by—by a certain being—and told to carry a private message to a king."

"What, just any old king?"

Miriam had to suppress a smile. "So long as I know his name."

"Do you know mine, then?"

"Your Majesty's name is Kuranes, I believe," said Miriam.

"Oh, that," said the King. "I thought you meant the other one. Never mind about that, then. Well, if the message is private, you may as well come forward and tell it to me."

Miriam curtseyed, and then mounted the seven steps to Kuranes' throne, bent, and in a low voice said, "The one who sent me here said that you're to take me to the Oracle of the Great Abyss, and then we're to go to the place of the flame. There's some kind of danger that—that I'm supposed to do something about. That's all I was told." She backed down the stairs, and curtseyed again for good measure before looking up.

The King was staring at her, aghast. He turned to the sages who sat to either side of his throne and in the language of Ooth-Nargai said, "Attend me." The sages hurried up the seven steps and clustered around the throne, talking with the King in low voices, for what might have been a long time anywhere but Ooth-Nargai. Finally they parted, and one of the sages asked her, "Lady Mee'ree'em, where did you learn the King's name?"

The language of Ooth-Nargai had no words for "fiction," "short story," or "book," so Miriam improvised. "From a legend I read in a scroll in the waking world."

The sage stroked his forked beard. "Even so," he said. "And this scroll—did it speak of another traveler from the waking world, a friend of the King, who is himself a king in the Dreamlands?"

"It did," said Miriam.

"Ah," said the sage, and turned back to King Kuranes. The sages clustered around the King again, talking in low voices, and then returned to their seats to either side, leaving Kuranes beaming upon his throne.

"My dear lady," said Kuranes, "I'm sorry to say that— through no fault of your own, I assure you—you've come to the wrong king. There was a day when I might have dared the Oracle of the Great Abyss, though even then—" He shuddered visibly, then paused and smiled again. "Fortunately I know the king that the one who sent you must have had in mind, and I shall send you to him at once, so that you can properly fulfill this errand of yours. He's an old friend and fellow-dreamer from the waking world, a very fine man, who now reigns six months out of each year in the city of Ilek-Vad above the Twilight Sea in the far kingdom of Rokol. I believe you know of him. His name is Randolph Carter."

SEVEN
The King of Ilek-Vad

The Street of the Pillars leads from the palace of the King past the turquoise temple of Nath-Horthath to the great harbor of Celephaïs, where ships from the far corners of the Dreamlands unload their cargoes and take on freight for distant ports. Night and day people throng it, not only folk of Ooth-Nargai, but travelers from a hundred lands. Onyx merchants from Inquanok in coats of felted yak wool, sailors from Oriab in silken robes, dark pilgrims from Thraa and Ilarnek, laughing leather-clad mercenaries from Thorabon, traders from Teloth and Hlanith, lutanists from Oonai, flautists from Drinen, dancers from the Liranian Desert who leap and whirl for a handful of thrown coins: to walk down the length of the Street of the Pillars or sit on the great turquoise steps of the temple is to see all these and more, for Celephaïs has the finest harbor upon the Cerenerian Sea and stands close to the center of the Six Kingdoms.

Through all of this, clad in the white sleeveless dress of a woman of Ooth-Nargai, Miriam Akeley walked. It was late afternoon; the sun's rays glowed on the onyx pavements, prayers echoed from the temple of Nath-Horthath, and a brisk wind brought the sea's scent up the street. Before her went a herald in livery of red and gold, and behind her came six servants in pairs, each pair with a sea-chest between them. Passersby stepped out of her way, onlookers gawked and gossiped. Miriam found it all entertaining, and wondered if her academic robes and hood would have suited the occasion better than the plain woolen garb of the Tanarian Hills.

At the foot of the Street of the Pillars the sea wall of Celephaïs stretched out for most of a mile to either side, and the harbor side of it was thronged with ships and cargo. The herald turned and led the way past a dozen crowded wharves to a three-masted galleon with a gilded mantichore for a figurehead and a tall forecastle behind it. As burly longshoremen hauled crates and bales and oaken casks on board to stow in the holds, the herald called to the first mate, who climbed deftly down a rope ladder and talked with him in a language that seemed to be half that of Ooth-Nargai and half some nautical jargon Miriam didn't begin to understand.

Still, they settled matters promptly. A parchment roll changed hands, and the first mate turned to Miriam. "My lady," he said in the language of Ooth-Nargai, "welcome aboard *Windstrider of Ullan*. The King has arranged for your passage to Ilek-Vad and all else that's required. If you'll go aboard, one of the ship's boys will take you to the steward and your cabin."

Miriam thanked him and then the herald, who made off, leaving the servants to pass their burdens to the longshoremen. A gangway with a rope railing on one side brought her amidships; guessing where her cabin would be, she ducked past the sailors and went aft. The ship's boy met her at the foot of the great sterncastle, and led her up to the quarterdeck and in through the door to a room within, where the steward was busy. By the time they'd exchanged more than a few words, sailors lugging her chests came in, and so she and her luggage were installed in her cabin nearly at the same moment.

"You'll want to stay here below until we've left harbor and gotten under way, my lady," the steward told her.

"I know," Miriam said, smiling. "I've sailed before, though not on a ship such as this."

"Indeed?" One of the steward's bushy eyebrows went up. "'Tis well. I'll come let you and the other passengers know once it's safe to go on deck."

She thanked him and, once the door to her cabin was shut, set about inspecting it. It was a trim little space with its own porthole, a bed aft with space for her sea chests beneath, and a little table, chair, and washstand made fast to the bulkhead forward. The sea chests held mostly clothing—King Kuranes had ordered her provided with supplies for the journey, and she was pleased to find not only shifts and sleeveless dresses but also garments for colder weather, thick warm gowns with sleeves, heavy woolen mantles, leggings, and socks shaped to wear under sandal-straps. In Ooth-Nargai it is always spring, but she knew she'd have no way of predicting the weather elsewhere in the Dreamlands until *Windstrider of Ullan* sailed back into time.

Clatters and thumps, footfalls on the sterncastle deck above, and now and then voices as passengers came aboard and got settled in their cabins: that went on and on, and then the thumps and clatters stopped and the shouts changed indefinably. Miriam glanced out the porthole and noticed that the ship berthed at the next wharf seemed to be sliding forward. A second glance showed that it was *Windstrider of Ullan* that was in motion, backing slowly out from the quay. She looked aft, and caught sight of a longboat full of sailors leaning into the stroke of their long oars, pulling a cable that she guessed was fastened to *Windstrider's* stern.

Stroke by stroke they hauled the ponderous mass of the

galleon free from the wharves and then south a short distance, so that Miriam had her first view of Celephaïs from seaward, all marble and bronze aglow in the afternoon sun. More clatters and thumps followed—she guessed that the cable had been brought back in and the longboat hauled up to its place amidships—and then a different force caught the ship, tipping the deck beneath her slightly and pulling the ship northwards to the harbor entrance. The first sails were up, she knew at once, catching the wind off the Cerenerian Sea.

She watched, entranced, as the steersman threaded a path past the hundred painted galleys riding at anchor in the harbor, then swung hard to port to the entrance of the harbor between great stone breakwaters. The end of one breakwater slid past, and long before it was out of sight the sea had *Windstrider of Ullan* in its grip, lifting her up on great rolling swells. The deck slanted further—more canvas had been spread before the wind, Miriam knew—and the galleon's sedate pace picked up. Another turn, to starboard, and Celephaïs came into sight again, drawing away beyond a widening stretch of open water.

A crisp rap on her door announced the steward. "My lady, you're welcome to go onto the quarterdeck if you like," he said. She thanked him, and he went on to the next cabin as she went forward to the door and stepped out into the open air.

White canvas curved above, straining at the yards and the rigging; clouds scudded past, and sky-blue gulls wheeled about, calling to one another in high desolate tones. Off to starboard, Mount Aran loomed up, and the golden light of early evening blazed on its snowy peak. Ahead, to port, and astern, the Cerenerian Sea reached to the horizon, dotted here and there with sails.

Other passengers joined her on the quarterdeck: a slender golden-haired girl of eighteen or so in an ornate blue gown

trimmed with ribbons, who stared at everything in amazement; a brown-haired girl of the same age who wore a plainer
gown and followed the first girl like a watchful shadow; a
gray-haired woman in a gray dress, who seemed to be watching them both, and didn't look at all pleased to be on the
water; and a pair of middle-aged men in drab tunics and hose
who chatted about the vagaries of trade in woolens and dried
fish. Though she knew she'd need to make friends with her
fellow passengers shortly, Miriam ignored them for the moment and walked to the forward rail.

Barefoot and bare to the waist, sailors hauled at ropes on
the deck below, while others scrambled aloft. On the sterncastle deck behind and above her, the captain shouted orders.
The sea rushed past, Mount Aran kept watch, and beyond
the mountain's southern shoulder, the purple ridge of the
Tanarian Hills slipped gradually out of sight.

As it vanished, a faint trembling seemed to pass through
the ship, and a stillness Miriam hadn't noticed before made
itself known by its absence. Something she could feel but
not see rushed past her, implacable as the wind, driving her
onward willy-nilly toward some unknown fate. A moment
passed; she felt it pass, and realized that she had returned to
time.

THE VOYAGE TO Ilek-Vad took twenty-six days in all: a good
voyage, the captain told all and sundry, though not the swift-
est he'd known, and the one stop they made in the port city
of Ogrothan to take on provisions and fresh water went with
admirable dispatch. Miriam found it easy enough to adjust to
the rhythms of shipboard life. She'd sailed on Michael Peaslee's big yacht, the *Norma Jean*, south to Florida and north
to Newfoundland more than once, and one golden summer
joined him, his husband, and a few mutual friends to cross

the Atlantic to Portugal and back. On board *Windstrider of Ullan*, she kept to the quarterdeck in good weather, stayed safely below in foul weather, and made sure to keep out of the sailors' way at all times.

She did not want for company on the trip. The two middle-aged men, merchants from Teloth, quickly determined that she had no family of importance and no interest either in trade or in politics, and thereafter sedulously left her alone. The blonde girl was another matter. Her name was Serin ban Eshe-Mathil, and she was the daughter of one of the great houses of the city of Thran in the kingdom of Sydathria; she and her maidservant Aysh, the brown-haired girl, were going to live with her father in distant Ilek-Vad, where he served as Sydathria's ambassador to the two kings of Rokol; she had never been further from home than the cities of Teloth and Hlanith and the jasper terraces of Kiran, and was half thrilled and half petrified to be sailing to the easternmost of the Six Kingdoms.

Miriam learned this in disjointed scraps at first, mostly at meals, which were served by the steward in a room aft of the passenger cabins on the quarterdeck. The two merchants sat at one end of the table and talked only to each other; the young woman and the old one, whom Miriam gathered was her governess, sat at the other, while Aysh sat in a chair by the door or helped the steward serve the meals. Miriam sat toward the middle of the table, and though the governess directed suspicious glances at everyone at table but her charge, and now and again hissed something to the girl that apparently amounted to "Mind your manners, young lady," Serin would at times get a look variously sly or mutinous on her face, and make as much conversation with Miriam as the governess would permit.

The language of Ooth-Nargai was the only tongue they had in common, and that posed certain difficulties when the girl asked Miriam what sort of person she was, for there were no words in Ooth-Nargai for "professor" or "college," or even for "learn" or "teach." After a certain amount of fumbling with roundabout descriptions, though, Serin taught her suitable words from other languages of the Dreamlands, and Miriam was able to explain that she taught history and literature in a large school for those who were no longer children.

That was apparently not a foreign concept in Sydathria, for Serin's face lit up, and the old governess abandoned her suspicious expression and regarded Miriam with a kind of envious respect. From Serin's enthusiastic chatter, Miriam gathered that she'd just come from such an institution for girls, a very ancient and famous school of its kind, which she'd entered on her thirteenth birthday and left on her eighteenth. Her course of study there was not quite the sort of thing Miriam was used to—the curriculum included fencing with dagger and buckler and shooting with the bow, as well as civil and religious law, espionage, the proper compounding of perfumes, incenses, medicines, and poisons, and a great deal of the practical theology necessary for dealing with the stern and capricious gods of dream—but it also included no small amount of history and literature.

The governess, concluding that Miriam was both a respectable person and one whose conversation might benefit her charge, stopped hissing injunctions at Serin. This was just as well, for three days out of Celephaïs, *Windstrider of Ullan* ran into heavy weather. The gale wasn't too bad, or so Miriam thought as she looked out at the gray churning water and the flying spindrift, but it was more than enough to leave the poor governess flat on her back with a wretched case of seasickness.

Miriam promised to accompany Serin at meals, for it was not to be thought of that the daughter of a great house of Thran would eat unchaperoned in the presence of strange men. As it happened, the precaution was needless at first, for both the merchants holed up in their cabins and requested nothing from the steward but dry bread and water until the storm blew out. For five days, the company in the stateroom consisted solely of Miriam and Serin, with the steward waiting on them and Aysh perched attentively on her chair near the door, eating from a bowl in her lap, listening to the talk with a little smile on her face and saying nothing.

The fourth day, Serin looked decidedly queasy herself, and Miriam said, "Not seasickness, I hope?"

"No, it is—" She stopped, looked baffled. "I cannot believe that they have no word in Ooth-Nargai for the, the blood, that comes with the moon—oh, you must know what I mean."

"I do," said Miriam, "but as far as I know, they have no word and no need of one. There is no—" She fumbled after terms for pregnancy and childbirth, which the language of Ooth-Nargai also lacked. "No making of children there, and no letting-out of them."

That got her an astonished look, and then Serin blushed and started laughing. "How very convenient for the maidens," she said.

Miriam choked, and started laughing too, hard enough that she only just managed to keep her bowl of stew from landing in her lap when the ship pitched suddenly to starboard. Serin helped her catch the bowl, and the two of them sat there laughing while Aysh, eyes dancing, pressed one hand to her mouth and tried not to join in.

From that moment Miriam found herself adopted as surrogate aunt, and custodian of the embarrassed confessions and rarely spoken hopes of an eighteen-year-old's heart. Though the storm blew itself out, the seas remained rough, and the governess stayed in bed—"Poor Neleth," Serin said sadly one morning, "it was as much as I could do to get a little bread and water down her. I hope we have gentler seas soon"—and so it became Miriam's far from burdensome duty to go with Serin onto the deck once the skies cleared. A brisk north wind had set in, sending spray flying from the crests of the waves and stretching the galleon's sails out into great straining arcs of white. The two of them stood by the leeward rail, holding tight to the smooth polished wood, while the captain paced the sterncastle deck above and the sailors labored. To either side, the high pale crags that flanked the Straits of Stethelos rose above gray unruly waters; *Windstrider of Ullan* was passing from the Cerenerian Sea into the Twilight Sea.

They had been talking about her father's house in Ilek-Vad, which Serin knew only from letters: a great sprawling pile of a place that was already standing a long age ago, when the doomed city of Sarnath still ruled the land of Mnar. The house was thronged with servants of every description, and Miriam wondered aloud why Aysh had been sent with her.

That got a look of astonishment from Serin. "But I could not possibly be without Aysh! It is a custom of ours in Sydathria. We had the same wet-nurse, and played together as children; when we were in school she had as much to study as I, for she will have the management of my household, and will guard me with a spear when I shoot the bow in war; if the gods give me children, she will be the midwife; if a man should lay violent hands on either of us, the other has the privilege of helping her flay him alive; and we will rest in one tomb." Then, with a sudden look of doubt: "But I suppose things are done otherwise in your land."

"They are," Miriam said, "but your custom seems good to me."

Serin glanced at her with a bright smile, and a little later a squall drove them belowdecks.

On days when the rain hammered the portholes they

holed up in Serin's cabin. Serin and Aysh settled comfortably on the bed, Miriam sat in the chair, and they told stories to each other. Apparently professors of literature in Thran included storytelling in their professional repertoire, for Serin assumed as a matter of course that Miriam must be a bubbling fount of tales, and Miriam found to her surprise that with a little effort she was able to live up to expectations. She lifted material by turns from Homer, Shakespeare, Sir Thomas Malory, an assortment of world mythologies, and the pages of *Weird Tales*, depending on the weather, her mood, and the moods of her accidental charges.

Serin repaid the debt by recounting stories of the Dreamlands, mostly old legends of Sydathria and the lands around it. One story Serin told, though, dealt with stranger matters: a land in the uttermost west, beyond Hatheg-Kla and the Bnazic desert, where flame rises eternally in the temple of a forgotten god. "They say that everything in the Six Kingdoms and beyond them is born of that Flame," Serin whispered, "and if ever the Flame is extinguished, everything will vanish away like mist in the sunlight." Aysh shuddered and beamed; Miriam nodded slowly, but recalled words she did not speak aloud: *you will go to the place of the Flame.*

TWENTY-FIVE DAYS OUT from Celephaïs, late in the afternoon, *Windstrider of Ullan* turned in a great arc from east to east-southeast. Miriam and Serin were on the quarterdeck just then, and so was Aysh, standing just behind her mistress. With the wind nearly abaft, the galleon ran swift before it. The sun hung low to starboard, its rays streaming across from horizon to horizon and sending the shadows of the sails far to port. Serin flung her head back and drank in the salt air. "Oh, it seems so short a while since we sailed from Thran," she said, "and shorter still since you came aboard, Miriam.

You have been so very good to me! When we come to land, will you come with me to my father's house? He and his wife will gladly make you welcome, and give you any help you might need while you are in Ilek-Vad."

"Thank you," Miriam said, touched. "But I have an errand to one of the kings of Rokol, Randolph Carter."

Serin's eyes went round. "King Randolphcarter!" she gasped. "Oh, I did not know! Have you met him, then?"

"No, but King Kuranes of Ooth-Nargai sent me to him, and we are to travel to a place of which I know nothing."

Serin took that in. "They say there is nowhere in the Six Kingdoms that Randolphcarter has not been, and few places beyond them," she said. Then: "If you can, once your errand is done, will you come? Please promise me you will!"

"If I can, I will," said Miriam. "I promise."

The next morning the coast of Rokol was just visible in the distance to the south, a dim line on the horizon's edge. Hour by hour it grew closer and took on definition, until Miriam, leaning over the rail to look past the foresail's edge, could see dark headlands rising above the rumpled surface of the Twilight Sea. She and Serin watched the shore draw near, until they could both see the spires of the High City of Ilek-Vad, perched upon its cliff of black glass, and the crowded roofs of the Low City surrounding the two harbors just west of it.

"Time to go belowdecks, my ladies," the steward said then. "With the wind as lively as it is, it'll be tricky work getting into the Inner Harbor, and the crew'll need free run of the decks."

They went aft, and Serin busied herself helping Aysh with the governess and their gear. Miriam went into her cabin and sat on one end of the bed. With the voyage almost done, her mind flailed between uncertainties about the task she'd been given, stark memories of the people she'd left behind in Arkham, and questions about what might be happening there. Whether Miskatonic University had fallen into Clark Noyes' hands, or the hands of whatever might be behind him—she had not forgotten Will Bishop's evasive words; whether Will had managed to get Amber to safety, and how the little creature was doing; whether Carl Upham had survived his beating, and what he and the other professors might or might not be doing about Miskatonic's future; whether any of them would ever find out what had happened to her; whether she could do whatever it was she was supposed to do at the Oracle of the Great Abyss or the place of the Flame— those circled in her mind, unanswerable.

Clatters and thumps, officers shouting orders, footfalls on the sterncastle deck above: the sounds seemed comfortable and familiar now. The galleon heeled hard as it turned to port, and turbulent swells surged beneath it; then the water calmed, and the galleon righted itself and glided ahead. A glance through the porthole showed wharves close by and sturdy stone buildings beyond them, and she knew that *Windstrider of Ullan* had come safe to port.

Then sailors leapt down onto the wharf and hauled on cables, bringing the galleon to her berth. A crisp rap on her door a few minutes later announced the steward, come to tell her that it was time to disembark. By the time she'd donned a cloak and come into the passageway, the others were spilling out of their cabins. The two merchants hurried past. When they were gone, the old governess Neleth thanked her profusely for taking care of Serin, and picked her way uncomfortably toward the door; Serin threw her arms around Miriam and said, "Come as soon as you possibly can," and scampered after the old woman; and Aysh took one of Miriam's hands in both of hers, pressed it to her forehead, murmured a word of thanks, and followed her mistress.

On deck the wind rushed past, and the blue gulls wheeled

and cried out high above. Miriam climbed down to the main deck, found the gangplank and crossed to the wharf. A carriage pulled by four black horses was just then leaving the wharf, and Miriam was nearly sure she saw Aysh's face pressed against one of the windows, looking back at her, just before it rolled out of sight. The merchants had already gone somewhere else, and an assortment of carts waited on the wharf, presumably for luggage as well as whatever cargo the galleon had carried.

Standing on the great timbers of the wharf, Miriam suddenly realized that she'd made no plans at all for her arrival in Ilek-Vad. The houses of the Low City stood before her, but if any of them were inns, she could see no sign of it. A moment later it occurred to her that she had no money for an inn—or did they even use money in the Dreamlands? She realized she had no idea. She turned toward the long arc of the city, roof above roof around the Inner Harbor past the glassy black crags above, to the turreted High City around the citadel of the kings of Rokol. If I have to walk up there, I have to walk, she told herself, and turned to leave the wharf.

As she did so, another carriage arrived at the wharf's end: smaller than the one that had taken Serin away, with only two wheels and a single pair of horses drawing it. It stopped, and a young man in a leather jerkin, knee-length trousers and high boots climbed out of it and came down the wharf toward her. He bowed and said, "Lady Miriam?"

"Yes."

"It is well. I am the King's messenger Amandanil. His Majesty has received word from his friend the King of Ooth-Nargai, and wishes me to convey you to the citadel. Will you come?"

"Gladly," Miriam said. "But I have things still on board."

"Of course." He turned and called to one of the ship's officers in a language Miriam did not know; after a brief exchange of words, he turned back to Miriam. "Your baggage will follow us promptly. If you will come with me, my lady."

ONE BROAD AVENUE led in a single smooth curve from the Inner Harbor to the gates of the citadel of Ilek-Vad close to a thousand feet above the sea. The carriage clattered along its length, past little narrow streets and sturdy half-timbered houses. The town reminded Miriam at once of unspoiled corners of New England port towns, the half-medieval city of Vyones in France where she'd gone on sabbatical, and Lisbon's old Alfama district under the towers of the Castelo de São Jorge. People moved briskly through the streets— Ooth-Nargai's unhurried pace lay many leagues behind her. Most of the men she saw wore, as Amandanil did, leather jerkins over plain white shirts and loose knee-length trousers; most of the women, embroidered blouses and woolen skirts falling between the ankle and the knee; both wore calf-high boots of soft leather with toes that curled up to points, and hooded woolen cloaks against the weather.

Miriam considered all this and said nothing. The young man next to her seemed content with that, and the cloppety-clop of the horses and the clatter of the wheels on the cobbled avenue kept the silence from becoming oppressive.

Finally the carriage passed through a tall archway into a courtyard, and rattled to a stop. Amandanil opened the door and leapt down, then offered her his hand. She took it, descended to the cobbled pavement. High walls of dark stone rose on all aides, pierced by paired windows with many-colored glazing; half a dozen other carriages stood here and there amid the courtyard, and off to one side a spirited mare tossed her head and neighed as a rider swung into the saddle.

"This way, my lady," said Amandanil, and led her to a stout double door up two steps from the pavement. Inside was a room paneled in dark wood, and women in the costume of Ilek-Vad . Amandanil spoke to them in a language Miriam did not know, then bowed and made off.

"You come from Ooth-Nargai, my lady?" one of the women asked her in the language of that country. When Miriam assented, she smiled. "It is well. Be welcome to the palace of the kings of Rokol. You are come from a sea voyage, yes? A bath, then, and all else that is needful. King Randolphcarter will send for you when he may, perhaps this afternoon, perhaps in the morning. He has many duties to complete before his brother king returns."

Miriam accepted that gratefully—since her return to time, the absence of hot water for washing aboard the *Windstrider of Ullan* had become a noticeable burden—and followed another of the women to what she gathered would be her chamber for the time being, a large airy room in one of the palaces' many turrets, with windows looking north across the Twilight Sea toward far Thorabon and west over the jumbled roofs of the Low City to the gray shoreline cliffs and dark forests of Rokol. The promised bath made its appearance, and before that was over her sea chests had come up from the harbor and she was able to dress in clean garments. A meal followed: brown bread, an onion soup that would have passed muster at the Restaurant le Frenaie, and poached fish in a delicate white sauce, washed down with a white wine that the woman who served her assured her came from the vineyards of Nir in far Sydathria.

All in all, she felt a good deal less disheveled when the servants of the King came to summon her to his presence that afternoon, and her reflection in the tall mirror in her chamber—silver hair neatly brushed, skin lightly browned by sunlight on the Cerenerian Sea, stark elegance of the white sleeveless dress of Ooth-Nargai with its cord binding—made her think of Greek priestesses in vase-paintings and marble statues. The king's servants bowed low and led her through a maze of corridors and chambers where courtiers gave her glances by turns startled and speculative, and then to a tall double door, where one of the servants knocked, entered, and then returned after a moment, saying, "My lord the King awaits you."

She thanked him and went through the door.

The room on the other side didn't look at all like a king's chamber. It looked remarkably like the study a Boston author of the 1920s might have had in his home, with tall bookshelves, a big oaken desk strewn with papers, half a dozen chairs scattered all anyhow around the walls, afternoon light streaming in through small-paned windows, and two big black cats sprawled in seemingly uncomfortable positions, one on the desk and the other on a cushion on the floor. The man who sat at the desk, turning in his chair to regard her, didn't look like a king, for that matter. Dressed in a loose white shirt and the baggy knee-length trousers and soft boots of Rokol, he had the black hair and lean harsh-angled face she remembered from the newspaper photograph, all but untouched by further age, and his movements had a decisiveness that made it easy for her to imagine him dodging bullets in the trenches of the First World War or climbing the sheer slopes of Mount Ngranek in search of unknown Kadath. "Your Majesty," she said in English, curtseying, as the door clicked shut behind her.

"So you're the woman who had poor Edmund in such a cold sweat," said Randolph Carter. Seeing her blank look: "Sorry. He goes by Kuranes here, but I knew him in the waking world as Edmund Trevor-Fitzwilliam. Please have a seat."

Miriam settled on the front edge of one of the armchairs, unsure of the proper way to sit in the presence of a king of

Dreamland. Randolph Carter seemed to sense that, and gave her a wry look. "Oh, for heaven's sake, make yourself comfortable. When I've got my crown on, and the rest of the kit, you can bow and scrape as much as you like, but here and now—no. I think you know who I am and what I was—though of course you have the advantage of me there."

"My name's Miriam Akeley," she said. "I'm—I was—a professor of history of ideas at Miskatonic University."

"Pleased to meet you. So Miskatonic hires women professors now? That's good to hear. I took my bachelor's degree there, you know."

"I did know that, actually."

He considered that. "Perhaps you'll tell me how you heard of me. It's got to be close to a century since I left, and I'm not fool enough to think that anyone still reads the stuff I wrote."

"Your novels are all still in print, as far as I know," Miriam said. "But I read of you first in the stories of your cousin H.P. Lovecraft."

Randolph blinked, and stared at her. "Howard? You've even heard of him? He had plenty of talent, no question, but the last I heard, he could only get his stuff published in amateur journalism or those wretched pulp magazines." He shook his head, obviously amazed. "Have you by any chance heard of the city of Thran—is it Dr. Akeley?"

"Yes," said Miriam. "And yes, one of the other passengers on the ship that brought me here is from Thran."

"That would be Raban sen Eshe-Mathil's daughter, I imagine. She'll be presented to me five days from now." Then: "But the guards at the gates of Thran have a custom, when a mortal dreamer comes to the gates, of requiring him to tell three dreams beyond belief before letting him enter. If you ever go there, tell the guard that you came to Ilek-Vad, went to the king, and talked with him about the forgotten literary ambitions of one of his poor cousins back in the waking world, and that'll do for one."

"But Lovecraft hasn't been forgotten," Miriam said, surprised. "He's considered the most influential American horror writer of the twentieth century. I teach classes on Lovecraft's stories, and most of my professional publications have been on his fiction."

That got her a look of thorough astonishment. "Literature classes and scholarly articles on Howard's stories? Have Shakespeare and Milton dropped out of fashion, then?"

"Not at all," said Miriam. "How many original articles do you think it's possible to write on Shakespeare and Milton?"

"Quite a few."

"They've all been written—most of them a dozen times over."

He took that in, and started laughing. "Fair enough. Tell the guard that the poor cousin of the king of Rokol has become famous in the waking world, and his tales are the subject of learned discussion among scholars, and you'll be two-thirds of the way into Thran."

"I'll keep that in mind," Miriam said, laughing also.

Randolph considered her, then, and went on. "Before we talk about the message that put Edmund into such a swivet, I hope you don't mind if I ask a question or two about the girl you traveled with, Lord Eshe-Mathil's daughter. Romantic young women—and a few romantic older ones, shall we say—come here from time to time with ideas about what they can hope from the kings of Rokol, and there have been painful scenes. I'd prefer to avoid another."

Miriam gave him a puzzled look, then thought she understood. "She certainly didn't say anything about wanting to fling herself at your feet, if that's what you mean."

"That's good to hear."

"You're unmarried, I take it."

His eyebrows went up. "I gather there's a good deal you don't know about Rokol." In response to her questioning look: "A very long time ago, the people here had no end of trouble because kings so rarely pass on their talents to their children, and so they made a law making the kingship elective and limiting it to those whose pastimes, shall we say, weren't likely to produce an heir."

It took her a moment to realize what he was saying, and by the time that happened, a memory had stirred. "Your cousin Lizzie's granddaughter mentioned in a letter—how did she put it?—that you weren't the marrying kind."

Randolph laughed. "So Lizzie finally pupped! That's good to know; you'll have to fill me in on the details another time. But as to the other—yes. Does that disturb you?"

"Not at all," Miriam replied. "My closest friend in the waking world, another Miskatonic professor, is—did they even use the term 'gay' in your time?"

That got her another surprised look. "Now and then," he said. "'Pansy' was a good deal more common; 'fairy,' likewise; 'Uranian,' among the educated; and of course 'temperamental.'"

"Temperamental?" she repeated, blinking in surprise.

"Yes, that was for personal advertisements—you could say that, or 'interested in Greek culture,' and the newspapers would print it. Of course there were plenty of uglier words." A quick shake of his head dismissed them. "But I hope your friend the professor hasn't had any trouble about that."

"Not at all," said Miriam. "He brings his husband to faculty events."

Randolph stared. "I assume you mean 'husband' metaphorically."

"No—Massachusetts was the first state in the Union to legalize same-sex marriage."

The king's mouth fell open, and he tried to speak, without immediate success. "Massachusetts!" he finally forced out. "You must be joking. Blue-nosed, hypocritical, holier-than-thou *Massachusetts*? Letting us *marry*?"

"Things have changed quite a bit," said Miriam.

Randolph stared at her a moment longer, then began to laugh. "Dr. Akeley, you've just earned your way into Thran." Then: "Well, that's definitely shaken me down to the core—though I'm glad to hear it. Very glad, in fact. I don't even want to think about all the misery that could have been avoided if the Commonwealth of Massachusetts had displayed that kind of common sense a century or two earlier." He shook his head. "There were plenty of reasons why I decided to leave the waking world for the Dreamlands once I had the chance, but that was one of them. You've read Howard's stories about the Dreamlands, I imagine?"

"Many times."

"There are plenty of dreams he was too much of a prude to write about, and those are here." Considering her: "Those, and much more."

EIGHT

The Lord of the Great Abyss

Evening in Ilek-Vad fell gray and golden, with lights gleaming in ten thousand windows between the cliffs and the restless sea. Back in her chamber, Miriam leaned on the windowsill and watched the daylight fade. She'd given Randolph Carter the message she'd received from the being she'd seen in the darkness that separated the circle of elms from the Tanarian Hills, and had him regard her for a long moment through slightly narrowed eyes. Thereafter the air of casual amiability with which he'd regarded her vanished; he asked only a few more questions, and then summoned a servant and sent her away with a suddenness that was almost brusque. Baffled, she made no protest, let the servant lead her to her chamber.

An hour later, another servant came with a message and a gift. King Randolphcarter, the young woman told her, would be in seclusion for at least two days, busy in a certain high tower of the palace about which it was not well to ask. In the meantime, Miriam was to consider herself free to walk throughout the palace and its gardens, and could take her meals in her chamber or with the courtiers and dignitaries in the Hall of Ordinary Festivity as she wished. While she waited, the king was pleased to lend her certain books. Miriam thanked her, inquired about the timing of dinner and the location of the Hall of Ordinary Festivity, and took the books.

There were four of them, neatly bound in cloth, and once the servant had curtseyed and departed, Miriam carried them to a table that stood against the seaward wall of her chamber, and opened them one at a time. Unexpectedly, they were in English, printed—she gathered that the sort of letterpress that had made Ben Franklin's fortune had found its way to Ilek-Vad, for the pages had that slight texturing she'd encountered in handprinted books before—and proved to be novels of Boston life written by Randolph Carter, unpublished in the waking world.

The first chapter of one novel kept her well entertained until it was time to prepare for dinner. The same young woman who'd brought her the books came thereafter to lead her to the Hall of Ordinary Festivity and showed her to her place, above the salt but noticeably far from the throne where the kings of Rokol were wont to sit at mealtimes. The throne was empty when she arrived, and stayed that way while others arrived and took their places and the great crystal gong sounded to announce the beginning of the meal. An elderly woman in an ornate gown—a priestess, Miriam guessed—recited something, prayer or incantation, and then everyone sat.

To one side of Miriam sat a man with long narrow eyes and a pointed chin, dressed in felted wool garments; to the other, an odd-looking person in a turban that rose to two points in front, and a mouth that seemed improbably wide. The man in felt garments, after the first course was on the trenchers, turned to her and said in the language of Ooth-Nargai, "I hope the gentle lady will forgive my curiosity, but I suspect you are not of Celephaïs, though you wear the garments of that place."

"And I suspect," Miriam replied with a smile, "that you're of Inquanok. But you're quite correct, and I'm curious about how you knew."

"The gentle lady is perceptive," he said. "Yes, I am Darhaneb of Selarn, a poor merchant of that land."

He didn't look poor by any definition, but Miriam let that pass, and introduced herself. "Even so," he said. "As to my knowledge—or rather my guess, for it was no more than that—I trust I will give no offense if I mention that silver hairs are not seen in that land, nor have the people thereof quite the cast of face I see before me. And the source of your knowledge?"

"The cast of face likewise," said Miriam.

Darhaneb laughed. "So often do our faces betray us! And your companion on the other side—I imagine you can name his homeland."

Miriam turned. The odd turbaned person smiled and, in a voice that didn't quite sound human, said, "Can you?"

"I believe," Miriam said, "that you're from the Plateau of Leng."

The smile broadened. "That is so. Rhu'u'lhau is my name, Miriam of Arkham."

"We came here on the same ship," said Darhaneb then. "That surprises you? The folk of Leng commonly sail from Inquanok when they go abroad."

"I had read," Miriam said cautiously, "of certain—tensions, perhaps?—between Inquanok and Leng."

His gesture dismissed them. "Between any two lands anywhere, such things arise now and again. Unavoidable, and with the blessing of the gods, unimportant."

"You are kind," said Rhu'u'lhau.

They talked companionably as the meal proceeded through its seven courses, and parted with courteous words once it was over. Then Miriam returned to her chamber and stared out the window at the last of the daylight. Her eyes followed the avenue that led from the gates of the palace down and around the harbor to the Low City.

Though the oncoming night had all but emptied the avenue, a lone figure strode up the hill. At first Miriam could see little, but as the figure kept climbing the slope she caught an impression of height, dark garments, a long swinging stride that devoured distance. Something about him sent a cold shudder down her spine. She backed away from the window, closed it, and tried to bury herself in Randolph Carter's novel until sleep took her.

THE NEXT MORNING dawned clear and bright. After breakfasting in her room, Miriam recalled a detail the servant had mentioned the day before, and asked about the palace gardens. A quarter hour later, perhaps, another of the palace servants opened a door and bowed, and she thanked him and walked out onto a gravel path edged by tall rosebushes.

A wall of dark stone with turrets at the corners surrounded the garden. Within, raked gravel paths traced ornate geometrical patterns among beds of flowers and herbs, some that Miriam knew and some she had never seen or imagined before. Roses, lilies, yarrow blossoms like snowbanks and tall aromatic rosemary bushes were familiar enough, but she wasn't sure what to make of the showy white blossoms with four little paddles like sea-turtles' legs under them, which swam here and there in a pond edged with irises, or the tall red trumpet-shaped flowers that blew, one after another, pale golden bubbles that floated away on the sea breeze.

Such curiosities kept her sufficiently intrigued that it was some time before she realized she was not alone in the gardens. The sound of footfalls on a gravel path not far away finally caught her attention. She looked up, to see a tall figure in black walking purposefully toward her. She didn't recognize him, and his face was anything but forgettable—lean and brown-skinned, with black eyes and a nose arched like a hawk's beak—but something in the far corners of her mind tried to tell her that she ought to know who he was.

"Dr. Akeley," he said in English as he approached her. His voice was deeper than she'd expected, with a faint accent she couldn't place. Many rings glinted on his hands.

Startled, she managed to say, "Yes. I don't think we've met."

That seemed to amuse him. "No, but we have mutual friends." Then: "It would be well for us to talk." He gestured toward a bench of wrought iron and pale wood not far away, in the shelter of a rose-arbor. "And by the way, you do know who I am."

Miriam gave him a startled glance, but crossed to the bench, sat on one end of it. He settled on the other, stretched his long legs out before him. Human though he looked, something profoundly unhuman seemed to hover within and around him, as though a mountain, a desert, or a wandering star had somehow briefly made itself look like a human being. That was the thing that convinced her that her first wild guess had been correct.

"You're Nyarlathotep," she said. "The Crawling Chaos."

He regarded her with the same amused look. "It's a pleasure to be recognized."

Details from *The Dream-Quest of Unknown Kadath* came absurdly to mind. "I would have expected to see you in prismatic garments and a glowing headdress of gold, or at least dressed in robes the color of scarlet flame."

Unexpectedly, he laughed aloud. "I see you're familiar with some very old lore. The headdress and the many-colored robes are only for certain important occasions, though. As for scarlet, I wore it for long ages in the past and I will wear it for long ages again—but until the stars are right, I wear black."

Miriam tried to make sense of that, failed. "Why are you—"

"Here? Because Randolph Carter called me, of course—though I admit I wanted to have a look at you myself, for reasons of my own. He had certain doubts about you and your mission here, which I was able to resolve."

"I thought you and Carter were enemies."

"You read that in H.P. Lovecraft," he responded, unperturbed. When she nodded: "I don't recommend trusting Lovecraft on that subject. He and I had our differences."

She stared at the Great Old One for a long moment. "You knew him."

"Of course. There are chapters in his life that never made it into the scholarly literature." Nyarlathotep considered her then. "Do you know who sent you here to the Dreamlands?"

"No, I don't."

"Nodens, Lord of the Great Abyss."

Miriam took that in. "What does he want me to do?"

"He'll make that clear in due time." He leaned fractionally toward her. "But you weren't chosen by accident, Dr. Akeley. Your private studies are known to us." She was about to claim ignorance when he smiled faintly and quoted, "'Memoirs to Prove the Existence of Cthulhu.'"

A silence passed. "I'd be interested in knowing how you found out about that," she said.

"Better ask how we could miss finding out. As it happens, you were once incautious enough to murmur a certain name aloud."

Cold fear stirred in her, but Nyarlathotep shrugged. "Speak the name of the King in Yellow aloud anywhere, even in a whisper, and he'll hear it—but if it hadn't been that, it would have been something else. We have various ways of knowing who studies our lore."

"What happens," she ventured then, "when you find out that someone is studying—that sort of thing?"

"That depends entirely on the motive."

"In my case, it was simple curiosity," Miriam said.

"That's usually how it starts," he said, "but that motive never remains for long. There are no neutrals in this business, Dr. Akeley. Sooner or later, anyone who learns about the Great Old Ones either aids them or opposes them."

"Are you telling me I have to choose sides?" she asked.

His laugh denied it. "You already have."

Then he was gone, as suddenly and completely as though he'd never been there at all. Miriam stared at the place where he'd been, then slowly got to her feet and found her way out of the garden and back into the palace, her mind whirling. What troubled her most was the last thing the Crawling Chaos had said to her, and it troubled her because she knew he was right.

LATER ON, SHE dined in the Hall of Ordinary Festivity in sight of the empty throne of Rokol, chatted with Darhaneb and Rhu'u'lhau, and buried herself in a second Randolph Carter novel when she returned to her chamber, seeking to still her thoughts in his amused and affectionate recollections of Boston life. She was dozing in a great overstuffed chair, the book in her lap and a many-wicked oil lamp of curious design glowing nearby, when a familiar chirring sound broke into vague disconnected thoughts.

She jolted awake, looked around suddenly. "Amber?"

All at once the little creature sprang onto her lap and climbed up onto her arm, chirring in delight. She let out a little cry, cradled her against her shoulder and let the fingers of one hand stroke Amber's back. "How did you get here?"

she asked, but the question answered itself; she could feel, through the little form clinging to her arm, an identical form curled up on a familiar towel in a cluttered, unfamiliar room. Of course, she thought. She's asleep, and dreaming of me. She set aside the book, sat there petting the creature for a long while, and went to bed with Amber still nestled in place.

She blinked awake to a sunlit morning; her hand was resting on her own shoulder, and Amber was gone. That was no surprise, but it left Miriam feeling lonely and miserable, thinking of all the people she'd never see again—friends, colleagues, former students, the threads that made up the fabric of her life in Arkham and the rest of the waking world.

Stop it, she told herself. Stop it. You were going to lose them soon anyway. That didn't help much, so she got out of bed and made herself ring the bell that brought the servants, and face the morning. She was still finishing breakfast when another servant came to tell her that the King had requested her presence as soon as was convenient.

She finished the contents of the leather flagon before her— like the English in the time of Elizabeth I, the folk of Ilek-Vad drank small beer with breakfast. "I'll need—" she started to say, and then stopped, for the language of Ooth-Nargai had no words for "just a few minutes." The servant seemed to understand, though, and waited in the hallway outside while she washed up, got her hair presentable, and gave herself a quick assessing look in the mirror.

A few minutes later she was being shown into the same study where she'd met Randolph Carter before. He glanced up from a leatherbound book he was reading, and waved her to a chair occupied by one of the black cats. "Good morning, Dr. Akeley. By all means move Alick; he'll get over it. I hope you'll forgive me for a certain curtness toward the end of our last meeting."

"Good morning." She picked up the cat and set it on the

floor. It gave her an unsanitary glare and then paced over to the cushion on the floor and started licking its flank. Miriam sat down. "Would it be fair," she ventured, "to ask for an explanation?"

He paused, and then nodded. "Yes. I had to be certain that you were what you said you were. If I were to mention an organization that calls itself the Radiance, would you have the least idea what I was talking about?" She shook her head, and he went on. "I thought as much. But the Great Old Ones, of course, you know about."

"To the extent that I can trust what your cousin and his friends wrote about them."

"Good," said Randolph. He leaned back in his chair and, regarding her, said, "Tell me this, then. Do you believe that humanity is the pinnacle of creation, the master of the forces of nature, the measure of all things?"

She gave him a startled look, but the expression on his face told her the question was meant in deadly earnest. "No," she said after a moment. "No, I don't."

"Why not?"

"That's a good question." With a sudden rueful smile: "It would honestly be easier for me to talk about the process by which that set of beliefs became popular in the Western world than it would for me to explain why I don't accept them. The curse of the professional scholar, I suppose." She paused for a short time. "I think it's because of their basic absurdity. All three phrases are sustained exercises in begging the question. There's no *prima facie* reason to think that creation has a pinnacle, or that the forces of nature have a master, or that all things have any common measure, and if you're going to claim these supposed honors for just one species that happens to be living at the moment on one out-of-the-way planet in one undistinguished galaxy out of trillions—well, you're going to have to answer a lot of very difficult questions first."

His angular face broke into a sudden grin. "Excellent!" he said. "I envy your students at Miskatonic. They must have had a lively time in your classes."

"Thank you," said Miriam.

"Now, the explanation," he replied. "The organization I mentioned does believe in these things. You mentioned the process that gave those notions their foothold in Western civilization. How long would you say that's been going on?"

She considered that. "Since ancient Greece," she said. "No, further than that. There were intellectual currents in Mesopotamia moving in the same direction a millennium or so before the Greeks got there."

"And if I told you that an organization founded in those very early times has been pursuing the goals I just named ever since?"

"I'd want to see some evidence," Miriam replied at once.

"Fair enough. There are books, but I have no idea whether you'd consider them reliable—and of course the name of the organization has changed many times over the centuries. But it occurs to me that you might have encountered the phrase *Dumu-ne Zalaga*."

"Yes, I have," she said after a moment. "What does it mean?"

"The Children of Light," said Randolph. "It's Sumerian, and it's the original name of the organization we've been discussing. In modern times, the usual term is the Radiance." He shook his head. "I had run-ins with them in the waking world. Their adepts are the most frightening people I've ever met: empty shells with no one there inside, and eyes like dead things."

Miriam stared at him, thinking of Clark Noyes, and slowly began to nod.

"So the issue," Randolph went on, "was figuring out whether you were what you claimed, or whether you'd been

sent by the Radiance to trap me. I settled that in the traditional fashion, by calling for guidance from a certain messenger
of the Great Old Ones."

"Nyarlathotep," Miriam guessed.

"Good. Yes, it was the Crawling Chaos."

"He met me in your gardens yesterday morning."

"I'm glad to hear that. I trust he mentioned that he was
able to vouch for you, and for the message you brought. That
latter was of some importance; it's one thing to seek the Oracle of the Great Abyss when summoned by its Master, and
quite another to do the same thing uncalled."

"King Kuranes practically turned green when I mentioned it," said Miriam.

"I imagine he did," he said, laughing. "Edmund really is
a dear person, but he's not the adventurous type. A timeless
realm where nothing ever changes is very much his style."

"But not yours, I suspect."

"Not mine at all. In fact, we'll be going to the Oracle this
afternoon."

Startled, she nodded anyway. "How far is it?"

"Very close indeed. You've heard of the gnorri? They're
the keepers of the Oracle. We'll proceed to the Low City after
lunch and approach them when the tide is right. And then—"
He shrugged. "What will happen will happen. The Oracle's
not without danger, Dr. Akeley."

EARLY AFTERNOON FOUND them ensconced in a carriage rat-
tling down the long curving avenue that linked the High City
to the Low City. Two horsemen with drawn sabers rode before the carriage and two more behind, and a pair of footmen similarly armed stood erect at the back of the carriage;
citizens of Ilek-Vad walking the streets turned to watch them
pass. Ahead, tall masts of ships in the Inner and Outer Har-

bors stood gaunt against the pale sky.

"Everything in Rokol is by twos," Randolph was saying; Miriam had asked him about the country's two kings. "In Ilek-Vad there's a Low and a High City, an Inner and an Outer Harbor; the country as a whole is divided into southern and northern moieties, with the Twilight Sea between them; every guild has two masters, every temple two priestesses, and so on. So of course there are two kings. Each of us reigns for half the year and must spend the other half outside Rokol's borders." Meeting her surprised look: "As I think I mentioned before, the people of Rokol had bad experiences with certain kings a long time back, and passed laws to prevent a recurrence. Myself, I don't mind at all; six months of relative quiet—my duties are mostly ceremonial—and then six months of travel suits me very well."

"Serin ban Eshe-Mathil said you'd been all over the Dreamlands," Miriam ventured.

"Oh, there are still places I haven't gotten to—the Dreamlands aren't easily mapped, or easily mastered. Did you know that there are six directions here?"

She gave him a startled look. "No."

"East and west, north and south, anth and ulth—all at right angles to one another."

After a moment, Miriam said, "That would imply four spatial dimensions."

"Excellent!" he replied. "Yes, it does. Those exist in the waking world, too, but there, humans can't perceive them. Here, we can." He glanced out the window. "Ah, here we are."

The carriage came to a halt, and one of the footmen jumped down, opened the doors, and bowed. Randolph sprang down to the cobbled street, extended a hand to Miriam and helped her down, then turned to the footman, and said something in the language of Rokol. Miriam had begun to pick up a few words of that language, and caught "wait" and "two or three hours."

"Yes, Your Majesty," the footman replied—Miriam had learned that phrase soon enough.

Ahead was the Inner Harbor and the stone quay that circled it. Randolph led the way to the water's edge, and then to a stair that led down to a landing where a longboat stood waiting, six oarsmen aboard her. "Here we are," he said. "I hope you're not prone to seasickness."

"Not at all," Miriam reassured him.

That got a pleased look and a nod. "Glad to hear it. We'll be in rough seas in a bit."

They climbed aboard the longboat and Miriam settled onto a thwart amidships. The king sat at the stern and gave instructions to the oarsmen, and a moment later the boat was free of her moorings and skimming across the harbor. Miriam threw her head back and drew in a deep breath of the clean sea air, and Randolph laughed. "I take it you're fond of being on the water."

"Very much so. The friend I mentioned to you, Michael Peaslee, has a sailboat, and trips aboard it are—were—the high points of my summers."

"You impress me. I knew far too many women back in the waking world who reacted to a bit of salt spray like a cat dropped into a bathtub."

Miriam laughed. "I know the type. I don't think they're as common as they used to be."

"That's very good to hear," said Randolph.

The longboat all but flew across the smooth water of the Inner Harbor, passed between the two stone breakwaters at its mouth, and angled across the Outer Harbor toward the glassy black cliffs below the High City. Outside the Inner Harbor's shelter, waves off the Twilight Sea rolled long and deep, and ships at anchor rolled with them. The westering sun shone through high clouds; to starboard, the Twilight Sea stretched to the edge of heaven.

Then the longboat rounded the point at the Outer Harbor's edge, and the wind picked up. Spray flew through the air as waves tipped with white foam surged around the little craft. Miriam took hold of the thwart on which she sat with both hands, kept her balance. The oarsmen strained at the oars. Randolph held his head high, as though being tossed like a wood chip on a rough sea was the best entertainment a king could ask for, and called out orders to the oarsmen; ahead of the longboat, the cliffs loomed higher. Mirian wondered for one cold moment if the oarsmen meant to drive the boat straight into the rock, then glimpsed the darker gap ahead.

A sudden surge, half the doing of the oarsmen and half that of a following sea, and the longboat shot into a sea cave. Beyond the narrow entrance, dim lights floating in the still air revealed a great open space hewn out by the sea, complex curves of a wave-cut ceiling high above, black water roiling and eddying below. The oarsmen, at Randolph's command, brought the longboat to one side of the cavern, where a great stone stair roughly shaped rose up out of the sea toward an archway high above, a stone post worn by cables alongside each step.

One of the oarsmen leapt onto the stair and made the longboat fast, and Randolph climbed onto the stair and helped Miriam off the longboat. He said something to the oarsmen that included the word "wait," and then turned to Miriam, motioned up the stair. As they climbed, he said, "Well, that brought back old times. Does Miskatonic still have a rowing team?"

"Yes, though I don't know a thing about it."

He laughed. "*Sic transit gloria mundi*. I was coxswain in 1893, when we handed the Harvard crew their heads on a platter at Poughkeepsie." With a shake of his head: "The experience has come in handy for me more than once, here in the Dreamlands."

The archway loomed black above them. They climbed, and in the darkness ahead, pale luminous eyes blinked open.

THEY REACHED THE top of the stair before Miriam could see anything but the eyes. A dim shape moved in the shadows, squat and ungainly; the pale eyes stared. Randolph spoke in a language that bubbled and choked, and all at once the eyes vanished. Miriam realized a moment later that the creature, whatever it was, had turned and was leading the way. "Come on," Randolph said, and Miriam followed his lead.

She could scarcely make out the walls of the tunnel around them by the faint flickering glow in the distance ahead. Of their guide she could only see faint glimpses: maybe half her height, humanlike enough to have two arms and two legs, but broad-shouldered beyond human proportion, and with something that looked like a long fin running down its back and its long thick tail. Its skin gleamed in the faint light, and its feet flapped on the tunnel's smooth floor.

The tunnel opened out finally into another great cavern, lit like the first by dim lights that drifted in the air. All around them were the gnorri: creatures like the one who had guided them, squat and powerfully built, with hands and feet splayed and webbed, and long spiny fins extending from the backs of their heads all the way down the spine to the tips of their tails. Each of them had a great bushy beard spilling down from the lower half of its face well down its body, and since they wore no scrap of clothing, it took Miriam only a glance to realize that the females were as lavishly bearded as the males. Their pale eyes stared at the two humans.

Randolph spoke to them in the same bubbling, choking

language, though, and one of them, a female with an especially impressive beard, responded in kind. After a conversation, she gave what seemed like instructions to the others, and one of the gnorri approached the humans. "They've agreed to take us to the oracle," Randolph told Miriam. She nodded, followed him and the gnorri toward an opening on the far side of the cavern.

Of the journey that followed, winding gradually downward through a maze of tunnels and caverns, Miriam afterwards recalled only fragments. Thoughts chased one another through her mind, stirred a wild assortment of hopes and fears. Finally, though, one last tunnel opened out onto a cavern greater than any of the others. The floor descended in broad steps to a pool of dark water. Here the guide made a crouching motion that seemed to be some kind of bow, backed away, and vanished into the tunnel.

"It occurs to me," Randolph said then, "that I haven't asked whether you can swim."

"Fortunately, yes."

"Excellent. I also hope your modesty won't be too greatly offended when I mention that bathing dress isn't worn in the Dreamlands."

She gave him an amused look. "Under the circumstances, that's hardly an issue."

His laugh echoed off the ceiling of the cavern. "Good! Very good. Well, then—the Oracle of the Great Abyss is at the bottom of this pool. All that's necessary is to swim down to it—and attend to the words of Great Nodens."

He stripped, left his clothes in a neat pile on one of the steps, and then took a running leap into the pool. She watched him swimming downward with powerful strokes until the darkness swallowed him, then took off her own clothing, and walked down to the edge of the pool. The dark water hid whatever lay beneath it. She drew in a deep breath, and dove.

Water rushed around her, cold and salt. She quickly found her rhythm, swam downward. The darkness became total, and then opened out into something else.

All at once she was falling, plunging downward through blackness as she'd done between the waking world and the Tanarian hills. She barely managed to stifle a scream. Air rushed past her, and then the darkness swirled and took shape. A vast hoary face the color of midnight bent over her, and eyes pale and huge as moons regarded her.

Something that was not a voice spoke: *It is well. You have come as you were bidden.*

Miriam tried to put her whirling thoughts into words, but before she could do so, the not-voice went on. *Attend. A grave peril has come upon the Dreamlands, as was long foreseen. One of the servants of the false and blinding light has passed through the same portal that opened for you. The guardians thereof would have turned him aside, but he bears the Blade of Uoht, and that is a cause for dread. He seeks the Temple of the Flame in the furthest west. If he comes there, he intends to turn the Blade upon the Flame and cause the Dreamlands to be no more.*

It is your task to stop him. He has reached the land of Sydathria in his journey, so haste is needed. Do you understand?

No, Miriam tried to say. I have no idea how to get there, or how to stop a man with a blade, or why you chose me—

It is well, said the not-voice.

An instant later the waters of the pool rushed past her, and she broke the surface and drew in a long and gasping breath. Blinking back salt water, she saw Randolph climbing out of the pool. She managed to get over to the edge, and he reached down, caught her hand, and helped her up onto the lowest of the stone steps.

"I'm sorry to say," he said, "that the Oracle does not pro-vide towels. One moment." He walked some distance away, well away from their clothing, and shook himself, for all the

143

world like a dog after a swim. Water sprayed in all directions. Miriam considered that and tried the same thing without much effect, then shrugged, went to her clothing, and donned the plain woolen garb of Ooth-Nargai.

By the time she was finished, Randolph was shaking out his cloak. Once he'd gotten it settled on his shoulders, she said, "Did you hear the—" Her voice faltered.

"The Oracle? Yes." He frowned. "That's dire news, no question. Still—" His chin rose. "We'll figure out something. Come on." He gestured toward the mouth of the tunnel. Miriam followed, and saw their gnorri guide come out to lead them back.

NINE

The Mountains of the Moon

The tide had risen by the time they returned to the cavern harbor, and the gap through which the waves surged looked uncomfortably low and narrow. Randolph talked to the oarsmen and then turned to Miriam. "We may have a bit of a rough trip back—the wind's picked up a good deal. Still, it shouldn't be too difficult. Shall we?"

Miriam climbed into the longboat, Randolph took his place at the stern, and the oarsmen pushed the boat away from the stair and rowed toward the mouth. They slowed in response to a command from the king, waited until a wave surged high in the cavern mouth, and then all at once leaned into the oars and sent the longboat shooting forward.

The outward ebb of the wave caught the boat and swept it straight through the cavern's mouth. As it leapt out from between the walls of the cliff, though, the wind howled, spray flew past, and another wave swept toward the bow, curling over at its crest. Randolph shouted orders above the wind's roar. The oarsmen strained, and the longboat shot up the wave's face, burst through the foam atop it, and slid down the far side.

A second wave surged up moments later, and this one broke sooner, dousing everyone aboard the longboat. Randolph handed Miriam an oddly shaped wooden scoop with a handle—she recognized it an instant later as an old-fashioned bailing scuttle—and shouted, "Bail for all you're worth!" A second wave broke over them, half flooding the craft. As the oarsmen fought to keep the longboat from being turned beam on to the waves and swamped, Miriam scooped water from the bilge and flung it overboard as fast as she could, but each wave added more. She kept bailing, tried not to notice the rising wind and the long ranks of spray-topped waves rolling out of the far reaches of the Twilight Sea.

As the longboat crested another wave, Randolph shouted something else to the oarsmen, and they brought the boat around in a tight curve as it slid down the back of the wave and rose up the face of the next. The longboat's stern rather than its prow burst through the crest, and then the oarsmen hauled on the oars as never before as the following wave picked up the craft and flung it forward. Glancing briefly forward, Miriam saw one flank of the black cliff looming up to starboard, and was horrified to notice rocks directly ahead. She kept bailing.

Another order from Randolph, and the longboat angled slightly away from the cliff and shot past the rocks with barely an oar's length to spare. Once they passed into the lee of the cliff, the wind died down and the waves slackened. The oarsmen strained, and a few minutes later the longboat was among the first of the ships at anchor.

"Enough," Randolph said, tapping Miriam on the shoulder to get her attention; she blinked, then handed him the bailing scuttle. Water still splashed over her feet. Soaked and chilled to the bone, she clung to her thwart and waited as the longboat sped to the mouth of the Inner Harbor, and then across it to the landing where they'd started.

A few minutes later Randolph sprang onto the landing and helped her out of the longboat. He turned back to the oarsmen—Miriam didn't need to know the language of Rokol to guess at what he was saying—and handed each something that glittered in the gray evening light. That done, he turned back to her and said, "Now let's get you wrapped in something warmer. That was a rougher jaunt than I'd expected—I hope not too rough for you."

"I'll be fine," she told him.

That got her a sudden grin. "That's good to hear."

He led her up the stairs to the quay, called to the footmen who stood by the carriage. One of them hurried over, unfastened his cloak, and settled it around her. "Now out of the wind," the king said, "and something hot to drink from the nearest tavern if you need it."

"Seriously, I'll be fine," Miriam said. The cloak was lined with fur, and took the chill out of her in moments. "I've been through a good deal worse."

Randolph nodded, but still made sure she got settled into the carriage as quickly as possible, then gave orders to the coachman and climbed in. As the door clicked shut, he said, "Tomorrow we can discuss what we'll do about the tidings of the Oracle."

"Is there anything we can do?" Miriam asked him point-blank. "If this person with the blade is already in Sydathria now—that's a month away by sea, and then as long as it takes to get to the Temple of the Flame overland. I don't see how we can reach it in time." *Nor what I can do about it,* she wanted to say; the thought of having to confront someone armed with a weapon left her feeling helpless, much the way she'd felt on the roadside northwest of Arkham.

"You don't yet know the Dreamlands," he said with a smile. "There's always a way. It's not a sure thing—if he's armed with the Blade of Uoht and has the least idea how to use it, it's going to be a challenge—but there'll be a way."

"The Blade of Uoht," Miriam repeated. "Uoht, as in The King in Yellow?"

That got her a sudden glance, and then a nod. "Excellent. Yes, that's the one—the blade with which Uoht avenged Cassilda and then turned on himself."

"That actually happened? I thought that was just a bit from Castaigne's play."

"Not at all." A sharp shake of his head denied it utterly. "The Kingdom of Alar rose and fell in the age between the destruction of Sarkomand and the rise of Sarnath. The Blade was taken by the King to Carcosa, and its nature was changed, as the nature of everything the King touches is changed. From there it passed to Yhe in the days of its power, from there to the isle of Poseidonis, and from there—well, that would be a long story, and not one I know well. The point now is to figure out how to stop it from being used by the Radiance."

The carriage rolled up the long slope to the High City amid a clatter of hooves. Miriam huddled into her borrowed cloak, and thought of the story Serin had told aboard *Windstrider of Ullan* about the temple of a forgotten god in the uttermost west. As the carriage reached the outskirts of the High City, though, Randolph suddenly started to laugh. "There's a way," he said. "Oh, indeed there is."

She glanced at him, startled. "What do you have in mind?"

"My dear Dr. Akeley," he said, "we'll travel from here to beyond the Bnazic desert in a matter of hours—by way of the Moon."

A HOT BATH, dinner in her chamber, two flagons of steaming mulled wine, and an early bed with a hot brick wrapped in cloth tucked under the covers at the foot: that was the Ilek-Vad way of handling a bad chill, Miriam gathered, and it certainly seemed to work. She woke up the next morning feeling little the worse for wear, and that afternoon was summoned again by the king.

"Feeling well? Excellent," he said. "I've made most of the arrangements for our trip. It will take two, maybe three days to arrange for our conveyance—there aren't enough cats here in Ilek-Vad to do the thing by themselves, so I've had to send out messengers throughout Rokol."

Miriam blinked. "So you weren't joking about the Moon."

"Of course not. I have excellent relations with the cats of the Dreamlands; I've done them favors from time to time, and they reciprocate—well, when it's not too much trouble. There's only so much you can ask from a cat. Fortunately, the cats here go to the Moon of their own accord all the time. Do you keep cats? In the waking world, I mean."

"I did, several of them," said Miriam. "Not for some years, though."

"Other pets?"

"Just one, and just before I came here. I had a strange little creature—I'm not sure exactly what she was, but she fits the old description of a witch's familiar. She quite literally fell through a hole in my ceiling one night, and we more or less adopted each other."

"Curious. I wonder what it was." Randolph cocked his head to one side, considered her. "I've noticed—do you mind if we use first names? Under the circumstances, it seems a little silly to stand on ceremony." When she agreed: "I've noticed, Miriam, that when you speak of your life in the waking world it's always in the past tense. Why is that?"

"I'm tolerably sure that I'm dead," said Miriam.

That clearly startled him. "That would surprise me," he said after a moment. "Perhaps you could tell me in detail exactly how you ended up here in the Dreamlands."

"Of course," she said, and recounted the whole tale. By the time she finished, Randolph was nodding slowly. "We'll have much to talk about in due time," he said. "First of all, though, you're not dead. The grove of the nine elms—that's a place I know well enough. An ancestor of mine vanished there back in the eighteenth century. It's a portal that leads to many realms, this one among them, and you passed through it body and soul."

Miriam stared at him for a moment, and then said, "Then there's another complication." In halting words—it was the first time she'd spoken of it to anyone but Dr. Krummholz—she told him about the cancer.

"That's an issue for the longer term," said Randolph once she was done. "Time in the Dreamlands isn't like time in the waking world; six months there might work out to centuries here—or it might not. But there's something else along those lines you should know. If you were simply dreaming, and died here, you'd wake up with nothing but a good scare. When you come here bodily, though, if you die here—" A sudden gesture. "Then you really will be dead."

"So that would also be true of you," she ventured.

"Exactly." A quick grin creased his face. "If that happens, I won't complain; I've lived a dozen ordinary lifetimes here, and though I'd happily live a dozen more—" He shrugged. "If I'd wanted to live forever I'd have made Edmund's choice."

He gestured sharply, dismissing the idea. "In the meantime, we have some preparations to make. I've already arranged for the Prince Chancellor of the Southern Moiety to take over my duties for the time being—it's going to be another two weeks before Etienne gets back from wherever he's been these last six months, and I don't propose to wait that long."

"Etienne?" Miriam asked, then realized what he meant.

"Of course. Your brother king." Then: "Etienne-Laurent de Marigny, by any chance?"

That got another quick grin. "I see you've done your biographical research. Exactly. I sent him a letter just before I used the Silver Key, letting him know in some detail what I was going to do. It took him six years to figure out another way of doing the same thing." He shook his head, laughed. "We were very close once. These days, we can spend about a week together before we get on each other's nerves, so the current arrangement works."

"My second husband and I probably should have done something like that," Miriam said. "Our cats would have ended up happier."

Randolph gave her a quizzical glance but let the remark pass. "One other thing needs to be settled. I grant that the clothing of Ooth-Nargai flatters you—"

"Thank you," said Miriam.

"You're welcome. It's not really suitable for the Moon, though, or for that matter the Bnazic desert or the road east from there—the cats can get us there but we'll have to make the journey back ourselves, you know. With your permission I'll have some of the ladies in waiting get you fitted for something better suited to the purpose."

Miriam agreed readily, and that evening before dinner was visited by a bevy of women, only one of whom spoke the language of Ooth-Nargai, and that only after a fashion. Nonetheless such communication as was needful took place, assisted by gestures and laughter, and before noon the following day the women were back with garments in the Rokol style—sturdy blouses and skirts, a hooded woolen cloak, a leather belt with a stout knife in a sheath, and boots with upturned toes that fit her well enough that they might have been made to her measurements.

She tried them on and considered herself in the mirror. Where the garments of Ilek-Vad made her resemble a Greek priestess, these gave her the look of a princess from the pages of *Weird Tales*. A well-aged princess, she thought with an amused smile, noting her silver hair and far from youthful features. Even so, that thought and the recollection of what she was about to attempt stirred something unruly in her. She'd noted in the past how often a wild craving for adventure slumbered uneasily in the most sober and scholarly heart; she'd felt it in herself, and tried to believe that sailing trips with Michael, Phil, and their friends satisfied it; but now here she was, about to venture across the breadth of the Dreamlands by way of the Moon, and the thought made her raise her chin and wish she knew how to use the knife at her belt for something other than cutting vegetables.

Meanwhile the cats gathered. She watched them now and then from her windows, lithe shapes pacing up the avenue from the Low City or bounding from rock to rock up the crags that raised the High City above the forests and fields to the east. They came first by dozens, then by hundreds, then by legions, until the palace grounds and the roofs of the High City were one great variegated mass of felinity. Well before the sun set, the king sent word that enough cats would be there by nightfall to do what had to be done. Miriam packed her clothing in a soft leather satchel the women had brought her, with a blanket roll strapped to the bottom of it, and tried to distract herself with one of Randolph's novels as the day drew on and she waited for the summons.

"HERE YOU ARE," said Randolph, handing her an oddly carved shape of translucent green stone on a leather thong, and motioning for her to put the thong around her neck. "The gnorri sent us these along with their best wishes. You don't recognize them? Talismans of Nodens. Any crossing from world to world is subject to his good will, so I'm glad to have them."

He and Miriam were standing in a broad open plaza to the east of the turreted palace of the kings of Rokol. Except for the places where they stood, every square inch of the cobbled pavement and the roofs, balconies, and windowsills of the palace was covered with cats. The Sun was down, and a few early stars glittered overhead; in the east, vast and golden, the Moon climbed steadily into the sky.

"In maybe a quarter hour," Randolph said then, "the Moon will be high enough, and then the cats will leap and take us with them. All you have to do is let yourself be carried with them. When we near the Moon, you'll feel them tense to land, and when that happens, flex your knees and hips, this way, and spread your arms out and forward, just as though you were jumping. Got it? Excellent. It'll be over sooner than you expect."

He crouched and talked to the cats in their language, and Miriam wondered who was giving final instructions to whom. One way or another, the colloquy was soon over, and Randolph and the cats turned together to watch the moon rise. A tense silence gripped the plaza and the whole High City.

"Shoulder your luggage, Miriam," Randolph said finally in a low voice, "and remember to let them carry you."

Miriam settled her satchel in place, as Randolph shouldered a larger satchel and a smaller bag, and got a sheathed sword poised on his hip. Around her, the cats crouched, and then sprang.

In the first upward rush, as she abandoned herself to the leap, it felt as though she and Randolph and the cats had all become mere cells in some immense cat-shape, huge and strong enough to make the leap between worlds. Then all thought went away in the terrible vertigo of the void, in a moment that seemed to stretch out into eternities. Finally

Miriam felt the cats near her tense for landing, and just in time, remembered Randolph's instructions and got her knees and hips flexed.

Then the ground came up beneath her, hard, and she barely managed to keep her feet. An instant later cats were pouring away to every side in a furry torrent. She blinked and tried to focus, then rubbed her eyes and tried again.

Randolph was nearby, crouching once again to talk to a few dignified elderly cats. The other cats bounded away in various directions, mostly toward one side, following the sunlight as it streamed almost horizontally across the landscape. There in the near distance rose somber mountains of gray stone half mantled in curious brown mosses, and topped here and there with low white sheets of ice. The wind blew cold, tinged with scents she didn't recognize at all.

What seized Miriam's attention, though, lay in the direction the cats weren't going. There, low in the sky, hovered a mottled-blue sphere a dozen times vaster than the full Moon, half of it brightly lit by the sun, the other half in shadow. Staring at it, she could make out the western end of the Twilight Sea, the Straits of Stethelos, the Cerenerian Sea beyond them, and a blob of brilliant white, where the coastline turned south, that had to be the snows on Mount Aran.

Her knees nearly gave way then. I'm on the Moon, she told herself. Actually on the Moon. The words barely hung onto their meanings. She glanced down, thinking of Neil Armstrong's bootprints on barren gray lunar soil, to find her own booted feet on a patch of golden-brown moss. A long moment passed, and then she laughed and shook her head.

"What is it?" Randolph asked. He had finished his colloquy with the cats, who had begun to stroll off at a leisurely pace, and came toward her.

"It's only just sunk in," Miriam said, "that this really is all a dream."

He nodded, gestured around. "Not the Moon you were expecting, I take it?"

"I read what your cousin had to say about it," she allowed.

"But it's another thing to stand here, I know." His quick grin caught the level sunlight. "The Moon in the waking world doesn't have air to breathe, or moss, or for that matter anything to entertain cats. I knew a fellow from Worcester named Bob Goddard who wanted to get there on a rocket, but I never could figure out why."

"They managed that in 1969," Miriam said.

"Did they? I bet they had to wear something like a deep sea diver's outfit there."

She gave him a startled look. "Fairly close to that."

"Must have been awkward. If we'd had to do that, we'd have had a long dull wait. As it is—" He shed his satchel, opened the smaller bag, shook out what looked for all the world like a big gingham tablecloth and spread it across a flat area of ground. The bag then disgorged a wicker picnic hamper and a bottle of wine.

Miriam started laughing again. "I'm impressed. A picnic?"

"Of course," he said, glancing up at her with another grin. "It's going to be several hours before the Bnazic desert comes under us, and I see no reason to spend the time uncomfortably. While I live, I live well, and if I die—why, I hope I'll die well." He motioned at the wine. "A little ice to chill that, and we'll be set."

MIRIAM'S KNIFE PROVED stout enough to pry chunks loose from the ice on the slopes of the nearest mountain. She had to wrap her hands in her cloak to carry the chunks back—the ice was cold enough to burn—but that was the only difficulty. By the time she went back to the picnic cloth and Randolph, he'd gotten everything else set out, and used a camp knife of his own to dig a hollow in the lunar soil to serve as an ice bucket for the wine. A moment later the wine was chilling nicely, and Miriam settled down on the picnic cloth. Randolph sat across from her, and behind him the huge disk of the Dreamland's Earth hung against a backdrop of brilliant stars.

"So what happens once we jump back down?" Miriam asked him.

"We go to the temple as quickly as possible. It should be close by the place where we land; I was able to find detailed information in an old book in the palace library. The cats will need to leap back up to the Moon once they get us where we're going—the Bnazic Desert's as cold as it's barren, and the Temple of the Flame contains certain dangers to which they're far too vulnerable—so we'll be on our own once we arrive, and it's simply a matter of doing what we need to do and then finding our way back to the Six Kingdoms. That shouldn't be hard; Parg is a few weeks' journey to the southeast, and once there we're in civilized country, with roads running to Sydathria and ships from Dylath-Leen going everywhere in the Dreamlands."

"Your cousin wasn't too impressed by Parg," said Miriam then.

Randolph gave her a wry look. "Howard and his idiot prejudices. Once when he lived in New York and I was visiting, I offered to take him to one of A'Lelia Walker's Thursday night at-homes down in Harlem. Everybody who was anybody went there, and I planned to introduce him to people who could have helped him get the literary career he wanted—but once he heard that Negroes would be there, he wouldn't have anything to do with it." He shrugged. "I went anyway, and got to hear Bessie Smith singing, so it was worth the trip."

"Bessie Smith the jazz singer?"

"Oh, you know of her? Yes."

"Very much so. I have—had—half a dozen recordings by her back in the waking world. I envy you that evening."

"Understandably so," he said with a smile. "But Parg— it's part of the kingdom of Oriab by ancient treaty, but you'll find few lands in the Six Kingdoms half as rich and splendid, and the Gamala of Parg's a monarch to reckon with by any standard. No doubt Howard came up with some contempt- ible notion instead."

They sat for a while in companionable silence, while the wind keened among the mountains and the disk of the Dreamland's Earth turned its face slowly away from the Sun.

"The one thing you didn't mention," said Miriam, "is what we're to do when we get to the Temple of the Flame."

"Whatever we have to do, to stop the person the Radiance sent," said Randolph. "I have no idea what that'll involve, but there'll be a way. The thing he has, the Blade of Uoht, is a weapon of quite some power—one of the three great trea- sures of Poseidonis, in fact, along with the Ring of Eibon and the *Ghorl Nigral*—but I very much doubt he'll know how to use it. The Great Old Ones wouldn't just have sent the two of us to deal with him if he did."

"I'm surprised that they don't simply stop him them- selves."

"They can't." Meeting her shocked gaze: "There's a long and ugly story behind that. The very short version is that cer- tain holy places were desecrated a long time ago, in order to keep the Great Old Ones from manifesting their power in our world. That's why the oracles fell silent, as Plutarch said, and why all the sorceries and wonders you read about in old books went away. Until the stars are right, the Great Old Ones have only a tiny fraction of their proper power, and for the most part they have to work through intermediaries."

Miriam took that in. "Prinn wrote something about seven temples," she said after a moment. "They were destroyed in the time of Alexander the Great, weren't they?"

"You've read *De Vermiis Mysteriis*? Good. Yes, that's what he was talking about. They weren't just destroyed, though. The Radiance—it had yet another name then, but it was the same organization—its adepts knew enough about the forces that flowed through the temples to work terrible rites of desecration in each of them, so that the voor, the life force, was turned back against itself, and what had been fountains of life turned into spreading pools of death. The Middle East wasn't always desert, you know."

"I read that somewhere," Miriam said.

"That's the reason why."

She nodded slowly. Randolph touched the wine bottle to be sure it was properly chilled, pulled a corkscrew out of the picnic basket, and poured them each a full glass. Fresh bread, soft cheese, and an unfamiliar rose-colored fruit that Randolph cut in thin slices, duly made their appearance, and Randolph raised his glass. "To our adventure. May it go as the Great Old Ones will." Miriam raised hers in response, and glass clinked on glass.

The wine had a tart clear flavor. Miriam sipped from her glass, enjoying it, and then asked, "Does all of this have anything to do with the drowning of R'lyeh?"

Randolph looked up suddenly from the loaf of bread he was slicing. "Why do you ask?" Something wary and perilous moved in his voice.

"You mentioned when the stars were right," Miriam said, baffled, "and one of your cousin's stories talked about how Great Cthulhu's power in the world was—well, limited, until that got around to happening." Then: "I take it that's not a good question to ask."

"In other company," said Randolph, "it's not always a

safe question to ask." He glanced up past her, where the last few cats in sight bounded here and there on the mountainsides, and then said, "Let's get the picnic sorted out first."

She nodded, still uncertain of her ground, and then helped with the plates and the food. When everything was set out—fresh butter, sliced meats, three kinds of fruit, a tossed salad with a dressing Miriam wished someone had gotten around to inventing in the waking world, along with the bread, cheese, and wine—Randolph sat back and said, "The desecration of the seven holy places wasn't the beginning of all this. Nor was the birth of the Radiance—they'd been around for most of a thousand years before they finally got their chance. This whole business goes back long ages before that, before our species was born. What happened was humanity's doing." His voice dropped away to a whisper. "But it wasn't just our doing.

"You know about Cthulhu." She nodded. "And you know about the King in Yellow. Do you know how those two are related?"

"They're supposed to be half-brothers, I think."

"Quite correct. Their father was Nug of the Silent Stars, their mothers two of the daughters of Shub-Ne'hurrath—you won't have heard of them; they ruled over life-waves that ebbed away long before the time of the first mammals. But the two of them, Cthulhu and the King, were meant to fill certain roles in the world. Not just the little world we experience—the great world, the one that bends away anthward and ulthward beyond human sight."

"Cthulhu is the high priest of the Great Old Ones," said Miriam, remembering that bit of lore and guessing that it was part of what Randolph had in mind.

"Excellent. Yes, and the other is their king. The one at R'lyeh, in sight of the anthern pole of the great world; the other at Carcosa, in sight of the ulthern pole; and the great world and the Great Old Ones held in balance between them. That was what should have been."

He sipped his wine, looked at her across the glass. "But that's not what happened. Once when I was in Ulthar—a lovely town, a place I could live in always if things had turned out differently—I visited an old friend, the patriarch Atal, and we talked about the deepest mysteries of the Great Old Ones. There was a considerable amount of wine involved." His voice dropped very low. "What Atal told me is that a quarrel rose between them—no ordinary quarrel, for it takes something truly grave to set eternal beings at odds. What it was, Atal didn't know, though he said his teacher Barzai the Wise hinted at it, just once, in words that left poor Atal pale and shaking for a week.

"I know little about the course of the quarrel, and I don't think Atal knew much more. I know that at one time the King actually renounced his kingship to keep the peace, and for a long age dwelt in Leng as a simple god of shepherds. But it could not last." In the lowest of murmurs: "Finally it came to war. The two of them contended with each other with all their might, the King triumphed, and Great Cthulhu perished—but of course he could never wholly die. So the King bound him in sleep in his city of R'lyeh and caused the seas to rise over him.

"And that's what opened the door through which the Radiance eventually entered. The Great Old Ones were estranged from one another—there were those who supported the one, and those who supported the other, and those who stayed aloof from both sides, and those divisions didn't heal—and only a high priest could call down forces from those who are above the Great Old Ones, as far as they are above us. So other things crept into the great world from the cold places outside and found human allies, or were found by them, and the Radiance was kindled."

Miriam considered him for a long moment. "And Great Cthulhu?"

"He dreams," Randolph said simply.

"Does anyone know what he dreams?"

That got her one of his quick grins. "You haven't figured that out yet?" His gesture took in the mountains of the Moon, the distant capering cats, the great sphere of the Earth half in shadow and half in sunlight. "You're inside his dreams right now, and so am I. The Dreamlands of Earth—those are the dreams of Cthulhu, as he lies dead yet dreaming in his house in R'lyeh."

TEN

The Temple of the Flame

Miriam stared at him for a long moment. Randolph met her gaze briefly, then turned his attention to the food. A silence passed; she finished her wine, and he refilled her glass.

"Are all our dreams inside his?" she asked at length.

"No, not at all. There was a time when that was the case, but—" He shrugged. "That was long ago, before the Radiance did everything in their power to block the way. Now it's children for the most part who come here in their dreams. I kept the trick until I was thirty, which is rare."

"I don't remember ever coming here," Miriam admitted.

"No doubt. The Radiance has gone to quite remarkable lengths to make sure that most people forget it."

A memory stirred, and Miriam recited half to herself a line from the poem Randolph had quoted in his letter: "'The hidden door of dreams, by some decree...'"

He gave her a startled glance. "You know Justin Geoffrey's verse?"

"Tolerably well."

"I'm impressed. I knew him, you know—a fascinating

163

man who deserved a much better fate. That poem's entirely autobiographical, and not many people recall as much as he did. Still, as you visit different parts of the Dreamlands, odds are you'll find someplace that sets off a chord of memory."

All at once Miriam thought of the Tanarian Hills and the curious sense of familiarity they'd stirred in her. It suddenly occurred to her that none of Lovecraft's stories described the far side of the ridge where she'd awakened, and yet she'd recognized it.

"People you'd never expect turn out to remember bits of the Dreamlands," Randolph went on. "During the Great War I met a young British lieutenant, Ronald something—I forget his last name—at a hospital in England, after I was wounded at Belloy-de-Santerre and he collapsed during the Somme. A pale little slip of a fellow, but he had this astonishing private mythology about fairies and gnomes and magic jewels, and he'd tell the most amazing stories about them if he was sure you wouldn't mock him for it. One night when neither of us could sleep, he told me that he'd gotten most of it from dreams he'd had as a child, when he'd gone to play in a cottage in fairyland." Randolph laughed, but there was no mockery in it. "I didn't tell him that I knew the place. It's just west of Kiran in Sydathria, near one of the gates to the waking world, and yes, quite a few children go there in their dreams."

"But that's not the only place they go," Miriam said slowly.

"No." Glancing at her: "You've remembered something."

"Well, not quite. I think I may have met myself in Ooth-Nargai." The little blonde girl who'd come with the others to help card wool, who'd perched by the fireplace and watched everything wide-eyed: the image hovered in Miriam's imagination, and merged slowly with pictures of herself she'd seen in old photos from her childhood.

"That's by no means impossible," said Randolph.

She took that in for a while, and spread butter on a slice of bread. "You said the Radiance tries to stop people from coming here. Why?"

"Oh, they hate dreams. Dreams aren't rational and logical, they won't do as they're told, they remind us of things the Radiance would like everyone to forget. Our own private dreams are bad enough, but Great Cthulhu's dreams, the dreams that flow into existence through the Temple of the Flame and sustain everything you see around you—those are memories of what was before the Radiance seized their stolen powers, and a promise of what will be, once the stars come round right again and the Radiance is a distant memory. Why do you think so many of the places in the Dreamlands are also places that existed in the elder world? They're places Great Cthulhu knew when he strode the waking world—Lomar, Leng, and the rest of it. And so every child who wanders in the Dreamlands reminds the adepts of the Radiance that their power is a passing thing."

Miriam nodded slowly. "If that's true," she said after another moment, "if all this is Cthulhu's dream, then what will happen to it when he wakes up?"

"Nobody knows," Randolph admitted. "Maybe the Dreamlands and everything in them will vanish in an eyeblink. Maybe they'll remain. Maybe something else will happen. My friend the patriarch Atal knows more about the Great Old Ones than anybody else in the Dreamlands—probably more than any human being anywhere—but when we've talked about it, he's told me that nothing in all his lore speaks to that."

He drained the last of the wine in his glass, got up, turned to face the great orb of the Earth. "Not much more than half an hour now," he said then. "The land that arcs down that way in the sunlight—the northern two-thirds or so is Sydathria, the southern third where everything's so green is Parg.

165

Oriab's the big island further south. Off to the west, the brown land? That's the stony desert between Hatheg and Hatheg-Kla. Further west, past Hatheg-Kla, is the Bnazic Desert, and our goal is further west still."

He sat back down, took the wine bottle, and refilled their glasses. In response to Miriam's amused glance: "Might as well enjoy it while we're here. We'll get back to civilized country in due time, but I can promise you a good many adventures before that happens."

"You're sure we'll get back?"

"Of course. This is all a dream, remember, and everything in it is governed by dream logic. When you came to Ooth-Nargai, someone was waiting in exactly the right place to meet you, and guide you to somewhere not too far away where you could get food and drink, and recover from the shock of arriving in the Dreamlands. Am I right?"

"Well, yes."

"That's the way dreams work. For the same reason, I know that we'll get to the Temple of the Flame in the nick of time to stop the person the Radiance sent; there'll be a way to stop him and recover the Blade of Uoht, though the cost may be terrible; when that's over, if we survive and go to the edges of the Bnazic Desert, a caravan or a band of wandering nomads will show up just in time to take us to the borders of Parg, where an old soldier will recognize me from the days when we fought side by side in the Gamala's armies against the wereworms of the uttermost west, and so on. That's just the way things are here." He grinned his quick grin. "Just as you've learned some of the deep mysteries of the Great Old Ones at a picnic on the Moon. Since you're here, you might as well get used to it."

THEY FINISHED UP the last of the food and wine, and Randolph got everything packed away into the hamper. "There we are," he said then. "I wish I could have brought something for the cats, but it would have taken the Ocean of Milk from that old Hindu myth to give them all a share." He laughed, and Miriam laughed with him.

He turned toward the mountains, then, and let out a fine caterwaul. A moment later the first cats began bounding down the slopes, and more followed, and still more, until the whole landscape became a sea of cats, circle on circle surrounding the two of them, with the blue light of the Dreamlands' Earth mirrored in their eyes. Randolph squatted and conversed with their leaders, gesturing from time to time at the great blue disk, and after a while stood again.

"Are you ready?" he asked Miriam.

"No," she admitted, "but I'll manage anyway."

That got her another of his quick grins. "That's the spirit."

She shouldered her satchel, drew in a deep breath, and surrendered herself to the cats as they flung themselves up from the Moon.

Once again the void spun around her in a moment that stretched out to the limits of time. Once again she felt the cats brace themselves to land, got her knees and hips flexed, and brought her arms forward. The ground came up hard beneath her, but she kept her balance.

Then all at once the cats leapt back toward the Moon. She felt them go, and glanced up in time to see a vast cat-shape springing out of sight against the darkening evening sky. An instant later it was gone, and she blinked and looked around.

She and Randolph stood on a long slope of dry soil dotted here and there with clusters of tough violet grass. Just behind them the slope crested and tumbled down into brown desert, then rose again in great rows of sinuous dunes tall as hills, with bleak barren mountains faintly visible beyond them. Ahead, the slope descended to a plain that had once been forested; the bleached snags of long-dead trees rose up from mostly bare ground. Windblown dust from the desert tinted the evening sky a dim gold, through which the Moon shone pale. These details barely registered in Miriam's mind at first, though, for before her stood the ruins.

They had been a city, or so she guessed from the shattered remains: a titan's city of red stone, fashioned in a stark rectilinear style of building she was sure she'd never seen before. Even in its long-abandoned state the city stood tall, tower above broken tower and wall behind crumbling wall rising up toward the golden sky.

"Here we go," said Randolph. "If we're lucky, we've gotten here ahead of our quarry, but we can't count on that. Eyes wide and voices low." He motioned with his head, signaling her to follow, and started down the slope.

The wind off the desert hissed around them as they walked. The dead trees loomed up, and beyond them the vast ruined gate of the city overshadowed all. Quick and wary, Randolph moved ahead, and she followed close behind, wishing she had some idea of what she was there to do, trying to pay attention to any sign that might alert her to the presence of the person they were supposed to stop.

Maybe half a mile on, as the bleached and broken remnants of a forest gathered around them, they reached a road paved in huge gray blocks of stone running straight toward the city gate. Randolph crossed it and ducked behind the long-dead trees on the far side, then moved parallel to the road, staying just in sight of it. Miriam tried to keep up and make as little noise as possible, and he glanced back at her, gave her an approving nod, kept going.

Nothing moved around them but the wind. If there were animals, birds, or even insects in the bleak landscape, Miriam did not see them. From the direction of the ruined city, though, came a faint vibration in the air. As she drew closer to the vast and crumbling walls, staying close behind Randolph, the vibration finally resolved itself into music: a high faint melody that sounded almost like a singing voice.

Randolph turned to her then. In a low voice: "Do you hear it?"

She nodded.

"I've got cotton wadding for our ears, once we get closer. That music's perilous stuff."

Miriam nodded again, for she'd already sensed something intoxicating in the strange shrill melody.

They hurried on. The gate loomed up ahead until it seemed to blot out half the sky. Finally the last of the dead trees rose up, and with a quick glance to either side, Randolph led the way across the narrow open space that separated the dead forest from the ruined gate.

Once they were under the shadow of the walls, he turned to her again. "This is where things may get risky. I'd recommend drawing that knife."

"I don't know how to use it," she admitted.

A quick nod accepted that. "Hold it like this, close to your body. Crouch a little—yes, like that. If he comes at you, face him—don't run—and stab, don't slash. Only amateurs slash. That might keep him at bay until I can cut him down."

"I'll do my best," Miriam said.

"Excellent." He drew his own blade, a long bright saber that looked sharp enough to shave with. "In we go."

They moved toward the gate. Wind hissed against the ancient stone, fell still once they were under the immense archway. Just on the other side, where the fading light of the sky still shone down from above, Randolph pointed suddenly to a place were sand and dust had drifted in across the pavement. A fresh bootprint showed there, and no cobbler of the Dreamlands had fashioned the sole, either. "He's already

169

here," Randolph said in a low voice. "Let's find a place to leave our gear behind for now. We'll need to hurry."

THEY STOWED THEIR satchels and blanket rolls in an intact stone guardhouse just inside the gate. Randolph took a leathern pouch from his satchel and tied it to his belt, and then they hurried on at a brisk walk. Even so, it took them something like two hours to reach the temple at the heart of the city. Partly that was a matter of sheer distance, partly it was because the city was not entirely empty. "Red-footed wamps," Randolph told her in a low voice as they hid behind a half-fallen wall, waiting for the soft heavy padding of some massive creature to fade into silence. "They're spawned in ruined cities, and have the same dietary habits as ghouls. Unlike ghouls, they'll take fresh meat when they can get it."

Once silence returned, they hurried on. The full Moon stood high above, casting a pallid light through the dust-clouded air on broken pylons, toppled obelisks, pillared porticoes that had tumbled to the ground countless ages ago. The music grew louder as they moved deeper into the dead city. Ahead, down a long straight street, something moved in the distance: another of the red-footed wamps? Miriam couldn't tell, but a moment later Randolph touched her shoulder and pointed ahead at the distant moving shape. "Our quarry," he murmured.

The night deepened, and so did the chill in the air. The two of them stayed in the shadows as much as they could, tried to catch up with the distant moving figure, and bit by bit succeeded. After most of an hour, Miriam could make out a recognizably human shape on the street ahead, catch enough of its movements to see it stumble, pick itself up, and hurry unsteadily on.

Finally they reached the edge of a vast central square just

as the figure hurried up the steps of an immense many-columned temple on the far side. Randolph made a gesture to stop, pulled something pale out of the pouch at his belt. "Cotton wadding," he said. "Stuff your ears with it, or the music will draw you into the flame. With any luck, he won't know about that."

She got her ears plugged, and then he motioned toward the temple The two of them hurried across the square and up the steps.

Beyond the outermost colonnade the temple seemed utterly dark at first. After a moment, though, Miriam could make out a faint shimmering light in the distance ahead. She clutched her knife more tightly, followed Randolph's lead into the near-darkness.

As her eyes adjusted, she saw a forest of columns stretching away into the distance ahead, carved with enigmatic bas-reliefs and dim hieroglyphic inscriptions. A flicker of movement between pillars showed her the location of their quarry. Randolph spotted it also, gestured, led the way with his saber. They hurried on, and the figure they pursued hurried ahead of them.

The light gradually increased as they went. Low dim shapes scattered about the floor took on definition. They were skeletons, Miriam realized, caked with the dust of countless centuries. Not one of them looked even remotely human.

Brighter and brighter the light shone, and the music rose in intensity with it. Something as imperious as it was seductive moved through the melody, at once summoning and alluring. The cotton in her ears seemed to mute the power of it as well as the sound, but even so it took an effort not to fling herself forward at a run, toward whatever waited at the source of the light.

By then they were nearly at the end of the vast pillared hall, and the light blazed out of the heart of an echoing dark

171

void beyond it. The one they had to stop was scarcely twenty yards ahead of them, weaving from side to side as though from exhaustion as he hurried onward. He was dressed in military-style clothing from the waking world, variously torn, slashed, and stained, and a makeshift bandage wrapped his left arm above the elbow. She felt rather than saw Randolph ready himself for the sudden dash that would bring their quarry down.

Then the man they followed happened to glance back over his shoulder, saw them, let out a sudden cry and sprinted ahead with speed born of panic.

Randolph darted after him. Miriam followed, running as hard as she could, but Randolph outpaced her easily and their quarry managed to stay further ahead still. A huge echoing space opened up around her as she ran; light streamed into her face, half-blinding her; she threw herself onward, toward whatever waited.

All at once Randolph stopped, flung out an arm, caught her as she came up to him. It took her a moment to shake herself free of the call of the music, and the first thing she saw was a vast shape looming up into the darkness high above her, unhuman but familiar, lit by a searing line of light before it. The bulbous head with its many tentacles and many eyes, the rippling muscles of the clawed limbs, the sweep of the folded wings: she knew at once whose temple this was or had been, and half-consciously murmured the archaic prayer to Great Cthulhu: *"Ph'nglui mglw'nafh Cthulhu R'lyeh wagh'nagl fhtagn."*

That brought sudden clarity, and Miriam realized why Randolph had stopped her where he had. Just beyond him, the floor ended at the brink of a huge circular pit that plunged down into unguessable depths. From the near edge of the pit, a narrow bridge with no railing reached straight out into the midst of emptiness, and at its end...

The Flame.

It seemed to float above the pit, its base just below the end of the bridge, its upper end a hundred yards or more above them in the vastness of the chamber, maybe halfway up the immense stone image of Cthulhu. A soaring fountain of fire, it looked white at first glance, but a second reminded her that white light is composed of all colors; hues no rainbow ever matched shimmered out of it. So did the music, and all at once Miriam understood what Randolph had said about its power. It seemed to invite her, command her, tempt her, to cross the bridge and fling herself into the Flame, and only the cotton in her ears muted the command enough to keep her from unthinking obedience.

There was another obstacle, though. At the foot of the bridge, the man they'd followed through the ruined city faced them with eyes narrowed and something thin and dark in his hand. White cotton showed in his ears—he'd known enough, Miriam guessed, to shield himself from the music of the Flame. It took her a moment to recognize the thing he held as a long dagger or short sword of unfamiliar shape, for the metal of the blade—if it was metal—was a blackness that swallowed every ray of light that touched it, and a sensation of terrible cold radiated from it.

It took her another moment to recognize something else, and then she gasped aloud. The face of their quarry was haggard and lined, and one cheek was scored with the tracks of claws and stained with half-dried blood. Even so, she recognized it at once: the face of the young man who'd introduced himself to her, back in the waking world, as Andrew Weeden.

"STAY RIGHT WHERE you are," Weeden said, his voice cracked with strain. "I know some of the powers of this thing—enough to kill both of you if you try to stop me." He shifted his grip on the hilt of the blade, held it low and threatening, ready to thrust.

Randolph said nothing, faced Weeden with his saber in his hand. Weeden glanced at him and then at Miriam. "You," he said. "I figured you'd come after me, once your masters told you I'd followed you. Do you realize that you led me here? That once you ran for your bolt-hole, we were sure to find it and send someone after you to close it up once and for all?

"The Dreamlands." He laughed; there was no humor in the sound, only bitterness and scorn. "The nightmare lands, rather—a nightmare of superstition and squalor. And your masters lure children into the nightmare, to they could blind them to the light of reason before they can be taught otherwise." In tones of utter disgust: "I bet you even enjoy it here."

"It frightens you that much," said Miriam.

"Don't be stupid," he snapped back. "This whole insane place has fought me every inch of the way since I got here—but I won. Now it's all going away. All of it, forever." Slowly, step by step, he began backing up the bridge, toward the white torrent of the Flame.

Randolph tensed to spring. All at once Miriam guessed that he was about to rush Weeden, and knew how unlikely it was that he'd survive the act. In that one frozen moment she thought of Anané, Ieloré, Serin, Aysh; thought of the little blonde girl she'd been, roaming the purple Tanarian Hills in dreams that had passed out of memory; thought of Randolph's words—"when I die, I hope I die well"—and she knew, or thought she knew, why the Great Old Ones had chosen her for this task, for there was one thing that might serve, one thing she'd spent most of six years getting ready to do in another way, and she knew that she could do it then and there.

Before second thoughts could stop her, she flung herself past Randolph and onto the bridge. She heard Randolph's low cry of surprise behind her but ignored it. Weeden had half turned toward the Flame, but he spun back around as she sprinted toward him. The Blade of Uoht flicked out toward her, low and threatening. As he thrust at her, she darted straight forward and threw herself onto the point of the blade.

Sudden cold burnt through her belly as it plunged into her. An instant later, as the point burst from her back, she seized his forearm in both hands with all her strength, and then—

A sudden step to the side, and she flung herself over the edge of the narrow bridge.

The sudden terror on Weeden's face told her she'd chosen the one move he'd failed to anticipate. He flailed in empty air, fought for balance, toppled after her. One outflung hand caught the edge of the bridge. For a moment they hung there above the abyss, and Miriam heard footfalls ring on the bridge as Randolph came sprinting after her.

Weeden shook his sword arm, trying to break her grip, and then drew up one booted foot to kick at her. She tightened her hold on his arm and tried to twist her body away from the kick. Then, suddenly, his hold on the bridge failed, and the two of them plunged together into the abyss. Weeden screamed, and from the receding brightness above came another voice, Randolph's, shouting her name.

Weeden screamed over and over again, wind and darkness howled past her, blood welled out of the wounds in her belly and her lower back, red lines of pain spread from the cold blade that transfixed her, but for the first time in longer than she could remember, Miriam Akeley felt at peace. She thought of Great Cthulhu dreaming in R'lyeh, and then of the statue in Arkham with the humble offerings she'd seen on the pedestal before it, and thought: I am an offering. A moment later: an acceptable one, I hope.

Around her, the roaring of the air past her ears turned into a hissing, and the hissing became words. The counsel they offered her seemed pointless, but it seemed just as pointless to refuse it, and after a moment she did as the wind asked, let go of Weeden's forearm and seized the quillons of the Blade of Uoht.

The hilt was slippery with her blood, and his grip slid loose. A moment later he was tumbling away from her, or she from him. His screams faded gradually, as though into some great distance, and Miriam puzzled vaguely over that, for it seemed improbable to her that they could have fallen so far apart.

Then her descent changed subtly. Though she was still falling, the tumbling motion had ceased, and she found herself lying on her back, resting on a vast and subtly curved surface that plunged downward as she did. Five great dim shapes rose like towers or standing stones past the edges of her vision, though a long moment passed before she realized what they signified, and knew that she rested in the palm of a colossal hand.

Darkness swirled and took shape: a great hoary face the color of midnight loomed above her, and eyes pale and vast as moons regarded her. *That was well done*, something that was not a voice said.

"Thank you," she mumbled in reply. Numbness spread through her from the blade.

Tell me this, the not-voice said then. *Do you desire to die here and now?*

The question seemed utterly abstract to her. "No," she said finally. "No, I think I'd actually rather live, but—" She tried to shrug, couldn't find the strength. A question struggled to the surface of her mind, and she asked the vast dark face: "What's going to happen to Weeden?"

Nothing, the not-voice said.

176

She blinked, puzzled, and it went on: H*e will keep falling. Perhaps he will go mad eventually, or find some way to kill himself; it matters not. He has passed into my realm, into the Great Abyss, and the fate I have decreed for him is that he shall fall through darkness forever.*

"And me—"

For you, I decree a different fate. Do you understand?

No, she tried to whisper, and only then realized that this was the answer Nodens wanted.

It is well. The colossal hand moved beneath her, and the void dissolved.

SHE WAS LYING on bare ground. Above her, tall shadows loomed against a pale sky. She tried to force her eyes to focus, but they refused to cooperate.

A man's voice, vaguely familiar, somewhere in the middle distance: "There she is." Footfalls whispered through the troubled air, hurrying toward her.

Another voice, female, that she almost recognized: "Oh my God."

"She's going to bleed to death," said the first voice. "Can you do anything?"

"I know a spell for bleeding." Movement, and then a vague pressure on her belly that slowly resolved itself into two hands. The second voice murmured words Miriam did not know, though its tones seemed more and more familiar to her, and a pleasant warmth spread through her belly. "Now— take the blade out."

A sudden movement, and the cold blade slid out of her. A silence followed, and then the first voice spoke, shaken: "That's—"

"The Blade of Uoht. Yes."

"To recover that—" His voice trickled to a halt.

"I wish she could have found a less dramatic way to bring it back," said the second voice, in tones that joined irritation, affection, and grief. Miriam finally recognized it: Jenny Chaudronnier's voice. She tried to speak, but the effort was too great.

"Old One," the first voice called out. "We've found her. She's alive."

A moment later a tall shadow blotted out part of her field of view. A third voice spoke, instantly recognizable as Nyarlathotep's. "Good. She'll need to be carried back to the car."

Hands lifted her. "Gently," said the first voice. "I don't want that wound to reopen."

"It won't," said Jenny. "Trust me—that's the first spell Abby Price ever taught me."

What seemed a long while later, she slid onto what felt like the broad back seat of a car. The leather of the seat, soft as the silks of Oriab, lulled her toward something that felt like sleep.

"We should get her feet up once she's settled," said the first voice.

"Easily done," said Jenny. Miriam's legs rose, settled back down onto what felt like someone's lap. "This way I can keep track of her condition."

"Thank you," said the first voice. Car doors slammed shut, and an engine roared to life. "Old One," the first voice said, "you're not going to hear me say this often, but—drive fast."

Nyarlathotep laughed. "That," it said, "I can certainly do."

The car leapt forward, and Miriam sank into darkness.

ELEVEN

The Treasures of Poseidonis

She drifted slowly awake, and wondered why.

The room wasn't one she recognized: high-ceilinged and square, with floral wallpaper above dark wooden wainscoting. A tall window divided into many small panes let morning sun stream down onto the covers of the big four-poster bed where she lay, naked beneath sheet and duvet, bandages wrapping her middle. Outside, muffled by the window glass, catbirds chattered.

"Good morning," said a voice she didn't recognize either.

She managed to turn her head, though it took an effort. A big overstuffed armchair sat next to the bed, and in it was a very old woman with stark white hair, who was smiling at her.

"Good morning," Miriam tried to say, and barely achieved a whisper.

"If you'd like some water, Jenny says that should be fine."

Jenny says? She tried to make sense of that, but the water was a more important issue just then. "Please," she managed to say.

The old woman got up, left the room, returned a moment

179

later with a glass. Miriam tried to bring one hand up to take it, but her arm felt limp and heavy, and the effort barely stirred it. The old woman helped her sit half up in bed, put the glass to her lips, let her drink.

"Better?" she asked.

Miriam tried to answer, but the words went spinning away into darkness, and so did she.

She woke again later—how much later, she had no way of guessing. The window curtain was closed. The same old woman was sitting in the same chair, reading a paperback by the light of a lamp. She glanced up at Miriam, smiled. "Awake?"

"I think so," said Miriam, in a voice that was a little closer to her own.

"You probably don't remember me at all," the old woman said then. "I'm Claire O'Malley, Jenny's great-aunt by marriage. We met at Jenny's graduation, in case that helps."

Dim images stirred in memory, and Miriam said, "Yes, it does. Thank you." A moment later: "Then I'm in Kingsport."

The old woman nodded. "In the Chaudronnier mansion. You've been here three and a half days, or pretty close. Do you remember anything about how you got here?"

Voices, shadows, pain: that was all that surfaced. "Not worth mentioning."

"You had a blade stuck in your belly. They'd gotten it out and stopped the bleeding before they brought you here, but it was still pretty bad."

"I know," Miriam said. Memories came tumbling back at once, vivid in the dim light: Randolph's voice shouting, the stark terror in Weeden's face as he fell, and the Blade of Uoht piercing her, the black length of it cold as ice on the Moon—

"The blade," she said, forcing her mind back to the one thing that mattered. "What happened to it?"

"Don't worry about that," said Claire. "Jenny recognized it, and she wasn't the only one. It's safe, and the Great Old Ones know."

"Nyarlathotep—"

"He knows," the old woman said. "He was there with the others when you came back from the Dreamlands."

Miriam tried to say something else, but the words would not come, and she let herself fall into the waiting shadows of sleep.

She slept, woke, slept, woke again, slept. More often than not, when she blinked awake, Claire was sitting in the same chair as before, though one morning it was a younger woman she didn't recognize, with curly brown hair and olive skin, and one night it was a mustached man with gray hair she thought she knew. After a while she found herself wearing her familiar sleep shirts—someone must have visited her apartment and come back with those. Broth came to supplement the water. They were worried about what the blade might have been done to her intestines, Claire explained, and Miriam gave her a blank look and then remembered: of course, they knew nothing about the other thing that was feeding on that part of her body.

Later, when she was strong enough to sit up in bed for a little while with extra pillows behind her, she asked Claire, "Where's Jenny? I'm a little surprised I haven't seen her."

"She's seen you," Claire said. "She's been very busy with everything that's happening in Arkham, but she's come two or three times a day. I don't know if she's free now, but I can let her know that you'd like to see her."

"Please," Miriam said.

The old woman pulled herself up out of the chair and left the room.

A QUARTER HOUR later, maybe, Miriam heard the door to the sitting room open, and a moment later Jenny came into the bedroom, looking troubled. "I'm sorry I didn't manage to stop by earlier when you were awake, but it's been a difficult time."

"Anything I should know about?"

"Not until you've recovered quite a bit more." Jenny gave her an assessing look. "This is probably a really dumb question, but how are you feeling?"

"Surprisingly well," Miriam answered, "all things considered." She stopped, then, trying to figure out how to say the other things that had to be said.

"You're wondering," said Jenny, "whether I'm going to think you're crazy if you talk about what happened to you. No, I won't. You went to the Dreamlands by way of a very old portal west of Arkham, where half a dozen other people have disappeared the way you did—your car's back in the parking lot behind your apartment, by the way, and we also managed to find your shoes and your purse. You came back not quite eleven hours later by way of the same portal. I don't know much about what happened in between those, but Nyarlathotep told me what you did at the Temple of the Flame, and—" She made a little gesture, palms up. "I'm awed."

"It really wasn't that big a thing," Miriam said. A skeptical noise in Jenny's throat told her what her former student thought of that.

But that brought up a point of immense discomfort. Somehow, Miriam knew, she was going to have to explain to Jenny that all the care that had been lavished on her had been wasted effort, a matter of a short reprieve before the inevitable happened. That reminded her of those last scans she'd seen, and all at once she noticed a certain improbable coincidence.

She placed her hand over the bandaged place where the

Blade of Uoht had pierced her. Yes, that was exactly over—
"That's odd," she said aloud.

"You shouldn't put pressure on that," Jenny said. "You still have a lot of healing to do in there." Then: "What's odd?"

Miriam glanced up at her, decided she was tired of hiding. "Jenny," she said, "I'm sorry. I have intestinal cancer; the doctor says I have maybe six months left. But the place where the blade went in—it's exactly where the primary tumor is."

Jenny's face went white. "You didn't tell me," she said in an ashen voice.

"I didn't tell anyone," Miriam admitted.

In sudden anger: "I could have done something. You knew that!"

Miriam tried to find something to say and had to settle for "*What?*"

The two of them stared at each other for a long moment, Jenny furious, Miriam baffled. Then Jenny's eyebrows went up. "You didn't guess?" she asked. "Five and a half years and you didn't guess—" She started laughing, a weak, shaken laugh, and sat down in the bedside chair as though her legs had suddenly given out.

"Jenny," Miriam said, hopelessly confused, "what are you talking about?"

Jenny looked up at her. "You spent five and a half years helping to train a sorceress."

Miriam stared at her, at a loss for words.

"Do I have your permission to show you something?"

Miriam managed a nod, and Jenny got up from the chair, murmured something under her breath, and pressed the back of her right hand against the older woman's forehead. Miriam expected to feel warm flesh, and was startled by the clear sensation of a cold smooth stone instead. Then Jenny drew her hand back, and Miriam caught sight of a ring on her index finger she had not seen a moment before: the band and bezel an improbably red gold, the great purple gem smoldering with a sullen fire.

Neither of them said anything for a while. "That," Miriam managed finally, "looks rather remarkably like the Ring of Eibon."

"It should," said Jenny. "Who's the last person you know of who had the Ring of Eibon in his keeping?"

"That was Luc le Chaud—" She stopped, realizing what the name implied.

Jenny nodded. "Uncle Martin can tell you exactly how many times great a grandfather Luc le Chaudronnier is of mine. But yes, this is the Ring of Eibon; it's been in the family since the twelfth century; and everyone's pretty much agreed that it's been at least that long, maybe longer, since any sorcerer or sorceress in the family has had as thorough a grounding in the philosophy and theory of sorcery as you gave me. So thank you."

"You're welcome," Miriam said, dazed. Then: "The ring—that's one of the three treasures, isn't it? And the Blade of Uoht..."

"You know about those, then," said Jenny. "Good."

"How did the Radiance get hold of the blade?"

The younger woman's eyebrows went up. "And you know about them. That's better—in a certain sense." Considering her: "It's an ugly story. Do you remember the night I graduated, when we dropped you off at your apartment?" Miriam nodded, and Jenny went on. "One of their negation teams tried to kill me maybe a minute after you went inside. They'd tracked us—probably with a drone—and had thirty men with silenced weapons waiting."

Miriam stared at her for a moment. "What happened?"

"I keep certain protections in place all the time," Jenny told her, "and I can call—certain allies—very quickly. So the bullets veered and missed, and a moment later the allies

I mentioned showed up and took the negation team somewhere else." Seeing the question in her eyes: "You really
don't want to know where."

Miriam nodded, and Jenny went on. "But the Radiance
had teams in Spain and Gabon too, and before I could send
a warning, the guardians of the other two treasures had been
killed and the treasures taken. You know what they did with
the Blade of Uoht. I don't know what they've done with the
Ghorl Nigral, the Book of Night. I imagine we'll find out the
hard way."

Neither of them said anything for a few moments. "I'd
like your permission," Jenny said then, "to use a spell to see
if there's anything I can do about the—the cancer. I'll need to
touch your bare skin; I hope that's not a problem."

"No," said Miriam. "Not at all."

"If you could—"

It took only a little fumbling for Miriam to push the covers down on her left side and pull her sleep shirt up, baring
most of her belly while preserving her modesty otherwise.
The place where the Blade of Uoht had pierced her still had
layers of gauze taped over it. Jenny came over to the bedside,
traced a complex pattern over the wound with her right hand,
then placed both hands palm down on Miriam's belly and
closed her eyes. Miriam watched her, fascinated by her look
of absolute concentration, until finally her eyes blinked open
again.

"That's really quite strange," Jenny said. "There was certainly a cancer there, but—"

"Was?" Miriam asked, baffled.

"Let me show you."

Jenny pressed a hand briefly to the older woman's forehead, murmured a spell, and then placed her palms again
against Miriam's belly. This time, Miriam's sight wavered,
and then showed her what Jenny was seeing: layers of skin

and muscle and viscera, the same patterns she'd seen in blurred black-and-white form in the scans Dr. Krummholz had sent her. Where the sprawling lumpy growths of cancer had been, though, she saw only shriveled remnants, and the primary tumor—that was gone utterly. The Blade of Uoht had apparently passed right through the middle of it, missing the organs it had pushed to either side, and now only a void remained.

The image vanished as Jenny opened her eyes. "I don't know what to make of it," Jenny said. "I can sense where it was, but—it's as though the Blade of Uoht cut it right out of you."

Then, finally, things made sense to Miriam. "It did," she said. "That's how dream logic works." To Jenny's baffled look: "Randolph Carter told me about that."

Her eyes went wide. "You met Randolph Carter?"

"He was with me at the Temple of the Flame."

That got a look of pure amazement, and Miriam smiled and went on. "He told me that everything in the Dreamlands follows the logic of dreams. If the Blade had gone through me in the waking world, it wouldn't have done that, but in the Dreamlands—that's how dreams work."

Jenny nodded slowly, and then let out a ragged breath and slumped back into the chair. Miriam rearranged her sleep shirt and the bedding. "I hope you're okay," Jenny said. Then, looking away: "My mom died of cancer."

"I didn't know that," Miriam said, appalled. "I'm sorry."

Jenny looked up at her. "We really have held each other at arms' length, haven't we?" With a fragile smile: "I'll try to do better."

"So will I," Miriam promised.

THEY SAT AND talked for maybe another quarter hour, and

Miriam got Jenny to promise that she'd let Will Bishop know she was safe—he deserved to know, and so did Amber; memories of the strange little creature twisted in her. Finally, though, Miriam's voice began to blur with drowsiness, and Jenny moved the extra pillows, saw to it that she was settled, and left. In the few minutes before sleep claimed her, Miriam tried to make her thoughts fit round the one future she'd failed to anticipate, a future in which she might just possibly have years left to live.

One task, though, stood uppermost in her mind, and for the first time since childhood, she mumbled a prayer: "Gods of dream, I need to find Randolph Carter and let him know I'm all right. Please help me." She was dozing by the time she began it and sound asleep before she finished, but the gods of dream are capricious and sometimes grant even the feeblest prayers, and perhaps the Lord of the Great Abyss intervened on her behalf. Whatever the reason, she sank into deep slumber at once, and not long afterwards found herself in the Dreamlands.

She was standing on a road paved with great gray flagstones and edged with low banks where flowers bloomed. All around her in the afternoon light spread the hedges, fields, and thatched roofs of a peaceful land, rolling down to a great river in the middle distance. She glanced down at herself, and found that she was dressed as she'd been on the journey to the Temple of the Flame: embroidered blouse, woolen skirt and cloak, and soft but sturdy leather boots with upturned toes, with her stout knife at her hip and the talisman of Nodens wrought by the finned and bearded Gnorri on its leather thong about her neck. Exhilaration surged in her. She flung her arms out to either side, drew in a deep breath of the fresh bright air of the Dreamlands, and spun in a circle, laughing in delight.

She had someplace to go, though. Not far ahead was a

town, a single broad street lined with half-timbered buildings, and beyond it a great stone bridge arched over the river. She headed that way, and—the logic of dreams being what it is—promptly came to a little house just outside the town, where an old woman sat in a chair on the porch, plying yarn with a spindle.

"Good day, grandmother," she called out in the language of Ooth-Nargai. "I fear I'm astray. Can you tell me the name of the town ahead?"

"Good day," the old woman said, "and you're astray indeed if you speak that language, for it's only because my father traded in Celephaïs that I know a word of it. This town before you, it's Nir, of course, and the river is the Skai. If you wish to return home, why, all you need do is cross the bridge, turn right on the far side, and follow the road down to Dylath-Leen, where unless things have changed utterly, you can get a ship to Celephaïs any month of the year."

"Thank you, grandmother," Miriam said. "I'm bound elsewhere, but you've already told me all I need to know to find my way. May the Great Old Ones bless you."

"Thank you, and likewise, to be sure," said the old woman, and returned to her plying.

Miriam went on through Nir, passed over the green and swirling Skai on the ancient stone bridge, and crossed the high road alongside the river that led south to black Dylath-Leen and north across the Karthian hills to the great entrepôt of Hlanith. Beyond the road lay a countryside of neatly fenced farms, little green cottages, and cats everywhere: pacing along the tops of fences, dozing in the sun on windowsills, or keeping watch from porches. She walked on, and soon came to a town built on rounded hills, where narrow cobbled streets zigzagged up the slopes, half covered by the overhanging upper stories of tall houses with peaked roofs. It was Ulthar, she knew, Ulthar where no man may kill a cat, and which

Randolph Carter had called the kind of place he could dwell in always. Of course he would be there.

How to find him, though? At first she was perplexed, but then remembered that she could trust dream logic. He would be in the first inn on the right, she guessed, and walked up the high street until a sign hanging over a door to her right told her she'd found the proper place. The public room was half in shadow and the rest in dim light filtered through diamond-paned windows. That early in the afternoon, it was all but empty; but there he was, sitting alone in the back of the room at a scarred oaken table, with his chin propped on his hands and his gaze fixed on a flagon in front of him.

"Randolph!" she called out.

He looked up suddenly, and then sprang from his place. Three long strides brought him to her, and he took both her hands in his. "Miriam," he said in English. "You're all right?"

"I'm fine," she said. Seeing the questions in his gray eyes: "Nodens intervened. He sent me back to the waking world in time, and friends of mine were waiting."

He let out a ragged breath, relaxed visibly, and released her. "That's very good to hear. And the Blade of Uoht—"

"Nyarlathotep has it."

"That's at least as good." He gestured toward the table where he'd been sitting. "But I'm forgetting my manners. May I get you something?"

"Please." She let herself be guided to the oaken table and settled onto a bench facing his. The barmaid, who had been watching the whole exchange in astonishment, came scurrying over, spoke to Randolph in a language Miriam guessed was that of Sydathria, went back and returned after a moment with another flagon of white wine. Miriam sipped it, said, "This is really good."

"The vineyards along the Skai are famous," said Randolph.

"Deservedly." She took another sip. "I have no idea how long I'll be here. I'm dreaming just now—my body's sound asleep in a bedroom in Kingsport."

"That's very good to hear." In response to her questioning glance: "There are plenty of less comfortable destinies."

She laughed. "True enough. With that in mind, should I ask how you got here?"

"Exactly the way I told you on the Moon," he said with one of his quick grins. Then the smile faded. "I waited beside the Flame until sunrise, on the off chance that something unexpected might happen. When it didn't—well, then I retrieved our packs, left the city, went to the edge of the desert, found some wood and lit a fire to make breakfast. The smoke brought a band of nomads out of their normal route; they were headed for Parg, as I guessed. A dozen days of hard travel and we got to the borders of Parg, where I met an old friend from Kadatheron and traveled with him by way of the Gamala's court at Rinar to Dylath-Leen. Since I still had plenty of time to spend before returning to Ilek-Vad, I sent a letter to Etienne by way of a Rokol merchant, and then wandered up this way to visit Atal and spend some time with the cats. I got here just this morning. And you? How did you find me?"

"I prayed to the gods of dream to help me," she said. "I owed you that much, and more."

He glanced at her and his face tensed.

"Randolph," she said. "On the bridge—you kicked Weeden's hand loose, didn't you?"

He met her gaze and nodded.

"Thank you."

"I guessed that was what you wanted."

"Of course. I'd have done the same thing for you, if it came to that."

Abruptly he sat back on the bench and laughed. "Miriam," he said, "you never fail to astound me. I hope you keep hold of the trick of entering the Dreamlands. I'd like to show you Oonai and Oriab and fallen Sarkomand, and roam with you past the cities of Mnar to the eastern deserts where Irem lies hidden. You'd be good company."

"Thank you," she said, touched. "That's high praise."

"And well earned." He raised his flagon. "To our future journeys together."

She smiled and repeated the words; the flagons tapped together, and she took a good swallow of the wine. It went straight to her head. She blinked, suddenly drowsy, and Randolph laughed again, took the flagon from her weakening hand, helped her forward to settle her arms on the table and her head on her arms, as the Dreamlands dissolved around her.

She blinked awake in the bedroom in Kingsport. Afternoon had come, and golden light splashed in through the window from the garden outside, edged with darker tones that hinted of an oncoming storm. I should get a good stout knife, she thought. And a talisman of Nodens, if those exist in the waking world—

She stopped, laughed, and told herself that she was being silly. It wasn't as though she would go wandering through ruined cities in the waking world, hiding from red-footed wamps.

Would she?

The Dreamlands, Randolph had told her, were a memory of what was and a promise of what would be. If the hints in von Junzt and some of the other old lore made the sense she thought they did, might she still be alive when Great Cthulhu awoke? She could not tell, but resolved to talk to Jenny about talismans of Nodens.

THE NEXT DAY Jenny made time to visit her right after breakfast—Miriam had been allowed toast, poached eggs, and tomato juice, which struck her as a great improvement. They sat and talked for most of an hour, mostly about the things Miriam had seen in the Dreamlands and the strange lore Randolph Carter had shared with her, though Miriam did not fail to ask about the Lord of the Great Deep and his talismans.

Just as she was beginning to feel drowsy, a precise tap on the door interrupted the conversation. It was the butler, Michaelmas, come to announce a visitor.

"Will? I'd be delighted to see him," said Miriam.

"Are you sure?" Jenny asked. "I know he'll be glad to wait a little if you need to sleep."

"I'm sure," Miriam said. "Whatever the news is, I'd rather know."

The butler made a measured bow and left the room. Miriam sank back onto the pillows, let her eyes drift shut for a moment. Jenny said nothing. Outside, the catbirds squabbled.

The door opened a few minutes later and Will Bishop came in, his canvas bag with him as usual. "Dr. Akeley!" he said. "It's good to see—"

A sudden high-pitched cry sounded from inside the canvas bag, and all at once a golden-brown blur flung itself from the mouth of the bag to the foot of the bed in a single leap. A moment later Amber had bounded the rest of the way and buried her tiny face in Miriam's shoulder, clinging to her arm and making little frantic chirring sounds.

"Oh thank God," said Miriam. "Thank you, Will." She stroked Amber's fur, felt an immense relief that the little creature was well. "I hope she didn't give you any trouble."

"Not a bit. You didn't tell me that she understands quite a bit of English."

Miriam nodded. "She's a clever little thing."

"Miriam," Jenny said then, "Where did you find that?"

Her voice sounded oddly unsteady. Miriam glanced up at her, and found that the younger woman was staring at the little creature with her mouth open, her wide-eyed expression blending more emotions than Miriam could easily count.

"She literally fell through a hole in my apartment ceiling," said Miriam. "The poor thing was starving—I don't know where she came from, but she had a very rough time of it." Then, considering Jenny again: "Do you know what she is?"

"Yes." She blinked in amazement; Miriam noted in astonishment that there were tears in her eyes. "I never dreamed I would see one." She drew in an uneven breath. "That's a kyrrmi: a relative of monkeys, I think."

Miriam tried to parse the name. "Where on earth is it from?"

"Poseidonis." Another ragged breath. "Their ancestors came from the rain forests of Atlantis originally, or so I've read."

"Hold it," Miriam said. "*Atlantis?*"

Jenny looked blank for a moment, then suddenly started to laugh. "Hasn't that sunk in yet? All of that's true, Miriam. Hyperborea, Atlantis, Poseidonis—those were real, as real as Rome and Babylon. My family came from Poseidonis originally."

Miriam stared at her, nodded after a moment.

"But the kyrrmis—maybe fifteen thousand years ago, when the rest of Atlantis was mostly under water, some bright soul in Poseidonis figured out that they could be domesticated, and trained to do all sorts of things. They're very clever, as you said."

Miriam considered the little creature clinging to her arm, ran her fingers through its fur again. "I wonder how on earth one got to Arkham."

"That's the easy part," said Jenny. "When the seas started rising again—that would be about eight thousand years ago—people fled from Poseidonis to Europe, Africa, the Americas, wherever there were Poseidonian trading posts and ex-pat communities. Of course they took kyrrmis with them, partly because, well—" She gestured at Amber, as the kyrrmi nestled affectionately into Miriam's shoulder; Miriam chuckled and nodded. "But also because they're useful in magic. There are whole branches of the old lore that you need a kyrrmi to practice, because of the way their nervous systems resonate with ours."

Miriam nodded again, more slowly. "So, witches and their familiars."

"Exactly. And that's why the Radiance set out to exterminate them."

Miriam gave her a horrified look. "That makes an ugly sort of sense."

"Doesn't it? They were very thorough—they usually are. They came up with diseases to which kyrrmis didn't have any resistance, all kinds of other nasty tricks, and of course they also just up and killed every one they could find. As far as we knew, the last of them died in West Africa about two hundred and fifty years ago. So the question that has me baffled is one of time rather than place—how on earth you found one still living."

Useful in magic, Miriam thought. She closed her eyes, tried to brace herself for the offer she knew had to be made.

"No," Jenny said at once, as though she'd read the thought. "If they're to work with a witch or a sorcerer, they have to be trained pretty much from the time they're weaned. So—" She shook her head, smiled. "It's enough to know that there's still one alive."

"If there was one in Arkham," Will said then, "there might be others."

Jenny and Miriam both looked at him. He'd settled on the armchair and pulled a stack of papers out of his canvas bag to read, but was watching the two of them over the tops of his half-moon glasses.

"That's true," said Miriam. "Though I don't know how you'd go about finding them."

"There might be a way," Jenny said then. "Maybe. I know it was tried before, but..."

Abruptly the younger woman got up and went to the door. "I need to talk to some people," she said, "and I imagine the two of you have plenty to discuss." To Will: "Don't let her strain herself too much, okay?"

Will laughed. "I'll do my best."

The door opened and closed.

"I WANT TO know everything that's happening at Miskatonic," said Miriam then. "Starting with Dr. Upham. Is he—"

"He's going to be okay," Will reassured her. "He got beaten up pretty bad, but some campus staff got him to the medical center right away, and he's home now recuperating. I've visited him—a lot of people have."

"Good," said Miriam; the word seemed hopelessly inadequate. "Do you know if they went after Dr. van Kauran?"

He gave her an amused look. "Yes. Did you know he's a Nam vet?"

"No, I didn't."

"Ex-Special Forces. Not the kind of guy you want to jump."

She looked up at him, suddenly uneasy. "What happened?"

"Nobody's saying. He had a couple of nasty bruises when I saw him in Dr. Upham's hospital room, but other than that he was fine. I've got a friend in medical school who heard from a friend at Salem General that they had three guys admitted there with serious blunt-impact trauma, really ugly

195

multiple fractures, like someone worked them over with a baseball bat. I'm guessing that walking stick of his isn't just for show."

She processed that. "I hope neither of them are backing down."

Will shook his head. "Dry day in R'lyeh. Upham's an old-fashioned New England gentleman, which means he's a cast iron bastard to anyone who tries to mess with something that matters to him, and van Kauran's the upstate New York equivalent, which I gather is even worse. They've both called me I forget how many times to find out if I've heard anything about you."

Miriam gave him a startled look, and he said, "Like I said, old-fashioned gentlemen. Beat them up, they're going to double down—beat up a lady, and they're going to make sure the people responsible get castrated with a belt sander. What do you want me to tell them?"

"Tell them I'm okay," Miriam said after a moment. "Tell them I got roughed up, not too bad, and I'm staying in a safe place with friends. Tell them I'm still going to fight this thing tooth and nail." Then: "And tell Denny and Dr. Peaslee the same thing. They'll be worried sick."

Will promised that he would. "Other than that, everyone's hunkered down waiting. Phillips left town and his office staff won't even answer the phone. There are people who aren't from the university, who have the Noology Department look, all over the campus. The Noology people themselves are still trying to talk to anyone who'll listen, but it's always the same spiel, practically word for word. It's really spooky."

"I can imagine," said Miriam. For a moment neither of them spoke.

"There's one more thing," Will said then. "You told me that somebody should try to follow the money, and so I decided to give it a shot."

Miriam blinked. "I meant a forensic accountant or some-one like that."

"You didn't say that," he replied with a grin. "So I started poking around, and—well, have a look for yourself."

He crossed to the bed, handed her the stack of papers he'd been reading. One of her arms was held hostage by Amber, who showed no interest whatsoever in letting go of it, but after a little fumbling she got the papers settled in her lap and began to read. They were printouts from document files and spreadsheets, she saw that at a glance.

By the time she'd finished the third sheet, her mouth had fallen open. "Will, where on Earth did you get these?"

"I went some places I probably shouldn't have," he ad-mitted.

"Morgan Hall?"

"Well, yes. I couldn't hack into the computers from any-where outside it."

"They'd have shot you dead if they'd caught you."

"They'd have tried."

She considered him for a long moment, wondering what he meant by that. In the wider world she'd fallen into, the baggy clothing he wore and the not-quite-right shapes of his body suggested an answer, one she wasn't sure she wanted to think about just then. Instead, she picked up the next sheet and read it.

By the time she got to the end of the stack she was shak-ing her head. "This is incredibly explosive stuff. If it got into the media, or better still, onto the internet—" She left the rest of the sentence unsaid. "Thank you again, Will. This just might help."

"I'm hoping."

She let herself slump back against the pillows, tried to think of the other questions she'd wanted to ask Will. Tired-ness, bone-deep, pressed her hard. No, she thought. No, I need to stay awake. I can rest later.

Amber raised her head, gave Miriam a long solemn look, and then nestled down again and began to make her low throaty churring sound.

"Amber!" Miriam said, instantly fighting to stay awake. "Stop that!"

The kyrrmi gave her a reproachful look and kept churring.

"I know who's going to win this fight," Will said with a grin. "You get some sleep, Dr. Akeley. I don't mean to be rude, but you look like you need it."

She heard the door open and close. "Little wretch," she tried to say to Amber, but was sound asleep before she'd finished the words.

TWELVE

The Gate of Ivory

She woke to Amber's chirring and the soft sound of a child's whispers. Morning sun streamed through the window, pooled on the bed. Evidently she'd slept the clock around, or close. Moments passed before her eyes cleared enough to see anything but brightness and blurs.

Amber was sitting up on her haunches on the side of the bed, holding a wedge of orange in her forepaws and nibbling at it. In front of her stood a girl maybe three years old, in a bright yellow dress. She had curly brown hair, violet eyes, and a face that seemed just a little familiar to Miriam, and she held a partly dismantled orange in one hand. She watched the kyrrmi with a look of utter fascination. Claire perched on the chair nearby, attentive.

"I think our guest is awake," Claire said then. "Good morning, Dr. Akeley."

"Good morning," Miriam said.

"Jenny thought your little friend would need a meal, so we begged fruit and nuts from the cook. You haven't met Asenath yet, have you? This is Asenath Merrill; Asenath, this is Dr. Miriam Akeley, your aunt Jenny's teacher."

The child gave her a wide-eyed look and said, "Hi."

"Pleased to meet you," Miriam replied.

"She's quite entranced by your kyrrmi—she's not the only one, of course." Claire laughed softly. "But she begged me and promised to be good as gold if I'd let her feed it."

Miriam nodded, and to the child said, "Asenath, her name is Amber."

That got her another wide-eyed look. "Oh, that's a pretty name," Asenath said, and after a moment: "She's the sweetest thing ever."

"She is, isn't she?" Miriam agreed.

The rest of the orange went into Amber's paws, one wedge at a time, and got neatly devoured. Finally, when it was gone, Amber let out a contented chirr, as though to say "thank you," and let Asenath pet her for a few moments, then padded up onto Miriam's shoulder and nestled down affectionately. "You should go tell your mother all about Amber now," Claire told the little girl then.

Asenath looked glum, but gave her a hug, said "Bye" to Miriam and "Bye, Amber" to the kyrrmi, and left the room. "If you need anything..." Claire said to Miriam.

"I think I can handle breakfast. Other than that, I should be fine."

"Glad to hear it." The old woman got up from the chair. "I'll let the maid know."

A few moments before the discreet knock sounded on the door, it struck her: Merrill. Asenath Merrill. The child's almost-familiar face, and a voice she dimly remembered, in the chaos and darkness between her plunge into the abyss and her waking in the sunlit bedroom—

She was shaken enough by the realization that when the maid came, their brief conversation about breakfast barely penetrated the surface of her mind. It wasn't until the maid returned maybe a quarter hour later with a tray that she was

200

able to shake herself out of the maelstrom of half-coherent thoughts to put what she needed to know into words. "If you don't mind my asking," she said to the maid, "is Owen Merrill staying here?"

The maid paused in the middle of pouring coffee, smiled at her. "Why, yes, ma'am. He's here with his family. A friend of yours?"

Miriam managed a nod.

"If you like, I'll let him know you asked after him."

"Please." With an effort: "Tell him I'd like to see him sometime soon."

"I'll do that." She finished pouring the coffee, got the rest of the dishes arranged on the table, gave her another smile and left the room.

HALF AN HOUR later, after the maid had come back and cleared away the dishes, a knock sounded at the bedroom door. It wasn't Jenny's light knock or the soft half-tentative knocks the maids used; it was a firm crisp tap-tap-tap that made Amber glance up sharply, and she knew instantly who it had to be. "Please come in," she called out.

The door opened, and there Owen was: broad-shouldered and sandy-haired, with a short beard and a face five and a half years closer to middle age, but still very much the Owen she remembered. "Miriam," he said. "It's good to see you."

She stared at him for a long moment, and then forced out, "I wish you could have let me know you were all right."

"I wish I could have, too," he said. "I'm sorry."

After another moment, she motioned him to the bedside chair. "So—there are reasons."

"There are rules," said Owen, sitting down. "We don't take risks. If Nylarlathotep hadn't vouched for you, Laura and I would have gone somewhere else for as long as you needed to stay here. That's how we do things."

"We," she repeated, with a raised eyebrow.

"The people of the Great Old Ones," he replied.

She took that in, then said, "It's good to see you, too." With a little laugh: "I hardly know where to begin. What happened, where you've been for five and a half years..." Her voice trailed off. Amber, who had been watching the newcomer closely, seemed to decide he was acceptable, and nestled against Miriam's arm and went to sleep.

"I'll start from the beginning," he said, with a grin so familiar it ached. "How much do you know about what the Noology Program was up to back then?"

"Not a great deal."

"They had people going into the restricted collection at Orne Library to take notes on the Necronomicon and some of the other major tomes. I happened to catch Shelby Adams at that one morning, and so they tried to kidnap me. I managed to get away—I'd already met Nyarlathotep and knew where to go—so I went to Innsmouth for a while, and some other places. I can tell you the whole story sometime.

"But the short version is that I ended up in Dunwich. It's a safe place for the people of the Great Old Ones, and I needed to be out of sight of—"

He paused, and Miriam guessed why. "The Radiance," she said.

"Yeah. So I settled down in Dunwich and got a job teaching the upper classes at the local Starry Wisdom parochial school—literature, composition, and history, mostly."

"That's an honest trade," Miriam said.

He grinned again. "Thank you. I'm not sure why I didn't consider education back when I was in college; it suits me, and I think I'm fairly good at it."

"But you also got married."

"I was getting to that. I met Laura at Innsmouth, and

after we both went to Dunwich, yes, we got married. You've met Asenath, of course—she's our oldest, and she has a little brother now, Barnabas. Laura's very talented; she's a priestess in the Esoteric Order of Dagon."

"Another honest trade," Miriam said with a smile. "Is she here? I'd like to meet her."

"Yes, she is," he said, "but I should warn you that you may find her a little unnerving."

Miriam gave him a baffled look. "What, does she have tentacles or something?"

"Actually, yes, she does."

She blinked. "Okay," she said after a moment. "I'll deal."

"I'll go get her," Owen said, getting to his feet. "Our rooms are just two doors down the hall from yours."

A moment later he was gone, and she lay back against the pillows. Amber made a questioning chirr, and Miriam said, "No, I'm fine. It's just—rather a shock." The kyrrmi seemed content with the answer, and settled back down.

A few more moments passed. Then, in the stillness, Miriam heard the quiet click of a door opening, followed by footfalls, and by something else—a soft rhythmic sliding sound approaching her bedroom. Just before the door opened, Miriam guessed what it had to be.

"Miriam?" Owen appeared in the doorway, and after him came a woman in her early thirties, in a white cotton blouse and a long skirt, with curly brown hair and a complexion Miriam couldn't quite place—a little too brown to be olive, with an odd greenish tone in there as well. A scent of salt water came into the room with her, as though she'd just been bathing in the sea. Miriam couldn't see the tentacles Owen had mentioned, but Laura's fluid pace and the sliding sound she made instead of footfalls gave away their location readily enough.

"My wife Laura," Owen went on unnecessarily. "Laura,

Dr. Miriam Akeley."

"We've met," said Laura, smiling and taking Miriam's hand. "Though I'm not sure you remember me."

Miriam blinked, and said, "I think I do. You were here one morning when I woke up for a little while, weren't you?"

The smile broadened. "I wondered if you were actually awake. Yes, I helped Jenny and the others take care of you when you got here, and we all took turns making sure Claire got at least a little sleep."

"Thank you," said Miriam, "on both counts." She waved them to seats. Laura settled into the armchair beside the bed with a motion too fluid for human legs to copy; Owen fetched a ladderback chair from across the room, brought it over, sat. "You've known Jenny a long time?"

"Just over three years now," said Laura.

Miriam tried to keep a sour expression off her face, didn't entirely succeed. "I probably shouldn't," she said, "but I feel..." She searched for a word.

"Lied to," suggested Owen.

"No, just—held outside."

"That's fair," Owen said. "But there's another side of it. Once Jenny ended up on—our side of the line, let's say—one of her main concerns was making sure you stayed safe. The Radiance will stop at nothing to keep its existence from becoming public knowledge, and let's not even talk about the reality of the Great Old Ones and the rest of it. So Jenny did what she could to protect you, and there were others who helped."

She glanced at him, and a sudden guess hinted at one of those others. "Will Bishop?"

Owen nodded. "He was a student of mine in Dunwich. He's got an extraordinary mind."

"I know," Miriam said. She considered them both for a moment. "But now I'm on your side of the line, to borrow

204

your metaphor."

"In more ways than one, I think," said Laura. "You have some kind of connection with one of the Great Old Ones, don't you? If you don't want to talk about that, of course, that's fine. I know it can be very private."

"Thank you," said Miriam, "but it's public knowledge in the Dreamlands." With an uncertain smile: "It seems— well, egotistical—to say so, but Nodens appeared to me on the way to the Dreamlands and he also brought me back, and—" She closed her eyes, and for an instant the Oracle of the Great Abyss hovered before her. "There's an oracle of his in Rokol," she said. "I went there."

"In the halls of the Gnorri below Ilek-Vad?"

Miriam's eyes snapped open. "You've been there?"

"No," said Laura, "but we know of it." When Miriam nodded: "Something you might consider—Jenny's people have a way of cultivating that kind of relationship, with one of the Great Old Ones. It's not something we do in the Esoteric Order of Dagon or the Starry Wisdom church, though some of us are thinking about it. We'll see what the elders say." She and Owen exchanged smiles, and Miriam noted that, guessed at the complexities that might be involved. "But you might find it helpful, now that you're on this side of the line."

"I'll consider it," said Miriam. "It's good to know I have friends here."

DAYS PASSED. SHE let herself move with the rhythms of her recuperation, tried not to notice the discomfort of dressing changes, put up with bedpans until she regained the strength to totter on Claire's arm out of the bedroom, through the little sitting room outside it, to the bathroom and back. She thought about Randolph's story of his hospitalization during the First World War, guessed that he must have felt much the way she did, sensing the ongoing conflict but forced to keep away from it for a time. Sunlight streamed through the window each morning with improbable brilliance, splashing on vases brimming with roses that the maids brought in each day and set where she could see them. Asenath came to visit Amber often; Owen and Laura dropped in when they could, and so did Jenny.

"I wish I knew more about kyrrmis," Miriam said. She and Jenny were sitting at the little round table in the sitting room, with a teapot and two cups between them—she had progressed to getting out of bed for an hour or two at a time. They'd finished talking about Nodens: a little statue on a sea-green silk cushion, a pair of tall candles, and a pair of bowls full of a potpourri in which rosemary and pine were dominant notes, had found their way onto an otherwise unused niche in the sitting room, and Miriam had copied down the details of the simple ceremony that, morning and evening, invoked the presence of the Lord of the Great Abyss.

"You seem to be very well informed about that one," Jenny said with a grin, indicating Amber, who was settled comfortably in her usual place on Miriam's shoulder.

"Granted. Still, you know what I mean. I don't even know how much English she knows; she's constantly surprising me."

"That I can answer," Jenny said. "Not a word. Kyrrmi were bred so that their nervous systems resonate with ours. You know the trick with two violins, where you play an open string on one and the same string on the other sounds?" Miriam nodded, and Jenny went on. "It's pretty much like that. She feels what you're feeling and sees every image in your mind's eye, so she doesn't actually need to know language at all."

"That's fascinating," said Miriam. "Does the old lore discuss them?"

"Here and there." She poured more tea for them both.

"We've got a book in the library by Johannes Aldrovandus—I'm not sure if you're familiar with him."

"Not at all," said Miriam. "Any relation to the Ulysses Aldrovandus who wrote the famous treatise on unicorns?"

"His son, I think. The family had a thing for sorcerous creatures. He has a chapter on kyrrmis, though, and it's pretty detailed."

"I'd like to see that."

"I'll have Michaelmas bring it up," Jenny promised.

Later, after Jenny had gone off to deal with the next stage in what Miriam gathered was an unfolding crisis in Arkham, and Miriam herself had slept for several hours, the butler came with a heavy leatherbound book of seventeenth-century date under his arm, set it on her table, asked after any other needs she might have, and left. Once he was gone, she got up, picked her way into the sitting room, and opened the volume. 𝕿𝖗𝖆𝖈𝖙𝖆𝖙𝖚𝖘 𝖉𝖊 𝕽𝖊𝖇𝖚𝖘 𝕻𝖗𝖆𝖊𝖙𝖊𝖗𝖓𝖆𝖙𝖚𝖗𝖆𝖑𝖎𝖇𝖚𝖘, the title page declaimed in black letter. She translated that and the subtitle at a glance: *A treatise on preternatural things, wherein are recounted the properties and habits of those beings, both monstrous and otherwise, that lie outside of nature; together with a description of creatures resembling human beings that dwell in forests, mountains, caverns, deserts, and oceans; collected from the best authorities, by Johannes Aldrovandus, professor of medicine and natural history at the University of Bologna, etc.* The engraver had surrounded the words with foliage, from which various creatures thrust their heads, and Miriam noted that one of the heads looked remarkably like the one on the little creature that peered down curiously from her shoulder.

It took her some while to find the chapter headed 𝕯𝖊 𝕵𝖆- 𝖒𝖎𝖑𝖎𝖆𝖗𝖎𝖇𝖚𝖘 𝕸𝖆𝖑𝖊𝖋𝖎𝖈𝖆𝖗𝖚𝖒, "On Witches' Familiars," but that was mostly because so many of the pages she turned on the way there went romping off into the most recondite corners of the old lore. She found a chapter titled 𝕯𝖊 𝕾𝖆𝖌𝖆𝖙𝖍𝖊𝖎𝖘 𝖘𝖎𝖛𝖊

𝔐𝔬𝔫𝔰𝔱𝔯𝔦𝔰 𝔍𝔫𝔣𝔬𝔯𝔪𝔦𝔰, "On Shoggoths or Shapeless Monsters," and another titled 𝔇𝔢 𝔍𝔲𝔯𝔪𝔦𝔰 𝔰𝔦𝔟𝔢 𝔖𝔭𝔢𝔩𝔲𝔫𝔠𝔦𝔠𝔬𝔩𝔦𝔰 𝔖𝔢𝔪𝔦𝔥𝔬𝔪𝔦𝔫𝔦 - 𝔣𝔬𝔯𝔪𝔦𝔰, "On Voormis or Cave Dwellers of Partly Human Shape." Here a chapter talked learnedly about cities under the sea and the not-quite-human creatures that lived in them, there half a dozen pages recounted bits of lore concerning beings descended from serpents who, Aldrovandus insisted, dwelt on the Earth long before the time of Adam. Unicorns came in for a full chapter of discussion—clearly the author had inherited the family interest in them.

The chapter on witches' familiars, when she reached it at last, was cut from the same cloth. Aldrovandus quoted a brace of respectable ecclesiastical scholars on the subject, calmly dismissed everything they had to say as abject drivel, and then cited passages from the *De Vermis Mysteriis, the Testamentum Carnamagi, the Liber Rerum Celandum,* and—Miriam blinked at this—*Bleis magister Merlini,* "Bleys the teacher of Merlin," whom Aldrovandus quoted more than once in a way that made it sound as though the two of them had discussed the subject in person. According to these, Aldrovandus pointed out, witches' familiars weren't demons in a random assortment of animal shapes, as the theologians claimed. Rather, they were animals of a particular kind that resembled a large rat, but had certain peculiar features that Miriam recognized at a glance.

He had no shortage of facts to recount concerning the habits of familiars, all of them accurate as far as Miriam knew, and so much to say about their care and feeding that she found herself wondering if the learned Johannes Aldrovandus had a member of the species perched on his shoulder while he wrote. Toward the end of the chapter, though, was a passage that made her stop, rest her chin in her hand for a time, and then read it a second time:

Of familiars it is also written that they have curious powers over dreams. Bleys the teacher of Merlin said that those learned in strange lore may, passing through the gate of ivory of which Homer speaks, enter upon kingdoms unknown to the waking world and adventure therein; further, that all travel to those lands in dreams in earliest childhood, until the world's wisdom, which is held as folly by the wise, bars their way; and still further, that certain means exist of reopening the ivory gate. Familiars are said to be among these means, and permit the wise dreamer to pass to many strange realms unknown to philosophers.

The chapter ended with a long and ornately argued disquisition on the place of witches' familiars in the great chain of being—Aldrovandus thought they belonged somewhere between apes and hedgehogs, which latter he esteemed highly—and the next chapter, 𝕯𝖊 𝕸𝖔𝖓𝖘𝖙𝖗𝖎𝖘 𝕮𝖆𝖓𝖈𝖗𝖎𝖋𝖔𝖗𝖒𝖎𝖘 𝖙𝖗𝖆𝖓𝖘 𝕺𝖗𝖇𝖊𝖒 𝕷𝖚𝖓𝖆𝖊 𝕮𝖔𝖑𝖊𝖓𝖙𝖎𝖇𝖚𝖘, described creatures like big pink crabs that dwelt beyond the circle of the Moon but occasionally descended to Earth. Another time, Miriam might have gone on to read that, but a thought had seized her. She nodded slowly, closed the book and set it on the table beside her, and got to her feet. Amber chirred at her, for all the world as though telling her to rest, and she laughed and said, "Yes, that's exactly what I had in mind."

Afternoon light filtered in through the window of her bedroom. The room was pleasantly warm, so she settled on top of the covers and let Amber nestle into the usual place in the crook of her shoulder. *Amber,* she thought at the kyrrmi, *I want to go to a certain place in my dreams, and I think you can take me there.* Then, as clearly as she could, she imagined the purple sweep of the Tanarian Hills, the grass and heather and low cedars hissing in the wind, and the long slope before her that ended in shining Celephaïs and the sea. *Here,* she thought.

She felt the little creature respond, puzzled at first, and then intent. The kyrrmi began making a sound that was nearly the low throaty churr Miriam knew, but not quite: unsteadily at first, as though she'd never done it before, and then with increasing sureness. Miriam fell asleep at once, and felt herself plunging through a curiously colored twilight realm in which none of the angles seemed to make sense and none of the shapes resembled anything she knew. Her own body did not have its usual shape, though she couldn't describe the shape it did have, and another being or thing went before her, guiding her—a shape like a polyhedron with surface angles that constantly shifted, gleaming with unknown colors.

Then all at once the twilight realm gave way to a scene she recognized instantly. She was sitting just past the crest of the westernmost ridge of the Tanarian Hills, where she'd slumped to the ground at her first sight of Celephaïs. The bees hummed in the heather, the wind brought fragrant scents up the slope toward her, the sun hung low and orange over the Cerenerian Sea: timeless Ooth-Nargai lay before her. In and around and through it she thought she could sense a distant shimmering music, the voice of the Flame.

A chirr sounded close to her ear, and she glanced that way, found Amber perched on her shoulder, looking around and sniffing with evident interest. "Thank you," she said to the kyrrmi.

She could feel the strain the plunge through the twilight void had placed on her, though, and while she wanted nothing more than to stay in Ooth-Nargai for what would be "a little longer" in a place subject to time, she knew better. She pictured the bedroom in the Chaudronnier mansion, then, and thought at Amber: we should go home.

The strange twilight realm with its unknown colors and uncanny angles opened up around her again. Space and time stretched improbably, and then she was back in her bed with Amber nestled down on her shoulder and the afternoon light turning toward evening outside the window.

Another day, when whatever still needed to be decided in Arkham had been settled once and for all, she knew she would travel further: down to Ieloré's cottage, first of all, to spend some timelessness with her friends there; later, across the sea to Ilek-Vad, to keep the promise she'd made to Serin, and then to go with Randolph to the far corners of Dreamland. Another day, she thought, and then drifted off into dreamless sleep.

MOST OF A month passed before Miriam finished recovering from the cancer and the rough surgery the Blade of Uoht had performed on her. It took an effort for her to keep from following her usual habits and pushing herself beyond her strength, for the news from Arkham was troubling. President Phillips still hadn't returned, but office space in Morgan Hall had already been assigned to the newly founded Office of Coordinated Studies, and the professors who were leading the opposition to the reorganization were beginning to feel the pressures that a university administration could bring to bear on recalcitrant faculty. More than once, Miriam brooded over the possibility of seeking a position at Brown or the Université de Vyones, though the thought left a bitter taste of failure in her mouth.

Her recovery would have taken longer if not for Amber, whose solicitous chirrs kept her from tiring herself. More than once, she slept twenty hours of the day, avoiding all but the commonest dreams, and the results were difficult to ignore: day by day, she felt a strength she had almost forgotten trickling back into her, and the circle of her world gradually widened from the bedroom and sitting room to the rest of the Chaudronnier mansion.

Her first journey down the stairs to the ground floor was difficult, though not quite so hard as she'd expected.

There was good reason for the effort; she'd called Dr. Gordon Krummholz' office a few days before to make an appointment, using a phone one of the maids brought up to her room, and Michaelmas drove her there—it irritated her that walking the twelve blocks was beyond her strength, but there it was. The receptionist gave her a look she couldn't read at all, and when the oncologist came into the examination room, the first words he said were, "I heard about what's going on at the university. Please tell me you didn't get beaten up."

She just looked at him, and he winced and said, "Okay, never mind. You've got someplace safe to stay? Good, good. What can I do for you?"

"Something a little odd has happened," she said. "I had some abdominal injuries." He winced again, and she went on. "The thing is, I've felt quite a bit better since that happened. I want you to run a new set of scans and blood work, and see whether something's changed."

He gave her a baffled look but agreed, with the kind of bland good humor that made her think he was used to such requests from terminal patients. The blood draw and the referral for the scans took a few more minutes, during which they chatted about nothing in particular, and then she headed back out to the waiting Cadillac.

Climbing back up the stairs to her room was difficult enough that she'd needed to lean on Michaelmas' arm for support, and the next day she scarcely woke at all. A few days later, though, when it was time to go to Salem for the scans, she managed the stairs herself without assistance, and two days after that she was well enough to have lunch with Jenny in the rose garden out back, sitting comfortably at a glass-topped table of cast iron and nibbling watercress sandwiches while bumblebees thrummed in the rose bushes around them and Amber, sitting at her own place on the table, feasted on mixed nuts and apple slices.

"You're going to end up spoiled rotten," Miriam told the kyrrmi, who responded with a contented chirr and picked up another hazelnut.

"And whose fault is that?" Jenny said, teasing.

Miriam laughed. "Ask Asenath and Emily. They were heartbroken that they didn't get to feed Amber her lunch today."

"Those two." Then: "I didn't know you'd met my other niece—my second cousin once removed, technically, but she calls me Aunt Jenny."

"Asenath introduced us." The memory woke a smile: the two little girls scampering down the hall toward her, and then stopping and doing their level best to imitate adult courtesies. "Your cousin Charlotte's daughter, I gather. Is Charlotte here?"

"Yes, she and Alain both, but she's shy in some odd ways." She poured them both more tea. "She's not an intellectual, and she's got some serious insecurities around that. It's silly; she's a very gifted person—but there it is."

Miriam nodded, thinking of undergraduates she'd had to help past the same issue.

"But you'll get to meet her soon one way or another. If you're feeling well enough, the family would like to have some of the other old Kingsport families over for a dinner party. I think everyone could use a break from the troubles up at Arkham, and quite a few people would like to meet you, you know."

"Would like to meet Amber, you mean," Miriam said, laughing. "Yes, I'm up to it."

"Well, yes," Jenny replied. "But not just her."

SHE WONDERED ABOUT that as she returned to her room that

afternoon, and kept wondering about it for the next two days, while preparations went ahead for the dinner party. The day before the party, though, one of the maids came up an hour or so after breakfast with a phone. "Dr. Krummholz, ma'am," she said. "He'll call back in a few minutes." Miriam thanked her while she plugged the phone into a wall jack, then waited for the ring.

"Miriam?" said the oncologist, once she'd picked up the handset. "Oh, good. You're still safe, no more trouble?" She reassured him that she was fine, and he went on. "I really don't know what to say. You were well into stage four, multiple metastases, and now..."

"Now?" she prompted.

"It's gone. That happens sometimes—it's called idiopathic spontaneous remission, which means we're idiots and we don't know why it happens. I've only seen one or two cases this far along that have done that. Not that I'm complaining, mind you."

"That's good to know," she said, laughing. "I really am feeling a lot better. Weak as a kitten, but better."

"That doesn't surprise me a bit. You weren't kidding about abdominal injuries. What did they do, stick a sword through you or something?"

"I don't know," Miriam told him. "I blacked out."

She could almost hear him wince. "Well, stay out of trouble. You're still off email, right? No prob, I can have a printout waiting at the desk if you want to send one of your friends around to pick it up. Just let me know."

They said the usual things and hung up, and Miriam sat there for a long moment staring at nothing. Despite everything, she realized, she hadn't quite let herself believe that her healing was real. Hearing it from her doctor, though...

She noticed, as though observing someone else, that she was shaking.

A questioning chirr sounded from the bedroom, and Amber came trotting out. "No, I'm fine," Miriam told her, and reached down an arm. The kyrrmi glanced up at her, chirred again, and then climbed up nimbly onto her shoulder. Miriam sat back in her chair and made herself relax until the shaking finally stopped.

Maybe twenty minutes later, when she was just beginning to think about doing something other than sitting there staring at nothing, a tentative knock sounded on her sitting room door.

"Please come in," Miriam called out, expecting one of the maids. The woman who came through the door, though, was vaguely familiar: in her late twenties, she guessed, with brown hair and a face that reminded Miriam at once of Martin Chaudronnier and little Emily.

"You probably don't remember me at all," the woman said.

That finished the process of identification. "Of course I do," said Miriam. "You're Jenny's cousin Charlotte, aren't you? We met after the graduation ceremony."

Charlotte relaxed visibly. "Yes, of course."

Miriam waved her to the other chair. "And I've met your daughter, too."

"I hope she hasn't been a bother."

"Not at all. For three-year-olds, she and Asenath are astonishingly well-behaved."

"Those two." Charlotte took the proffered chair, allowed a first faint smile. "They've been best friends since before either of them could walk."

They chatted for a little while about the children, and Amber helped things along by leaping down from Miriam's shoulder to the table, crossing to Charlotte's side, and accepting a tentative caress with a chirr of pleasure. Finally, reassured, Charlotte got around to the purpose of the visit. "For the dinner party tomorrow," she said, "Jenny and I wondered if you had an evening gown, or if you'd like to wear one from the family's collection—we've got more than a hundred of them, from the best designers."

"I haven't worn a formal gown since senior prom in high school," Miriam admitted. "I'd love to—but I don't know the first thing about how to choose one."

That got a sudden bright smile. "I can help with that. Let's get you measured first."

Miriam had never been able to afford bespoke clothing, but had some idea of what was involved, and so the range of measurements Charlotte took and noted down in a little notebook didn't surprise her too greatly. Amber watched the whole process with great interest. Finally Charlotte fished an assortment of fabric swatches out of her purse, held them against Miriam's face and hair and considered them with a critical eye, then made more notes in the notebook.

After that was finished, they talked for a while longer about little pleasant things, and then Charlotte excused herself. She was back the next afternoon, wearing an impressive golden gown, and accompanied by a maid who brought in a prodigious garment bag and a jewelry box. These opened to reveal respectively a gown of sea-green silk that dated from the nineteen-sixties, and an abundance of silver jewelry set with diamonds that was at least a century older. Miriam, recognizing that she was utterly out of her element, let Charlotte guide her through the intricate process of getting the gown and jewelry properly arranged.

"There," Charlotte said with a nod of satisfaction. "What do you think?"

Miriam turned to look at herself in the tall mirror by the bathroom door, and blinked in astonishment. The lines of the dress were classical in their simplicity, and the shimmering sea green of the fabric and the silver jewelry brought out unexpected nuances of color from her skin and hair. It was the overall impression that struck her most forcefully, though. "I look like a sorceress," she said.

Charlotte nodded, as though it was the most ordinary thing in the world. "You're lacking one thing for that," she said, and nodded at the little round table, where the kyrrmi sat, watching the proceedings with evident approval.

Miriam took the hint, went to the table and held out her arm. Amber climbed to her shoulder and chirred. "There," said Charlotte. "Now you look like a proper sorceress."

"Did the sorceresses in Poseidonis all have kyrrmis?" Miriam asked, surprised.

Charlotte gave her a look of equal surprise. "Yes, of course." Then: "If you're ready—"

"Please."

The carpeting on the corridor floor outside muffled the sound of her steps as she followed Charlotte's gesture, headed for the great stair not far away. Voices came up from below. When she got to the head of the stair she could see men in black evening dress and women in gowns at its foot. Jenny, resplendent in a ruby-colored gown, was on one side of the crowd, and a gray-haired figure that had to be Martin Chaudronnier stood at the bottom of the stair.

She started down the stair, and got halfway down before anyone noticed. Then faces turned to her, and low murmurs alerted those who hadn't yet seen. By the time Miriam reached the foot of the stair every eye was on her—or rather, she told herself, on Amber.

"Good evening, Dr. Akeley," said Martin.

"Good evening."

Amber greeted him with a chirr. Martin gave the kyrrmi an amused look and said, "Your small friend has excellent manners." Then, offering his arm: "May I have the honor?"

"Please," said Miriam, and took it.

217

THIRTEEN

Nyarlathotep's Ring

Late that night she climbed the stair to her rooms, closed the door behind her, sighed and rubbed her eyes. Amber, half asleep on her shoulder, blinked and gave her a questioning chirr. "No, I'm fine," she said in response. "That was—pleasant."

It was a good deal more than that, she reflected, as Amber climbed deftly down to the floor, waited for Miriam to open the door to the bathroom, and went about her business there. Fine food, fine wine, lively conversation, and the pleasant formalities of a bygone era: it had been an altogether delightful evening, made even more so by an attentiveness from Martin Chaudronnier that hinted at something beyond mere hospitality.

Well, what of it? she asked herself as she went into the bedroom and extracted herself from the jewelry and the gown. If something blossoms from that, she thought, why, we're consenting adults not otherwise attached. Besides, Amber likes him—and laughed, partly because it seemed absurd that the kyrrmi's opinion should matter, partly because it did matter.

She settled into bed maybe a quarter hour later, ran vague fingers through Amber's fur, and sank almost instantly into sleep.

Seventy steps of shallow slumber lead to the cavern of flame where the bearded priests Nasht and Kaman-Tha make strange offerings to the gods of dream, and seven hundred steps of deeper slumber proceed beyond that, but those steps lead downwards, and the steps Miriam climbed in her dream led up. They were of midnight-black stone, and they felt cold as the Bnazic desert beneath her bare feet. Amber was perched on her shoulder, though, and seemed to know the way. That comforted her as she climbed.

After a time, golden light came down the stair in a trickle, and as she climbed further, the trickle became a flood. Finally the stair came to a doorway and ended. Beyond was a balcony, and below the balcony a city blazed golden in the evening light. Houses and temples, colonnades and arched bridges of veined marble caught the glory of the setting sun's rays. To one side, broad streets lined with fountains, delicate trees, and urns full of flowering plants reached toward a harbor that glowed like hammered bronze. To the other, red-tiled roofs and old peaked gables climbed steep slopes, across which little lanes of grassy cobbles wound here and there.

The balustrade at the balcony's edge was veined white marble carved in strange shapes, some of which she recognized and some of which seemed to stir faint forgotten memories in the deep places of her mind. She paid little attention to them, though, for someone was standing at the balustrade, gazing down onto the city. Hands bright with many rings rested on the rail. Tall and slender, robed in prismatic garments in a style that was old before Atlantis first rose above the waves, and crowned with a pshent, the royal headdress of Egypt, that glowed inwardly with the colors of sunset: she knew him at once, even before the lean dark face turned back toward her and a motion of the head summoned her forward.

She crossed the balcony and stood beside him for a long moment, looking down at the glory of the sunset city. Greetings seemed superfluous. "I think I was here once," she said finally, "or will be here someday, but I don't know which."

"That depends a great deal on what you mean by 'was' and 'will be,'" said Nyarlathotep.

She pondered that for another long moment.

"You have a choice to make," he said then. "You've already risked more and achieved more than many who've devoted their lives to our service, and you've taken no vow that binds you to risk everything again. You've earned the right to stay where you are and let things fall as they will. Not even the King in Yellow will condemn you if you choose that."

"You're talking about Miskatonic," Miriam said.

He nodded fractionally, sending ripples of light through the pshent. "If it falls into the hands of the Radiance, that won't be the worst defeat we've suffered."

"Why do they want it so badly?"

"More reasons than one," he said. "There are things still in the library they would give much to keep out of our hands, and they suspect Abelard Whipple of concealing things from them—not without good reason. But there are deeper factors, woven into the deep places of the land itself." He faced the sunset city again. "You'll have read of the moon paths, the secret channels of voor that flow through the body of the Earth. Arkham sits atop a nexus where many moon paths cross—the most important such nexus in the eastern half of the continent. The Radiance seeks to control that. They almost did, once, before Belbury Hall burned. Now they seek to renew their grip on it."

"And you think I can stop them."

He glanced at her, said nothing, and all at once she realized what he meant.

Time passed, and the edge of the sun brushed the bronze sea.

"I honestly wish I could stand aside and let it go," she said finally. In a whisper: "But I can't. I just can't."

The Old One glanced at her again, allowed a faint smile. "Do you know what to do?"

"I think so."

He drew a glittering silver ring off one finger, gave it to her. "Then you'll want this. Use it at the right moment, and it might protect you."

She took it, tried to think of something to say.

Then all at once she was blinking awake in her bedroom in the Chaudronnier mansion in Kingsport, as the first pale light of dawn trickled in through the window. Amber was sound asleep against her shoulder, and something unfamiliar rested in one of her hands.

She blinked and tried to focus, but she knew what she would see long before her eyes finally came clear. In her hand, Nyarlathotep's ring glinted cold and strange.

It took her most of another week to make her plans and preparations. There were hard questions to ask about Arkham and the Miskatonic campus; the papers Will brought her also had to be copied, and the copies taken to an assortment of weird places and weirder beings. Only when Jenny told her that one copy was safe with the voormis in green-litten Dhu-shai, another had been taken by Owen to Dunwich, and a third had gone to a rendezvous at night with a tall figure in black in the hills north of Arkham, was Miriam ready to act.

First, though, another task waited.

At Jenny's request, she'd brushed Amber daily and hand-ed over the loose fur, and on a certain evening Jenny was absent at dinner: in a hidden place somewhere in the house,

222

Martin said, with a brief glance downward that hinted of cellars and secret vaults. The next day, tired but triumphant, Jenny reappeared, and in private opened a little bag of brown velvet to show Miriam a tawny crystal precisely the color of the kyrrmi's pelt. "This should do the job," Jenny said. "We'll see."

The following morning Michaelmas brought the Cadillac around to the carriage port. Miriam and Jenny, both of them in old clothes, loaded the trunk with shallow cardboard boxes, well-worn towels, and a full shopping bag from a Kingsport grocery. Will Bishop climbed into the front seat next to Michaelmas—there would be doors to open, and he had a packet of slender steel tools in his canvas bag for that purpose.

None of them said much as the car wove through the narrow streets of Kingsport and started up the road to Arkham. Amber, perched as usual on Miriam's shoulder, looked around with bright eyes. Abandoned farms slid past; then, unexpectedly, they drove by one that had found tenants once again, and had fresh paint on the farmhouse, chickens in the yard, and a cluster of goats chewing thoughtfully in the pasture next to the road. A few more empty farms, and then the stony hills closed in, green with willows and scattered pines, reaching on across a distance that was not measurable in miles.

On the far side of the hills, past the wreckage of an abandoned shopping mall, Arkham came into sight. Miriam half expected to see some terrible change already visible on the Miskatonic campus, off past the roofs of the ancient town, but the great cyclopean shapes of the university buildings looked as they always had. If the Radiance was guarding the entrances to the town—she'd discussed that possibility with Jenny and Owen, and made plans to deal with it—they were nowhere to be seen. Then Old Kingsport Road turned into Peabody Avenue, the sagging gambrel roofs of the town closed in around it, and Michaelmas turned onto a side street, drove past derelict buildings into the heart of old Arkham.

The Cadillac stopped at the corner of Pickman and Parsonage Streets, sidled over to a parking spot on Pickman Street. "Okay," Jenny said then. "Now—we'll see."

No one else was in sight, so Miriam let Amber stay on her shoulder as she got out of the car. She and Will took a box and a towel out of the trunk, along with the bag from the grocery, and followed Jenny over to the abandoned hulk of the fast-food restaurant that occupied the lot where Keziah Mason's house once stood.

Jenny took the brown velvet bag out of her purse, held it to her forehead, nodded. "Yes. Yes, I think so." Then, surveying the empty windows and the rubble inside: "I'm not sure what's the best way in."

Will grinned, climbed in through one of the shattered windows, and forced the door open from inside. Jenny and Miriam entered. Within, shadows hung thick in the empty space. The fixtures and furnishings were long gone, leaving a bare floor of broken tile with heaps of rubbish piled against the far wall, and a door gaping open to the former kitchen.

"You know what to do?" Jenny asked then.

They did. The bag from the Kingsport grocery disgorged a carton of milk and a pie plate. Once the latter was on the bare floor and half full of milk, Jenny walked a short distance away and began murmuring something in a low voice, tracing strange arabesques in the air with her right hand. When she nodded, Miriam turned her attention to Amber, pictured other kyrrmis hiding in the building, and silently asked her to call them.

Amber gave her a wide-eyed look, and then let out a shrill whistling call that sent echoes chasing one another into the darkness where the kitchen had been. Minutes passed, and then—

A faint scrabbling, like a rat hidden in the walls.

Miriam and Will froze. Jenny kept murmuring, and her right hand gestured. Amber sniffed the air, and made the same shrill cry.

A small moving shape appeared in the door of the old kitchen: familiar, but not quite familiar. It had Amber's yellow eyes and handlike paws, and its fur was the same filthy brown Miriam remembered, but it was older and more heavily muscled. A beard edged its face, and it had two sharp and visible canine teeth. It paused, gave them the guarded look of a creature all too familiar with danger and pain.

Amber jumped down from Miriam's shoulder in a single leap, and let out another cry, softer. The other kyrrmi came a little further from the door. Amber called again, and the other responded in a deeper, gruffer tone. The two held what sounded for all the world like a conversation, and then the other kyrrmi turned back to the door and called out.

Behind it, after a moment, three more kyrrmis edged warily out into the light.

One of them was a female, Miriam was sure of it, older than Amber but not as old as the male they'd seen first. She moved heavily, in a way that made Miriam put her hand to her mouth. With her was a much younger kyrrmi with visible canines and a first growth of beard—a young male, Miriam guessed—and another, half the size of the others, who stayed close to the female.

The old male in the lead, the four of them crossed the floor, eyeing the three humans uneasily. Miriam guessed why, and very slowly squatted down. Amber chirred at her and climbed deftly up on her shoulder, then bounded down again.

That was apparently enough to convince the other kyrrmis. They came over to the milk, sniffed it, and then three of them began to lap it up.

"Come on," Miriam said to the old male, in a tone she knew Amber found soothing. "You can have some, too."

The old male gave her a steady look and sat up on his haunches, and Miriam nodded. He would wait until his family was full; that was his way, and the way of kyrrmis.

When the three had finished, and looked noticeably wider in the belly than they had been, the old male did his best to lap up what was left. When he sat up again and considered them. Jenny spoke aloud. "Please come with us. You'll be safe and there'll be plenty to eat. Will you?"

Whether they understood her or not, Miriam never did find out, but Jenny seemed satisfied by the response. One by one, she pointed her left thumb at each of them and murmured a word in a language Miriam did not know. One by one, they blinked, nestled down onto the cracked tiles of the floor, and went to sleep.

The bag from the grocery also held rubber gloves. Miriam pulled on a pair, and so did Will. All four sleeping kyrrmis went onto the folded towel in the cardboard box, close to one another for comfort, and Will took the box and carried it back to the car.

"The female—" Miriam ventured.

"She's pregnant," said Jenny.

Miriam nodded. "I thought so."

"You have no idea what this means." Jenny shook her head slowly, as though stunned. "It's like watching the towers of Susran rising up again out of the sea."

"I know it makes a good friend of mine very happy," said Miriam. "That's enough."

Jenny gave her a troubled look, said nothing.

WHEN THE KYRRMIS were safely ensconced on the back seat

226

of the car, Jenny said, "Okay, give me a moment. I want to make sure we haven't been detected—and there just might be more kyrrmis somewhere nearby." She took the brown velvet bag from her purse again and pressed it to her forehead, closing her eyes. Opening them again: "Yes. This way."

The three of them, carrying the grocery bag and another box and towel, crossed the street and walked two blocks west along Pickman Street. There a building of soot-stained brick that once housed Arkham's largest department store rose six stories into the summer sky. Amber sniffed and chirred, and a moment later Miriam knew why: around the corner was the Yian Café.

"Somewhere well inside," said Jenny. "I wonder if there's a door onto the alley."

There was. It had a padlock on it as well as an ordinary deadbolt, but Will brought out his tools and made short work of both. They stepped into a great empty space dimly lit through dirty windows, followed Jenny across to a wall where something like a rathole, but larger, pierced the wall at floor level.

They repeated the same process: milk in the pan, conjurations in the dim air, and Amber's shrill call echoing in the stillness. A long silence followed, long enough that Miriam and Will glanced at one another, but then a faint scrabbling sound came from within the wall. Amber called again, and all at once a kyrrmi popped out of the hole and gave them all a bright-eyed glance. Beard and sharp canine teeth showed the gender, but he was evidently much younger than the fierce old warrior they'd found on the site of the witch-house, and bolder as well. He bounded over to Amber, who was perched on the floor near the milk, and the two of them had a brief conversation of chirrs and chuffs before the young male went back to the hole and called.

After a time, another appeared, an older male, scarred

and tough; then a smaller kyrrmi, with visible teeth but only the very first trace of a beard; and then others: eight in all, one of them an infant clinging to the fur of its mother's back. Five fed while two kept watch—the infant was apparently still nursing—and then the two older males went to lap up what was left. There wasn't much, and so Miriam, moving very slowly, poured more milk into the pan. All eight watched her solemnly, and then the two males went to the pan and lapped up their fill.

A few minutes later they were all asleep, having given whatever answer Jenny hoped to get to her question, and Miriam and Will got them settled in the box, not without crowding. They left the abandoned department store and hurried back to the car through the empty streets. All the way, Miriam saw Amber's gazed fixed on the young male who'd come so boldly out to them, noted a half-familiar giddiness in her expression, and blushed, guessing what was going to happen as soon as the two kyrrmis found a suitable opportunity.

Michaelmas gave the box of kyrrmis the closest thing to a startled look his unexpressive face could manage. "A considerable collection, Miss Jenny."

"I know." She was beaming. "Let's see if I can find any more."

She walked a short distance away, held the brown velvet bag to her forehead for a while, and then slowly nodded. "I think so," she said. "Just a few, and I'm pretty sure those are the last. We still haven't been noticed, so we can get them and—" She let the sentence drop. Will and Miriam got another box and towel, and followed.

This time she led them to a block of row houses, two on one end still inhabited but the rest abandoned. The roofline visible beyond them stirred something in Miriam's memory, though it was a moment before she realized why: the apartment house where she lived was only two blocks away.

Jenny walked down the cracked sidewalk, passing door after door, and finally stopped at one. "Do you think you can get us in, Will?"

"Piece of cake," he said. The delicate steel tools came out, the deadbolt clicked open, and they slipped inside. The interior was a mess, full of decayed furniture and debris—but before the door closed behind them, Amber started making loud agitated chirrs.

"She knows this place," Miriam said, sensing the kyrrmi's reaction. "She's been here before."

Before they could put down a pan of milk or do anything else, a faint scrabbling sound came from one of the other rooms, followed by a high quavering call. In response, Amber let out a high-pitched shriek, flung herself down from Miriam's shoulder, and bounded through the open door. Kyrrmi-voices tumbled over one another, excited, and then Amber came trotting back out into the living room with three other kyrrmis: an old female and two of Amber's generation, a male a little older than Amber and a female a little younger.

"It's—" Miriam had to stop and swallow, seeing the resemblance. "Amber's family."

"In that case," said Will, "they certainly deserve a treat." He set out the pan and poured the rest of the carton of milk into it. The two younger kyrrmis came straight over and began to drink, but the old female came up to Miriam, who squatted down and said, "Pleased to meet you. I've tried to take good care of your daughter. Won't you have some milk?"

The old kyrrmi may not have understood the words, but she seemed to sense something of the meaning, or at least the feeling behind them. She let out a soft little chuff, then went to the pan and drank her fill of the milk.

This time, Miriam sensed, the question was hers to ask. "I'd like to take all of you with me," she said, "to a safe place where there's plenty of food, and people who care for kyrrmis. Will you please come?"

All of them gave her solemn looks. Jenny, looking on, nodded and pointed her thumb, and three of the four blinked and settled on the floor and went to sleep. Amber sniffed them and made a fretful sound. Miriam imagined the three of them waking in the Chaudronnier house at Kingsport, with Asenath and Emily holding a bowl of fruit and nuts for good measure, and the image made Amber chirr with delight and bound back up onto Miriam's shoulder.

They left the pan of milk where it was, in case some stray cat happened by. "Sixteen," Jenny said in a dazed tone as they went down the steps. "I want to pinch myself to make sure I'm awake. That's more than enough to begin breeding them again."

"You may have some problems from inbreeding," Miriam cautioned her.

"There are incantations to Shub-Ne'hurrath that'll take care of that. Besides, now that we know they've survived, we can look in Salem, and some of the other places that had plenty of witches back in the day. There might be others."

They crossed the street and headed back toward the car. "The poor things must have lived on garbage, insects, anything they could find or steal," Jenny said. "Kyrrmis used to be delicate by all accounts, but these—they had to be tough to survive."

"Like the rest of us," said Will.

They got the third box of kyrrmis settled in the back seat of the car. "And now, Miss Jenny?" Michaelmas asked.

Jenny turned to Miriam. Tentatively: "We could go back to Kingsport."

"No." She'd wondered if her courage would hold up once the time came, but she didn't feel particularly brave just at that moment. There was something that had to be done, and that was all. "I'll need to stop at my place for a few minutes, and put on something a little more suitable than this—" She gestured at the dust-stained clothing she had on. "And then to campus. After that—we'll see."

Jenny nodded glumly, climbed into the car.

HALF AN HOUR later, Miriam got out of the car in the Lovecraft Museum parking lot and headed north, toward Morgan Hall. She did not let herself look back. The atmosphere in the car had been tense to the breaking point. As Michaelmas pulled up to a parking spot, Amber clung to her arm, making piteous cries, and had to be pried loose gently and handed over into Will's custody. Just a few minutes, she told herself, and then it will be over—

One way or the other.

She had on her trademark black dress and white sweater, the most expensive of her shoulderbags settled under one arm, makeup and perfume carefully understated. The whole thing had to be done just right. She'd considered and reconsidered the options, not neglecting Randolph's sound advice about how to do battle, and the only way she could be sure of the outcome was the way that risked the most. She'd watched Clark Noyes often enough to know that the least hint of anything but perfect confidence would be fatal.

She passed through the narrow space between Orne Library and the Armitage Union, slowed her pace fractionally as she started across the grass of the quad. Ahead of her, Morgan Hall's stark brick mass rose high.

It was not like those earlier times: the frantic plunge through the undergrowth, the sudden leap onto the bridge. Her pace measured, her mind cold and clear, she walked up to Morgan Hall's north doors, went in, and started up the big central stair.

On the third floor, off to the left, the doorway had already been lettered OFFICE OF COORDINATED STUDIES. She glanced at it, went forward, and the doors hissed open. "Can I help you?" said the receptionist at the desk beyond the door, a gangly young man in short-sleeved white shirt and black tie.

"I'm here to see Dr. Noyes," said Miriam, and walked past his desk without another word, into the office beyond. People looked up from their cubicles, startled, as she passed them by. She'd figured out already where Noyes' office would be—there was only one place on the floor that would suit the calculated conventionality of his taste—and went straight there. The sign on the door confirmed her guess, and so did the secretary sitting outside the room at an overpriced computer desk of glass and steel, a middle-aged woman with the same bland lack of expression Noyes always wore.

"May I help you?" she asked.

"I'm here to speak to Dr. Noyes."

"Did you have an appointment?"

"No, but he'll see me anyway. Tell him that it's Miriam Akeley."

She typed something, paused to read the response. "Dr. Noyes will see you now."

Miriam went through the door. Inside, Noyes was seated at an even larger and more overpriced desk with three computer screens on it. He waited until she'd closed the door before speaking. "Miriam," he said then. "I admit I'm surprised."

"No doubt," she replied, amused. "I'm sure you're very busy, so I won't waste time." She pulled out a stack of papers from her shoulderbag, set them on the desk, took two steps back. He took them, glanced at the first page, the second.

"A remarkable set of documents, you must admit," she said. "Payments made to President Phillips, and every member of the board of regents, that look remarkably like bribes. Off-book expenditures by the Noology Department, funded through some very dubious channels. Games played with the Miskatonic endowment fund by people whose connections to this department aren't hard to trace. Highly questionable financial links to six other universities, and two nongovernmental organizations I suspect you really don't want to see mentioned in print. Add to that the fact that two of the professors who led the opposition to your little scheme got beaten by thugs—with medical records to prove it—and there's quite enough to launch a media firestorm." Meeting his gaze: "And if that happens, it's just possible that the existence of a certain ancient and highly covert organization may become a matter of public knowledge."

Nothing had changed in the deliberate blandness of Noyes' expression, but she could sense the shift behind it, the cold murderous thoughts her words had roused. She smiled in response, and said, "There's more. By all means take your time and read all of it."

He read more, looked up again. "I'm wondering where you came by these."

"I'm sure you are."

"I'm also wondering what would happen if they were to disappear."

"Along with me?" She laughed. "Clark, do you really think I'm that stupid? There are copies of those in many other hands right now."

"They could be found," he told her.

It was then that she realized what gift the Crawling Chaos had bestowed on her. "One of those hands," she said, "gave me this." She took the ring from her shoulderbag and set it on the desk in front of him.

He recoiled. It wasn't a sudden motion; it was slow, calculated, cold. "Take that thing off my desk."

Her eyebrows went up. "Does it frighten you that much?"

"The fact that you have it," he said, "shows that you're a

traitor to the human race."

"An interesting claim." Miriam took the ring, returned it to her shoulderbag. "I don't suppose you asked the human race for its opinion on that subject."

Noyes gave her a bland empty look, and then said, "I trust you have something less nonsensical to say about these." A nod indicated the papers.

"Of course. I'm here to bargain."

"Indeed. I gather your side of the bargain is that these stay out of public sight."

"These and any others that happen to come my way. Out of the media, off the internet, and out of the hands of the state assembly and every member of the faculty who might find some use for it. Yes."

"And in exchange?"

"My own personal safety, obviously. Also that of my students, past and present."

"That's a great deal to ask," he interjected.

"I'm not done yet." She drew in a breath. "I want you, your department, and this whole misbegotten project of yours out of Miskatonic. I don't know why you chose this university and I frankly don't care. Choose another. Announce that you got a better offer elsewhere—based on what's in those papers, you could make that happen with a phone call. Blame it on the pigheaded intransigence of the faculty senate if you want to. Just go away, and let Miskatonic keep on doing what it was founded to do."

He considered her for what seemed like a very long time. "If you renege on the deal," he said then, "you and every graduate student you've ever taught will be dead within a week."

Miriam guessed then that she'd won. She said nothing, waited.

"Very well," he said then. "You'll have your university—

what's left of it, for the little while that it manages to survive."

"No reprisals," she warned. "Or the deal's off."

"Don't be any more of a fool than you have to be, Miriam," Noyes said. "This is the endgame—a fulfillment three thousand years in the making. I trust you don't expect us to exempt Miskatonic from consequences that will affect every other university on this continent."

"No," said Miriam. "I'll be content if this university shares the common fate—whatever that happens to be."

Noyes laughed. It was a ghastly sound, as though he had never heard a laugh before and had only the most theoretical notion of what one should sound like. "Whatever that happens to be? You amuse me. There's only one possible ending for all of this, and there never was any other. We'll win. We always do, in the end."

"The end hasn't happened yet," Miriam reminded him.

"You know as well as I do what I mean. Reason always triumphs."

"Keep telling yourself that," said Miriam. "I'm sure you'll find it very comforting when Great Cthulhu rises from the sea."

He regarded her for a long moment, with the same blank expressionless look as before. "I think this conversation has outlived its usefulness. You'll excuse me, as I have work to do."

"Of course," said Miriam. "I don't expect to see you again, Clark, but I can't think of any particular reason to wish you well."

Noyes said nothing more, simply sat there watching her with empty eyes as he waited for her to go. She nodded, turned, and left the room.

If she was going to die then and there, she knew, this was when it would happen. Noyes would alert someone in the office outside—a few lines of text or some other signal—and a bullet would fly out of a silenced gun, or some servant of the Radiance would wield some other means of immediate death: they had no shortage of options where that was concerned, she guessed. She did not let herself look at the secretary, the people in the cubicles, or the receptionist, though she could feel their gaze on her as she walked. She did not permit herself to hurry.

The doors to the Noology Department office hissed open and then closed behind her. The muscles in her legs were trembling, but she did not trust the elevators. She started down the great central stair of Morgan Hall. The sound of her footfalls echoed off the brick walls to either side, and she tried not to think about what each whispering sound meant.

Only when she went out the doors into the open air did she let herself begin to hope. Sunlight blazed on brick and grass, the wind tasted of the sea: all of it seemed charged with a beauty and a stark reality she'd never noticed before. She steadied herself, started across the quad toward the gap between Orne Library and the Armitage Union, and to the parking lot beyond it. The car would be there—

The car was there.

One of the rear doors flung itself open the moment she came into sight, and Jenny came pelting out of it, threw her arms around Miriam and then all but dragged her back to the car. Half dazed, half laughing, Miriam let herself be guided most of the way there, then stopped and said, "Just a moment. I have a promise to keep."

Jenny gave her a startled look, but let her go. No one else was in sight, and so Miriam walked over to the great bronze statue of Cthulhu, dug in her handbag, took out a silver dime and three perfect seashells she'd bought at a Kingsport shop, and set them before the statue with the other offerings. Then, curtseying, she murmured the ancient words of reverence: *"Ph'nglui mglw'nafh Cthulhu R'lyeh wagh'nagl fhtagn."*

236

She turned to find Jenny beaming at her, went back to the car, and climbed in. Amber flung herself onto her arm, chirring frantically. The door closed, putting its seal on the improbable reality.

"It worked," said Will, smiling.

"I think so," Miriam said. "We'll have to see if they keep their end of the deal. If not—"

"If not," said Jenny, "There's going to be a reckoning." She climbed into her side of the rear seat, adjusted the position of a box of sleeping kyrrmis. "If that happens, I'm going to have some of Owen's good friends take you and some others to green-litten Dhu-shai, where you'll be safe and out of the way, and then the Noology Department is going to find out just how big of a can of misery I can open up and dump on their heads." She slumped back against the seat. "That may have to happen sooner or later anyway, but if they try to cheat..." She left the rest unsaid.

Michaelmas, who had started the engine, turned half around in the driver's seat. "Where now, Miss Jenny?"

Jenny glanced at him, then at Miriam. "Kingsport—if you're willing."

"I don't want to impose on you," said Miriam.

Jenny gave her a look that might have been irritable if there hadn't been so much obvious affection in it. "Miriam, please don't be silly. You're welcome in our house whenever you want, for as long as you like." Then, seeing the expression on Miriam's face: "Besides, right now you know more about the care and feeding of kyrrmis than anybody else alive, and—" She gestured at the boxes and the sleeping shapes in them. "We're going to need a lot of help with these."

It was a transparent ploy, but Miriam laughed and nodded. "I'll have plenty to do in Arkham in a little while, but—for now, Kingsport. Please."

Jenny beamed and nodded to Michaelmas, who took the

237

Cadillac smoothly out onto Garrison Street. Miriam let herself sink back into the upholstery of the seat, listened to the soft little chirrs Amber made. Kingsport, she thought, calling to mind the salt-laced wind off the harbor and the great soaring cliffs beyond the town. All at once she remembered Ilek-Vad, with its own sea winds and soaring cliffs, and the sky-colored birds that wheeled around its towers.

Kingsport, she repeated to herself. For now.

Acknowledgments

LIKE THE FIRST three novels in this series, this fantasia on a theme by H.P. Lovecraft depends even more than most fiction on the labors of earlier writers. Lovecraft's own dream stories, in particular the novel *The Dream-Quest of Unknown Kadath* and the short stories "Celephaïs" and "The Silver Key," and his later story "The Dreams in the Witch-House," were of course the primary quarries where I mined blocks of onyx for my own edifice, but a great many of his other stories also contributed their share of building materials, as did the writings of Arthur Machen and Clark Ashton Smith.

Any of my readers who are startled or offended by my references to Randolph Carter's sexual orientation might want to reflect on the fact that H.P. Lovecraft was completely oblivious to the fact that his friend and literary executor R.H. Barlow was also gay. Given the amount of time Lovecraft spent brooding on the unhuman, it's probably no accident that he was none too perceptive when it came to a good many human things. The remarkable thing is that Carter, as Lovecraft describes him in "The Silver Key," is as perfect a portrayal of a gay man of his class and background as you will find in 1920s literature, and it seemed reasonable to take the hint, and portray him accordingly. George Chauncey's magisterial *Gay New York: Gender, Urban Culture, and the Makings of the Gay Male World, 1890-1940* helped me work out those details of 1920s gay culture that were relevant to this story

While Johannes Aldrovandus and his tome on preternatural creatures are both inventions of mine, his father Ulysses Aldrovandus is not. I am indebted to Odell Shepard's classic *The Lore of the Unicorn* for my introduction to the elder Aldrovandus, whose family name simply begged to be attached to a Lovecraftian tome.

My intellectual debts remain largely the same as before, though I owe a note of thanks to the authors of two websites that have provided assorted bits of inspiration for details in this story—Fred Lubnow's "Lovecraftian Science" (http://lovecraftianscience.tumblr.com), and Ruthanna Emrys and Anne M. Pillsworth's "Lovecraft Reread" (http://www.tor.com/series/the-lovecraft-reread/). If internet bookmarks showed wear, both of these would be fairly tattered on my computer. I also owe, once again, debts to Sara Greer and Dana Driscoll, who read and critiqued the manuscript, and to Shaun Kilgore, who as usual made the process of seeing this book into print much more pleasant than otherwise. I hope it is unnecessary to remind the reader that none of the above are responsible in any way for the use I have made of their work.

About the Author

BORN IN THE gritty Navy town of Bremerton, Washington, and raised in the south Seattle suburbs, John Michael Greer began to write as soon as he could hold a pencil. A widely read author and blogger, he has penned more than forty non-fiction books and seven novels. He lives in Rhode Island with his wife Sara.

43082337R00149

Made in the USA
Middletown, DE
19 April 2019